Sing Me
Who You Are

Elizabeth Berridge

First published in 1967

This edition published in 2023 by
The British Library
96 Euston Road
London NW1 2DB

Cataloguing in Publication Data
A catalogue record for this publication is available from the British Library

ISBN 978 0 7123 5487 5
e-ISBN 978 0 7123 6860 5

Text design and typesetting by JCS Publishing Services Ltd
Printed and bound by CPI Group (UK), Croydon, CRO 4YY

Contents

✣

The 1960s

- **1960:** World population is above 3 billion for the first time.
- **1963:** The Ministry of Housing sets out mandatory requirements for council housing standards, compulsory from 1967, including minimum floor area, heating and a flushing toilet.
- **1963:** The 'compact cassette' is introduced by the Philips Corporation, marketed as a dictation recording device and eventually replacing reel-to-reel recorders for most domestic use.
- **1964:** A revision to the Married Women's Property Act allows women to be legal owners of the money they earn and to inherit property. Prior to this revision, everything a married woman owned or earned belonged to her husband.
- Throughout the 1960s, the average age at marriage in England and Wales slowly and steadily falls, from 28.3 for men and 25.3 for women in 1960, to 27.2 and 24.8 in 1969.
- **1967:** *Sing Me Who You Are* is published.
- **1967:** 193,300 council houses are completed in the UK, the highest number after the post-war peak of construction.
- **1967:** The Abortion Act legalises abortion in the UK for women up to 24 weeks pregnant, if two doctors agree that continuing the pregnancy will be harmful to the mother or baby.

⌘ ⌘ ⌘

- **1967:** The Forestry Act 1967 requires anybody felling a tree to apply for a felling licence.
- **1968:** The average weekly wage for a woman is £10, compared to £21 for a man.
- There are approximately eight domestic cats per 100 people in the UK throughout the 1960s. The number of pet cats steadily rises to 16 per 100 people in the early 2000s, overtaking the number of pet dogs in the mid-1990s.

Elizabeth Berridge (1919–2009)

Elizabeth Berridge was born in south London on 3 December 1919, the daughter of a land agent who specialised in administering large estates. As Harriet Harvey Wood noted in her *Guardian* obituary, 'she may have inherited something of his eye for property, for her descriptions of houses and localities, especially of the growth and development of the southern suburbs where she grew up and lived for large parts of her life'.

Berridge was educated in London and Geneva, and in 1940 married Reginald Moore, the founder of the literary magazine *Modern Reading*. They moved to Wales, where they raised their children, Lawrence and Karen. In 1945, Berridge's first book was published – a slim novella called *The Story of Stanley Brent*. Over the next two decades she wrote several novels and many short stories, appearing in literary magazines including the *Cornhill*, *New Writing* and *London Magazine*, as well as a short stint working in publishing.

Her novels met with some success when they were originally published: 1964's *Across the Common* won the *Yorkshire Post* Novel of the Year Award, and other novels were translated into various languages and adapted for BBC radio dramas. She wrote several television plays, a children's book called *That Surprising Summer* in 1972, and in 1974 edited the early diaries of Elizabeth Barrett Browning, but didn't publish any novels for adults after *Sing Me Who You Are* until the 1980s, perhaps spurred on by her 1960s novels being reprinted by Abacus. Berridge also reviewed novels for various newspapers for twenty-five years, and was

❊ ❊ ❊

a judge for several literary prizes including the Katherine Mansfield Short Story Award and the Dylan Thomas Short Story Award.

When one of Berridge's stories was included in *New Writing vol.4* (1995), it's said that editors A.S. Byatt and Alan Hollinghurst thought its inclusion would encourage 'other young writers' – and were surprised to find, at the launch party, that Berridge was in her seventies. Her final novel, *Touch and Go*, was published the same year, and she died in December 2009, the day before her 90th birthday.

Preface

Following the death of her mother, Harriet Cooper is able to make a fresh start. She sells up and leaves London for rural Cambridgeshire and the unusual home she has inherited from her aunt – a single-decker bus in a field belonging to her cousin. Seemingly she has burnt her boats, but has this move been made too early? After all, she is only in her late thirties! And what of all the investment she had made in her profession as a librarian? Decisive, determined, self-reliant yet vulnerable, Harry discovers the past can be misinterpreted, knowledge may be incomplete, and memory imperfect. There are secrets and lies, things hidden or unspoken by family and friends alike. Whose version is most accurate, or do differing accounts combine like the turning of a kaleidoscope to form a picture of sorts? And how will she find out who she is and what she really wants from life?

The Second World War throws a long shadow over this story set in the 1960s – in the memories of prison camp and of lives and loves lost – yet the novel also reflects the rapid changes of that period. Social attitudes and subtle class distinctions are set against a desire for greater personal freedom. An element of the plot examines the post-war need for housing development and conflicting responses to urban expansion. Along the way there are 'ructions', machinations, intrigues, accidents, resentments and resolutions.

Elizabeth Berridge had a critical eye and honed her own writing by editing and reviewing the work of others. From the opening

❇ ❇ ❇

pages, packed with arresting images, her vivid descriptions of colour and setting draw the reader into the landscape. Her delineation of distinctive characters, defined by small gestures and speech patterns, makes them leap from the page. She is a wry and witty recorder of human foibles and a deft creator of striking similes.

Her novel explores the constraints for a single woman without stable financial security (still depressingly familiar today) and raises questions about memory, relationships, identity, change and new beginnings which are relevant for us all.

Alison Bailey
Lead Curator, Printed Heritage Collections 1901–2000

�֍ �֍ �֍

Publisher's Note

�֍

The original novels reprinted in the British Library Women Writers series were written and published in a period ranging, for the most part, from the 1910s to the 1950s. There are many elements of these stories which continue to entertain modern readers, however in some cases there are also uses of language, instances of stereotyping and some attitudes expressed by narrators or characters which may not be endorsed by the publishing standards of today. We acknowledge therefore that some elements in the stories selected for reprinting may continue to make uncomfortable reading for some of our audience. With this series, British Library Publishing aims to offer a new readership a chance to read some of the rare books of the British Library's collections in an affordable paperback format, to enjoy their merits and to look back into the world of the twentieth century as portrayed by their writers. It is not possible to separate these stories from the history of their writing and as such the following novel is presented as it was originally published with just a few minor edits. We welcome feedback from our readers, which can be sent to the following address:

British Library Publishing
The British Library
96 Euston Road
London, NW1 2DB
United Kingdom

Sing Me Who You Are

Death speaks to the shepherds:
'Your sheep are gone, they can't speak for you.
I must have your credentials, sing me who you are.'

(Eclogue by a Five-barred Gate)
Louis Macneice

Part One

One

✤

Mrs Everett was the first to see the overladen Hillman inching up the lane from the road while she was busy at her long blowing lines of washing. Two small boys, collecting pegs as she dropped them, stood behind her as the noise of the engine, chugging up the steep rutted lane in low gear, drifted with the autumn wind over the hedge. The children called:

'It's her, back, mum!'

They swooped to the hedge, nipped under it, ran waving down the crotchety lane that ruined dodgy springs. It was not as if they particularly liked the woman behind the wheel of the labouring car, for all adults were suspect; but they were curious, and nothing much happened on the farm unless they made it happen. They noted the new luggage-rack on top, with boxes tied across and across, as if the owner were going to sea, or moving house. The inside of the car was loaded up to the windows.

From behind the wheel Harriet Cooper saw the boys, but she was concentrating too much on the pot-holes and scattered stones to do much more than give a brief wave. She came on slowly, past the notice their father had painted and put up by the gate in the hedge.

CHILDREN PLAYING DRIVE SLOWLY PLEASE

Awkward white capitals on a daubed green plank.

'She's got specs on,' said the youngest, staring after the car.

'She's got a cat with her, too. A cat. It was lookin' out the winder.'

They ran back to tell their mother, but a great gust of wind had taken a sheet she was unpegging and wrapped it around her so fast that she had no time to shout, stare, or even to move. It was aggravating, and Mrs Everett fought, making smothered cries of rage. The two boys, seeing this white pillar before them, ran round her as round a maypole, unwinding her with shrieks of joy.

'Here, stop it, that's enough!' Gasping, she stepped out of the trampled, spoiled sheet at last. 'That's one of the Hall's sheets and she don't want it looking like a football field. Drat! And I'd given it a nice clean blow, too. It'll have to be washed again.'

She ran with the crumpled sheet under her arm, cuffing her children, flushed with hostility, and stared away across the curving hedge of her garden after the now invisible car, listening to find out which way it was turning – up through the gates to the Hall, or along the bumbling track through the woods. The boys could find out soon enough, she told herself, heaving up the laundry basket with her strong arms, banging the ballooning sheets into shape as she passed. Either way it all added up to trouble. Mrs Everett liked things to be clean and proper and she smelt ructions. Why on earth had *she* come?

❧

Harriet stopped the car in the spinney, under the neutral trunks of the tall beeches. Through her driving-mirror she had caught sight of Mrs Everett wrapped in the sheet like Lot's wife and she gave a tight little smile.

'I bet she's smelling ructions already,' she said aloud as she opened the door and got out. But what was a ruction? How did it smell? Hot and pungent like smoke from a dying fire of rags and bones, or had it the sharp bite of newly scythed nettles? It wouldn't be like clean woodsmoke, that was for sure, not if she knew Mrs Everett.

After the buffeting wind outside, the calm and silence of the spinney offered the same relief as an unexpectedly warm patch of sea gave to an exhausted swimmer, and Harriet stood mentally treading water to subdue an odd lurch of fear. For it was something – well, wasn't it? Arriving at a place knowing it to be the last one. After this move, there was no other. But if you weren't careful you arrived at your last place too early in life. Like getting on a train at eighteen and jogging through unremarkable outskirts until the big city showed itself through a tangle of junction rails.

That station was marked PENSION and you were fifty or sixty years old and the hand on the carriage door was an old hand with rising veins and to your surprise the city outside was demolished.

Harriet found that she had been standing with her hands pressed against the smooth grey bark of a tree, thinking these things. Now she jumped back into the car, hearing the sharp, annoyed cries of her two cats. Both now had their wedge-shaped Siamese faces pressed up against the window: to them all unknown territory was hostile precisely because there was no past or future to be carried in their egocentric intelligences.

To soothe their mounting hysteria, Harriet said comfortingly:

'You'll be able to hunt, just for the look of the thing. Gregg doesn't allow traps on this farm, and I expect you can deal with the dogs.' But the blue eyes of her cats blared in distrust.

'Even if Aunt Esther only meant it as some kind of joke, or challenge, it hasn't misfired yet. And it means that I've jumped off that damned train before my dotage.' But she was afraid of good luck, and her voice trailed away as she drove slowly through the spinney and emerged from the tunnel of tall trees and elderberry bushes out on to a wide sloping field that swooped and fell to what was really no more than a hidden half-town. Beyond, the land surged up again in fawn and yellow rectangles to the blue horizon.

She brought the car to a stop by the side of a nut and blackberry hedge. The long green single-decker bus stood broadside to the top of the field; old, shabby and out to grass. A lonicera hedge, which Harriet had herself planted some years ago, protected the bus from the winds that drove off the Cambridgeshire plains. Between it and the spinney stretched a long untidy garden which she had wrested from nettle and ground elder. Her late roses still lolled, pansies still bloomed and michaelmas daisies of all colours spilled carelessly over the uncut grass.

Harriet's mother had said bitterly that it was a pity Esther hadn't left her a decent sum of money, not this old ruin. And not even the land it stood on, she had added. Land meant something, as Harriet's father had realized. If you had an interest in property or food you were well set up, otherwise—

Oh, phooey!

She let the cats out of the car. Bella went first, standing quite still on the unfamiliar grass, tail up and twitching. Her enormous blue eyes in the black mask of a face looked once at Harriet, waiting. Then the still un-named kitten, fast growing into lean cat-hood, jumped down crossly, giving a yell of annoyance as its mother batted it with a nervy paw. They started warily for the hedge, sniffing, ears flattened, bodies crouched, hating unknown open spaces.

Wading through the still-dewy grass – for the bus lived in shadow half the year, and this was autumn – Harriet went through the wooden gate set in a gap in the hedge and up on to the step. She unlocked the padlock and pushed open the door, which folded inwards down the middle. Stepping inside she became aware of the musty smell of disuse. How long, a month, six weeks? Enough for damp to invade this thin shell. She would open windows, light a fire, banish it. The small kitchen, converted from the driver's cab, was neat and clean as she had left it. But there was mould on the curtains and a mouse had gnawed at a candle-end, left forgotten on the draining-board. Her lamps had lost their brightness, but they stood ready, filled. Coffee and tea and essential tinned food were all in the cupboard. A yellowed page on the uses of herbs in cooking curled on the wall where her saucepans hung.

Before she went up the step into what she had made her main living-quarters, she ran the tap to get rid of the taste of the plastic pipe that carried the water from a pump in the middle of the field. Then she darted round to the back to turn on the Calor gas: the container was shrouded by giant mint clumps, and she rubbed a leaf between her fingers and sniffed. Many summers, many pleasures, revived in that action.

While the kettle boiled she opened windows and only then sat on one of the upright wooden chairs that faced the five long windows and allowed herself to look out.

Thurber once wrote a nice piece about being shortsighted. For days, he said, he had watched a dog crouched on the porch of a house over the way, and was alarmed when it at last blew off into the road and turned itself into a yellowed old newspaper. In the same way, the outdoor colours of trees, bushes, ploughed land and sky, ran into one another as Harriet absorbed the pattern. This she did slowly, greedily, as if filling herself with nectar like a bee. Sometimes she amused herself by putting on her glasses and looking out. At those times she was amazed to pick out yellow gleams from straw bales, catch a glimpse of a lark or a church tower, note the reddening of berries in the hedges, the precise shape of a yellowing elm. But mostly she preferred, as today, to let the whole lovely greenery-yallery space unfold in front of her. Even the sky, the thin blue wash swept about by a late September wind, was on the move.

Last time she had come, the mustard field in front of the bus had been in full bloom. Gregg had told her that it attracted pheasants from miles around, much to the chagrin of his neighbours. More so as he didn't care to shoot the birds in great numbers. Now the mustard was ploughed in, and she could watch hares leap across the furrows. She knew it by heart, and yet, when she closed her eyes, could never see it clearly in her head when she was away from it. Perhaps, she thought, when she was very old, out to grass somewhere herself, she would recall all this as clearly as the house in the suburbs, the chipped garden roller leaning against the fence; her father in his monkish dressing-gown, sloping off for a Sunday morning smoke in the woodshed.

Not yet, though. This was the present. The past she had done with, sold up; chairs that had been too much sat in, tables too much eaten off, pictures gazed at until they became invisible. The kettle boiled over. She made tea in a mug with a couple of tea-bags and a sugarless tablet. At thirty-seven she was too fat and knew it, as she knew all her other boring shortcomings.

She walked out of the bus, her only inheritance, out of the gate; a tallish, near-sighted woman with fading red hair and a bully-boy assurance. She should have been big and jolly; once she had been; a child with an open clear look. Now, landing where she had chosen, she felt lumpish and sad and deflated by the finality of arrival. And she walked alone in the field that had once blazed with yellow mustard followed by her two cats, who leaped over the ticklish grasses on the verge, fearing abandon. So she was not quite alone.

They saw each other at the same moment, although to Harriet the man coming up delicately around the edge of the field was a blur. They shared the same feelings of intrusion and annoyance. Meirion Pritchard, emerging over the rise, instinctively checked his pace. He loved the twelve-acre curve of this field, it gave him a sense of space and of privacy. He had to remind himself of his right to be there, for he had few rights. All at once he saw something pale run up the woman's body to sit on her shoulder and felt the same shiver of disgust as when, in a country pub, a ferret had poked its head out from a farm labourer's shirt and the man had watched his face and laughed.

Who the devil could it be? She was scarcely Venus rising from the foam with that figure. She was lighting a cigarette, she had risen from a straw stack, bulky in jeans. He would like to have been inspired, for he was always on the look-out for inspiration, in the manner of your sporadic poet. He would have liked to start off in the manner of a good minor poet, which was what he considered himself to be:

> 'I met a girl in a golden field
> A golden girl with head aflame ...'

And all he saw was a redhead (yes, the lowering sun had picked out that much for him) with a cat on her shoulder, standing near a disintegrating straw heap. Even that discrepancy might be turned to something; he must make a note and work on it.

When he was about twenty yards away he called out, 'Good evening' with the careful courtesy of the townsman trying to belong. She did not move, stood waiting for him like a farmer in an orchard lying in wait for small boys scrumping apples. She looked down and clicked her fingers, and another cat – good God, how many more? – ran up her leg with sickening familiarity. It sat on her other shoulder, so that as he drew level there were three pairs of eyes, two pairs of slanting and unblinking blue, and one pair of reddish brown, all watching him.

She spoke the words he had been thinking, flinging away two tea-bags from the mug she carried. Her cigarette was held with a man's firmness between middle and third finger.

'Who the devil are you?' she asked. 'This is private land.'

A deep voice. What one might call a 'good' voice. Stung, he answered her as an equal.

'I'm aware of that. I'm dining up at the house.'

'Oh. Are you a friend of Magda's or Gregg's?'

A cool directness, the intimate knowledge that hinted at superiority, brought back his stammer.

'Well, you c-c-could say of Mag, of Magda. She and I are on the same committee. Of course, I know Gregg, too. He—'

Tricked into over-explanation, he felt a fool, felt murderous, and abruptly shut up.

Harriet's antagonism evaporated in the face of such unease. She said almost kindly, unhitching the smaller cat from her shoulder without a wince, 'I'm Harriet Cooper. Magda's cousin. Somehow I never expect to see anyone here.'

'I always walk up this way. It's usually so peaceful.'

He had not forgiven her and made to move away, but to his astonishment she burst out laughing, and turned with him to walk back up the field.

'You're a bit early for dinner, aren't you? It's barely six.'

She must be in her thirties, he thought, and yet her easy manners and near rudeness were those of a teenager. Coltish. Nervy. When she was older she would twitch. This judgement gave him back his self-respect and he watched her as she walked near, but not by, his side. He was repelled by her careless mannish stride, for he was a small, swiftly moving man, half a head shorter and at least a stone lighter. While he made detours around the nettles and bumpy fawn clumps of rye grass she stepped unconcernedly through them. The detour took him some way from her and he saw the laden Hillman parked beside the open bus.

Harriet watched him stop and look and wonder. She noted the quality of frail obstinacy that informed his movements, the manner in which he held his hands out from his sides as he walked: ridiculous or touching, according to your nature, or of course the degree of your intimacy. Briefly, for no reason, she wondered whether he was Magda's lover.

'Yes,' she said, moving swiftly up beside him, pleasure deepening her voice. 'It's mine. Actually, I've had it for years.'

'I've passed this old bus so often, I wondered ...'

'I'm moving in. In fact, I've just arrived.'

Meirion added one more adjective to his summing up. Vulnerable. As if this quality offset her brashness, and gave him the right to speak, he repeated:

'Moving in? Now? But it will soon be dark.'

'There'll be a moon,' said Harriet, with absolute certainty.

'As I'm early – yes, I am early, you're quite right. Co-could I give you a hand, unless you're expecting G—'

'They don't know I'm here. My movements are my own. So thanks very much, Mr —? I don't know your name.'

'Pritchard. Meirion Pritchard.'

She nodded, and at once, without coquetry, put out her hand like a well-brought-up child. So now we are formally introduced and have shaken hands, firmly and politely, I may help her unlash those formidable objects. There's a hint of Magda there, thought Meirion, watching Harriet's unhurried efficiency as she started unloading the car.

'Boxes on the floor by the table and blankets and things on the divan you'll see behind the curtained-off cabin at the end of the main room. I'll sort them out tomorrow. This is very good of you. Of course, it might have rained in the night.'

Meirion watched her coil the ropes around her small brown hands until a heap of neat circles lay on the grass. She had method, he could approve of that. He looked about for some sort of clue, for he liked to know everything about everybody. Why had she come here? Did she paint or write? He rather hoped not, for he had had his fill of amateurs. Perhaps she gathered herbs by moonlight, attended by her cats ...

'Deck-chairs and garden tools in the shed at the back of the garden.

Then I'll give you a hand with these boxes. They're heavy. I'll take this in. It's full of bottles, and odds and ends of food.'

At last the car was empty.

'Do you leave it outside?' asked Meirion.

'For the moment, yes. I'll see Gregg about stowing it in a barn as the weather gets worse. We'd be bogged down in the mud otherwise. Come in and have a drink. You deserve it.'

Harriet lighted two Aladdin lamps, one standing in front of an antique mirror which reflected the light, and the other swinging from a hook on the wall. At once the outside air seemed to darken and the inside of the bus became a small retreat of light and uncertain warmth. She bent down and put a match to the prepared fire, throwing on handfuls of dry twigs from a box standing next to the old black stove. Then she pulled a bottle of whisky from one of the hampers and found two unexpectedly beautiful glasses.

Seeing him looking at them with surprise, she said, 'If you pare yourself to the minimum, that minimum must be absolutely pleasing, don't you think? One can't drink good whisky out of plastic mugs, after all.'

She had added water to his whisky. He preferred soda but could not say as much, and all at once the closeness of the place, and Harriet's propinquity, made him desperately ill at ease. He suffered from an almost frightening degree of empathy, and was aware that his own tentative personality was constantly in danger of melting and mixing in with another's, if it was stronger and more positively coloured. He was aware now that she regretted asking him in, could scarcely believe that a stranger to her was sitting uncomfortably on a pile of blankets on a bunk bed, drinking whisky and trying to make small talk. Yet he believed in this small rite of celebration; her first night here. It must be significant.

'One must appreciate life's significant moments,' he said suddenly, after two long gulps at his whisky. She looked at him in astonishment. To take her mind off his presence, she was examining the blue-and-white matting on the floor, thinking that she must brush it thoroughly tomorrow and put it out in the sun to air.

'Isn't that an old wind-up gramophone?' he asked, scarcely aware that she had not made any comment. 'I suppose you have a store of 78's. But then if you're going to be here alone you'll want a radio as well.'

'I like to be independent,' said Harriet. Surely he wasn't getting drunk on half a glass of whisky? 'The only thing I rely on from outside is water.'

'But you could fix up electric light. Look, the fittings are still there in the roof He gazed up at the curved ribbing outlined in blue and white. It was pretty. 'You could run it off a car battery, or fix up a sort of windmill.'

'I prefer oil lamps,' said Harriet.

There was silence. The intimacy engendered by working together had suddenly died: as he divined, she was furious with herself for allowing him to invade this place, her place, as well as her field. What did he do? She didn't care enough to ask.

Bella had jumped up on the table and was patting at a large moth that flew like a crippled aeroplane around the lamp. On the curtain near by a queen wasp laboured out into the warmth.

'Leave it, Bella, you'll have the lamp over,' said Harriet, and reached out for the moth, cupping it in her hands and putting it out of the half-open window. Then she knocked the wasp to the floor and put her foot on it.

'They love it in here,' she said. 'But now that's one wasps' nest less for the summer.'

'You don't mind things like that,' said Meirion, finishing his whisky. He had had no lunch and the whisky – a large one – made him less cautious than usual. He had forgotten that he should leave: Harriet's certainty about what to preserve and what to destroy filled him with a curious excitement. 'You're not afraid of storms, alone up here?' Voicing a private fear.

Harriet half-glanced at him, refilled his glass and her own, lighted a cigarette and absently fed the fire. 'I'm not afraid of anything much,' she said. 'I think women are better at being alone than men. A woman can find so many trivial things to do that time simply flies. At least, that's what people tell me.'

Stung by the edged tone, he said quickly, 'I said, alone. In a storm. I'm not supposing that you are lonely. That would be presumptuous.'

At once she smiled. Where did presumption start or end?

'I see. The storms up here,' she said forgivingly. 'They're marvellous. Terribly old testament, with God's wrath cracking open the sky. You can see all the way round, yellow and pink and green. You can almost hear the gnashing of teeth and rumbling of celestial turns. The cats hate it.'

'You should have lived in covered-wagon days,' said Meirion, his face fiery with whisky and admiration. He stared down tipsily from his high perch. 'Perhaps you did. Do you believe in reincarnation?'

But she was never to answer this question, for it was drowned by a commotion at the door. A very big man, having to bend his head, blundered in from the dark outside, stumbled up the step, swore, then shouted urgently:

'Harry! Hi, Harry! You here?'

This was one question that could be answered, and to Meirion's astonishment, his reluctant hostess leapt to her feet as if an electric current had vitalized that heavy body. She moved with incredible lightness and speed and in a moment was being hugged by the intruder.

'Gregg, you ass. You know the door folds down the middle.'

They stood looking at each other, Gregg's large hands dropping to his sides. He was nearly six foot four and made Harriet look almost slender. He was running to flab in his early middle age, but his blue eyes and grey hair still gave him the deceptive appearance of a tough old soldier. He looked past Harriet and over at the piled boxes, and then saw Meirion sitting neatly on his pile of blankets, cross-legged, hugging a whisky glass.

'Good God!' he said. 'What's all this? Place looks like a warehouse. Are you and Meirion settling in together? Congratulations, hope you'll both be very happy.' He came forward, laughing, felt for a chair, lowered himself into it. 'I walked down to meet you, old boy. Somehow thought you were coming up to eat with us. Got waylaid, eh?'

Meirion made a scared move. Magda hated people to be late for meals. How could he have forgotten? He waited for Harriet to explain. To his horror she evidently saw no need for explanations.

'Well, now you're here, let's drink a toast,' she said, pouring another generous measure of whisky into a glass. 'I've moved in, Gregg. I bet you couldn't get everything you possess into a place this size.'

'I can hardly get myself in,' said Gregg. 'You're mad. And I'm strictly off this stuff, but hell, who wants to live for ever?'

Meirion watched them, fascinated. His instinct told him that they didn't either of them care about spoiling Magda's meal. He was the one who would have to do the placating. While he moved carefully down from the mound of blankets it seemed as if the two of them were going into some sort of familiar routine.

'So how are you?' asked Harriet, spreading her hands.

'So how should I be? A clown in clover.'

'Why don't you ask me how's business?'

'So how's business?'

'Terrible. Don't ask me.'

They roared with laughter.

Outside, the last of the sunset had been swallowed up. An owl hooted. And outside, too, crept one of Mrs Everett's small boys, watching the uncurtained windows. He saw the two men, one laughing, one not. One sitting, one standing, with the tall red-haired woman in between holding a bottle of whisky. And as he darted like a fieldmouse home through the spinney he was pursued by a wild burst of singing. There would be plenty to tell his mother, and the smell of ructions would be as the savour of herbs to her nose.

Two

�֎

The next morning Harriet woke up at dawn with a hangover and the sensation that she had somehow been left out in the rain.

Although she was very bold about whisky, she knew she had overdone it after the two men had gone the night before, so that early morning was a bad time, waking with guilt souring her mouth. Magda's dinner must have been spoiled, for whenever Gregg started to drink he never wanted to stop. That meant that she could expect a visit from Magda when the rain lifted. If it ever did. Just now it rattled on the roof and sounded like a battalion of iron-shod birds running across. Rain spurted in on her from the half-open window above, and she reached up blindly to shut it.

She couldn't at first pin down her discomfort. Where the hell was she? On waking she had, from habit, looked towards where the half-open door should have been; the door into her mother's room, wondering if she had called for her. Then she saw the curtain, carelessly looped. Of course, she had rolled on to this bunk in the cabin, heaving aside the gramophone and unidentifiable tied-up bundles. The cats had crawled into her sleeping-bag when the fire went out, so that now she could not move at all.

Turning her aching head to see the pale sun hanging miserably in the white sky she could almost hear her mother's voice:

'I don't know how you can sleep in that thing in the middle of a field. You could have done with her money instead. That's Esther all over, she always was mean. The more you have the meaner you get. I've never had much, but I'm not mean.'

No, mother had never been mean. Only careful. Tearing up vests for polishing cloths, pulling old woollen socks over worn-out mops; mixing margarine and butter. All the same, Harriet knew that in a strange way her mother had enjoyed Aunt Esther's meanness. It vindicated her. For whenever her sister-in-law had driven up in her car to take them out for a surprise picnic, she could not enjoy herself until Esther said, at some point out on the downs, 'I hope you've brought your purse with you, Daisy. I never carry much money on me and we may need some petrol on the way home.'

At which Mrs Cooper would give Harriet a sharp nudge and say calmly, 'I always come prepared, Esther.' She always paid up, too, so that in the end the picnic cost her more than she could afford and she had to go short for some days afterwards. Harriet realized that her mother was only really happy when she was denying herself something; the word forgo had dominated her childhood. What she found most exasperating was that the more her mother disliked people, the more she felt she had to do for them.

Aunt Esther would arrive with boxes of windfalls from Uplands: apples, plums, pears.

'I thought if I provided the fruit and you the sugar, we could share the jam,' Esther would say, not mentioning who was to make it.

'She does it because she thinks Bertie gives us money,' Mrs Cooper told her daughter one summer day when Harriet found her in the scullery stirring a pan of bubbling jam. Outside the temperature was over eighty degrees. 'Now don't be in a black rage. Try to understand her. It's her way of getting it back. She feels guilty, too, at Bertie suddenly making money: she can't bear to see us struggling, but at the same time she hates to give people anything. What *is* she to do, poor thing? I suppose it's only natural to want some return.'

While the jam cooled in the jars, Mrs Cooper sat and drank iced coffee under the garden's one tree and said something that surprised her daughter. It was as if she carried on the conversation they had started half an hour before.

'It's like those lumps of bacon-fat on pieces of string that sailors swallow to cure them of seasickness. They swallow the fat and bring it up again on the string ... that's the sort of present Esther likes to give.'

Harriet never forgot this nauseating analogy and often got into trouble for suppressing a giggle when Aunt Esther came sailing towards them with her gift face on.

'Forewarned is forearmed,' said Harriet's mother comfortably, having put Esther and her money in the proper place.

Harriet lay uncomfortably in her sleeping-bag, wondering whether to get up and light the fire, make some tea. The cats purred as she moved, stretched their claws luxuriously into her back. The wind drove the rain hard against the roof and windows. Both were proof against anything that came, she knew that. Last summer she had spread sacks over the roof and slurped great dollops of black Aquaseal over the whole lot. She had enjoyed crawling about on the top while her mother sat in a deck-chair below, complaining about the wasps.

She couldn't get her mother out of her mind this morning.

'If only Esther had left you this field to go with it!' she had said querulously, for now she was old. 'This field would suit us nicely. We could build a bungalow here. I like hearing those church bells – such a natural sort of music. Suppose Magda sells the field? I wouldn't put it past her.'

'Nonsense, darling. It's one of the most fertile. Gregg got £400 worth of barley off it last year. That's not bad for just over twelve acres. Anyway, where else could we move this bus? It'd drop to bits.'

Her mother's momentary silence condemned the bus.

Then she said obstinately, 'All the same, your father would say I was right.'

Harriet's father had been Clerk to the Council and had quietly bought up ten acres of derelict allotments just before the war. When he died he had left his wife and daughter comfortably enough off to discomfort Aunt Esther, because his ten acres had turned out to be suitable building land. Aunt Esther did not have such a pleasant old age as Harriet's mother. People said that it was a tragedy that her charm and fire should have been whittled away into mere eccentricity. But Harriet had retorted that eccentricity was never mere. Others went farther and said that poor Esther had gone off her rocker. But splendidly, countered Harriet. At least Aunt Esther had died full of panache.

By mid-morning the rain stopped. The sun had been out over the other side of the spinney for some time, and now it showed over the tall beeches. At once Harriet put out the blue-and-white matting as she had planned and got down to scrubbing the floor. The boxes were still piled high on chairs and bunks, but the disorder was rational. There was order in it.

She was rinsing the kitchen floor when she heard the barking of dogs. Magda was on her way. Now she knew how the fox felt.

It was Magda's habit to walk her six dogs each morning through the woods, along each of the several rides. As she walked she would mark a tree she thought should be felled. This gave her an almost sexual quickening, because she knew that Gregg hated trees to be cut down, and the argument they would have about it later was the nearest they came these days to consummation. She liked treading about her land, and although she was a small woman, at these times she walked with a bossy trudge, constantly calling the dogs to heel. Earlier on she had stood at the highest point of her estate, above the spinney that protected Harriet's old converted bus, looking down over the woods and field that drifted gently to the little town below. At this time of year she could see a long way, beyond the town and over at least six counties. But all she had noticed this morning was the smoke from that absurd chimney of Harriet's bus. The smoke rose unhurriedly from beyond the trees, for the wind which had chased the rain away had itself gone, leaving a still, damp autumn day. Harriet's smoke irritated her, as if her cousin was deliberately writing sky signals asserting her presence on this land. And Harriet was someone whom you couldn't very well order off, like gipsies or tramps. However much you wanted to, you couldn't do that to poor old Harry.

Sometimes Magda wondered how she would feel if Uplands belonged to Gregg and not to her. She liked to say to herself as she leaned on a gate watching Everett on the red tractor, away over a harrowed field, 'I am Mrs Witheredge of Uplands. I own two hundred and fifty-five acres.

A farmhouse, two woods, and the rest arable. I own a factory and the business is doing well.' But she never added, 'I wish I had a child to leave it all to.' It was enough for her to know that it was all hers and that she was in her prime.

She started purposefully down the hill, skirted a field in which pigs were rooting about, cut through an apple orchard, went round the farmyard with its long barn, through the spinney and emerged on to what Gregg annoyed her by calling 'Harry's field'.

The cats fled in at the door of the bus when they heard the dogs, and leapt up on to one of the boxes, stiffening like pointers, growling softly in their throats, tails bushed. At once Harriet went out, closing the door behind her.

'Hullo,' said Magda, waving her dog-whip, 'I saw your smoke from the high paddock. May I come in?'

Dogs foamed around Harriet, their tails waving high. Two dalmatians, two dachshunds, a yellowish labrador and a delicate whippet. This last Harriet loved and she called it to her.

'Petronella! Beautiful girl, how are you?'

She squatted down to stroke the long sensitive head, but the bitch was nervous and sprang away.

'She's pregnant at last, thank God,' said Magda. 'Working for her keep, good girl.'

'Can you leave them all outside?' Harriet asked, as the whippet cocked her leg against the buddleia.

'Oh dear. Yes, of course, your cats. You've brought them with you, then?'

'They're my kith and kin. Come in and have coffee and hear my apology for last night.'

After several sharp commands to the dogs Magda followed Harriet indoors. At least the floor was clean, but Harriet felt very much the unmerry peasant being visited by the lady of the manor. Magda found herself a chair, stealthily brushed her finger over it for dust, found none, and risked her caramel-tweed-skirted behind on it. She examined the bus with frank curiosity while Harriet, busy with coffee making, quietly observed her.

Magda had not so much disintegrated, she saw, as set, into middle age. She was half a dozen years older than her cousin and her face had that furry, collapsed look of so many women in their early forties. But her skin was fine and clear, and one felt that this far she would allow age to touch her but no farther. She had 'a little woman' up in town who did her face and massaged her body once a month – soon to be once a fortnight. Lying there under the skilful, slippery hands she allowed herself to be worked on like a grubby Old Master, being stripped and retouched.

She dressed as she talked, with a fitness to the occasion. Now she was very much the moneyed countrywoman and landowner, her tinted blonde hair and its casual flipped-up ends blending with her neutral cashmere sweater. She looked born to wealth, which in fact she had not been. Perhaps it was her Jewish ancestry (for Esther, her mother, was half-Jewish, of a Hungarian mother and an Irish father) that made her take such care of her looks. She carried out all the beauty aids tipped by those ageless, indefatigable advisers in women's magazines: when she wore gloves they were spotless, she smiled a lot to keep her muscles from flagging, she wore light chiffon scarves at the neck, like her mother, and kept her lipline clean. In the circumstances Harriet thought her tenacity admirable. In addition, she possessed the kind of sensibility that has been defined as the faculty for knowing oneself in relation to events, or to people outside oneself. But knowing is rather different from understanding: it seemed to Harriet that, without humility, sensibility of this kind became only self-satisfaction, a grosser sort of self-indulgence.

But then Harriet had always been jealous of her cousin's good looks, for they had been brought up together, and it had always been Magda who looked English and delicate and attracted notice. Harriet found it gave her a special kind of pain to look too long at her cousin. So it was with pleasure that she now noted that as usual Magda wore an absurd gold charm bracelet. She had always made mistakes about jewellery.

'Here's your coffee,' said Harriet now, ashamed of herself. 'It's only instant, d'you mind?' Betrayed as usual into a half-apology.

'My dear, of course not, when you're so busy.'

'I'm really sorry I spoilt your dinner-party last night. I wasn't expecting to see anyone, it was all rather a surprise.'

'You were naughty, Harry. I'd made a special spinach soufflé for Meirion, and it was ruined.'

At once Harriet's mood lifted. To hear Magda say perilous words like 'special spinach soufflé' took her right back to childhood when she would beg her to try 'She sells seashells by the seashore' just to hear that lisp.

'Oh dear. Did you give them a terrible talking-to?'

Magda laughed, and blinked innocently.

'You're lucky to be able to afford to give them so much whisky. Meirion doesn't drink, you know. One Dubonnet and he'll recite half "The Ancient Mariner".'

'I thought he behaved a bit oddly. Queer little man.'

'He thought you were a bit queer, too. He kept asking me where you kept your canvases.'

Harriet raised her eyebrows.

'He's convinced you must be a painter or something. You know, coming down here to live. At least, that's what he said. Are you truly going to live here, Harry? Here, let me help you unpack that case.'

Together they took out cups and saucers and dishes, wrapped in newspaper. Magda assessed each one shrewdly as she wiped it over with a cloth and put it on the table.

'Your mother left this bus to me. Why shouldn't I live here?'

Magda shrugged and shook her wrist. The charms tinkled.

'You'll be off back to London when the snow comes. You've never lived in the country in the winter. And this isn't even a proper house.'

'I can't go back to London. I've sold the house. Didn't I tell you?'

All the old banked-down antagonisms of adolescence sprang up in the look they exchanged. If they had been schoolgirls Magda would have leapt on Harriet, fists pulling that flaming hair, screaming, 'How dare you? it isn't fair!' And Harriet would have kicked out at the vulnerable shins, spitting out 'I'll do what I like! I'll do what I like!'

But middle age being what it is, a strong Bastille for youthful devils, Magda merely caught her breath, dropped her eyes and said:

'You never tell me anything until you've done it. So you've *really* sold the house. What about the furniture?'

'I brought some with me. Sold the rest. The good things, that is. I need the money.'

'Money! You can always get a good job with your qualifications.'

Harriet turned away to control herself.

'Has it ever occurred to you that I'm bloody fed up, having a job? I was stuck in that damned library for fifteen years, and half of that was working at exams. I want to feel free and think about what to do.'

'Oh Harry,' said Magda, with real feeling. 'I do wish you'd married. You might have had children.'

'I suppose I might just about have them now, if I'm quick,' laughed Harriet. 'Find me somebody. How about Meirion?'

This was unfair and she knew it. But Magda looked genuinely surprised. 'Oh, he's a confirmed bachelor. He looks younger than he is. Anyway, you'd eat him up. By the way, what did you do with Aunt Daisy's gorgeous Rochester dinner-service?'

'Sold it. You know I've a small income, Magda. But I want some capital as well, in case, oh, I don't know. I might – but for the time being, I'm here, if it's all right with you.'

'I should think by now you have squatter's rights. How would *you* feel if *I* sold Uplands without a word to you? Aunt Daisy's house was home to me when I was little. I do think you should have told me. And anyway, Harry, she said she was leaving me that rosewood dressing-table. I haven't anything of hers to remember her by.'

Magda always returned to a grievance, Harriet reminded herself. She had been let off the spoiled soufflé only because now there was a bigger and better issue.

Harriet started to screw in cuphooks, and without a word Magda handed her the cups she had wiped.

'You'll want a piece of wood nailed to that shelf to stop the saucers slipping,' she said at last, when they were hung up. 'You could do with another shelf, too, for the plates. Perhaps Everett could fix it for you. Gregg's useless.'

This was an old grudge of Magda's, Gregg being useless about the house, so Harriet merely said, 'I can do it myself. I'm going to put up some shelves this afternoon for my books.'

And sharply, Magda said, 'Oh, your books. I don't suppose you could bear to get rid of any of those.'

'Mother wanted to give you her sewing-machine, but you didn't want it,' said Harriet, ignoring these lethal words. 'I'm sorry about the rosewood dressing-table, Magda. I decided everything in such a hurry at the end that I forgot.'

But she hadn't forgotten. She had been offered such a good price that she couldn't resist taking it. Now she felt wretchedly guilty, for Magda's desire for the dressing-table might conceivably have been sentiment, not acquisitiveness, and in this light her own action was mean. When you had very little money, meanness was somehow even more inexcusable. Had she been thinking about those picnics on the downs, taking a late revenge on Aunt Esther?

'I've got a modern sewing-machine, with a built-in light,' said Magda sulkily. 'Aunt Daisy was like a mother to me. I was fond of her.' Almost reverently she said, 'It was rather wonderful, her dying in church like that.'

'It was very quick,' said Harriet dryly. 'But it wasn't in the middle of her favourite hymn. That would have been better still, I suppose.'

Magda had unearthed a pair of tall brass candlesticks from the bottom of the box and set them up on the table before her. They had stood on Harriet's father's desk, and matched a heavy brass inkpot with a handsome cover. She could not leave them alone.

'Mother took such a time, dying,' she said, her hands running up and down the twisted stems. 'She had every sort of minister to see her, but she could never make up her mind who to be saved by. That's what I admired about Aunt Daisy. She made a decision and stuck to it.'

Harriet kept her back firmly turned on her cousin. It was wicked to lure Magda into these Goonlike exchanges, but all the same she wished that Gregg was with them. The innocent humourlessness of her cousin had both protected her against her own mother's alarming excesses, and the teasing of Harriet and Gregg. This had been their common ground for years.

Harriet said gently, 'Mother didn't plan to die in church, Magda. She was just lucky, if you want to see it that way.'

But there were tears in Magda's eyes and she held fast to the candlesticks. Such a respectable end, and no trouble to anybody! That is, after the first awful embarrassment for poor Harry.

'Oh,' said Harriet, wretchedly. 'Look. Do take those candlesticks. I've got the inkpot somewhere. You can put them all on your lovely mahogany desk in your dressing-room. Of course you must have something from the house, from the family. Do have them, Magda.' Then, feeling this little ceremony lacked something, she added some wholly inaccurate words, 'Mother would have been so pleased.'

Harriet's mother had died in the middle of Hymn No. 270 (*Ancient and Modern*). Her high, tuneless soprano had stopped abruptly and she had dropped forward over the back of the pew in front, hymnbook still open in her hand. Her peppermints, gloves and collection money (two sixpenny pieces, to make a modest jingle) had dropped off the shelf and rolled out into the aisle. Her chin had hit the wood, and her shiny straw hat, a new one, was jerked forward violently over her reading-glasses. All around the singing had grown ragged, heads turned.

It had been horrible. All the more so as this sort of behaviour would have horrified Mrs Cooper herself. (If the woman didn't feel well, why hadn't she stayed at home? Such a commotion, so unfeeling.) She must have died at once, Harriet saw, as she picked her up, for there was no realization of any outrage on her face. There was no expression at all.

Harriet looked up the hymn afterwards, to wring some significance from it. Her mother had died with the words 'panoply of God' strongly on her lips. Maybe it was God's way of whispering a private word in her ear. She deserved it at the end of a hard-working, undistinguished life; a life, Harriet had often thought of as idiotically devoted to others. Surely this God she had sung to so vigorously for so many years could give her some comfort?

'Poor little soul,' thought Harriet now, as she stared at the newly polished brass tap over the sink. 'She was good, and silly, and put-upon. By me as much as anyone.' And she didn't need to be reminded, by

Magda or anyone else, that her mother would not have approved of her *selling* up the *home*, as she would have put it with dramatic emphasis. But like a cicada, after her death, Harriet had determinedly crawled up her stalk and split the case of a long-drawn-out grubhood. A cicada spent seventeen years underground: she had spent many more. It was time to dry out her wings in the sun. How long did a cicada live in the free air, with wings and all? A season? One summer season. Silly insect.

'Are you sure I can have these?' Magda was saying, fully recovered. 'I've always admired them. I must say they'd look well on my desk, especially with the inkpot. I do a lot of local Council work now, you know. And they're really far too valuable for you to keep in this old bus, Harry. Anyone could break in and take them. I know, I'll look out some china ones for you, in exchange. You'll need candles down here, until you get electric light fixed up. Everett—'

'Look, Magda, I *like* lamplight. I like having to fill lamps and trim the wicks. I'm not going in for any mod. cons. at all, you never know where they'll lead to.' She looked sharply at the door, for she had heard a clumsy scratching and snuffling. 'Your dogs are getting restless. I'd better rescue the matting from the garden before they make it filthy.' In her mind's eye she saw them sending their disgusting yellow jets of urine over her roses and the bit of grass she was coaxing into a lawn. She suspected that the dachshunds – which she had never liked – were rootling about on the rockery with their washerwomen's paws.

As she stepped out of the bus, clutching the candlesticks, Magda said, 'We're both alone now. It's funny, isn't it? Come up and have a meal with us tonight. I've lots to tell you. I want to talk to you about Gregg.'

Tapping her dog-whip against her smooth thigh, she called the dogs like Santa summoning his reindeer.

'Come, Leon and Panda, Gog and McClusky! Wooster! Petronella! Out now, hup!'

And away she went, not one of the dogs daring to jump up. They spread out in front and behind her like an escort; a poor little fairy princess whose wishes had somehow got bent in the granting.

Harriet watched the cortège, and the cats came too to watch with her. Their eyes still turned to the way through the wood long after the last sharp bark had died away; then Harriet went in to hunt through boxes for the inkpot. In expiation.

Three

❈

Harriet spent the afternoon putting up bookshelves. She had not intended to do this yet, for there were other, more urgent, things to attend to. But she had said to Magda that this was what she would be doing, and some exactness in her nature drove her to do it.

The wooden partition that divided the cabin at the back from the main part of the bus was the obvious place. It took four shelves on either side of the opening, and she did the job properly, with wall brackets screwed, not nailed in. These she had brought from home, with the shelves already measured and cut to size.

Then she sorted out her books.

There were three boxes. And of all the key decisions that had to be made in a lifetime, deciding which books to keep and which to get rid of (Harriet could never say' throw away') came third in order of conscience and heart scouring. Numbers one and two varied with each person, but they usually had to do with sex and duty. Books were a constant, and when one was done with sex and duty the battlefield could be surveyed from a comfortable distance. If one was wise, and Harriet hoped that one day she might be, old age could be a listening-post of vicarious satisfactions. Then, if you were lucky enough to keep your sight, you could indeed 'read all abaht it'.

Harriet was temporarily free of sex and duty. As this thought occurred to her, she said aloud to the cats, 'Temporarily'. To stop any thunderbolts that God might be fingering.

Sentimentality or sentiment – near neighbours these – had made her keep Arthur Mee's *Children's Encyclopaedia*. Time has outpaced that admirable man. What educator nowadays would start off a series of ten volumes with the ominous words, 'It is a Big Book for Little People and it has come into the world to make your life happy and wise and good'?

Harriet did not feel that she was happy or wise or good, and somehow she doubted whether many of Arthur Mee's devotees were either, in spite of the strong moral tone of his contributors. Perhaps, like herself, they had merely been given a wider range of prejudices to rearrange from time to time. Coping with that index had certainly made her tenacious in her search for knowledge. It had undoubtedly helped her while she was doing Cataloguing and Classification for the Intermediate part of her Library Association exams. By correspondence, too. Once you had tried to track down, Milton, say, through the list of cross-references in the *Children's Encyclopaedia*, you could tackle anything.

She remembered, as she hauled out the heavy, shabby blue volumes, how pleased she had been to discover a grammatical slip in *The Areopagitica*. How pedantic she had become up in her cold bedroom, with the patterns from the oil-stove reflected on the ceiling, working away in her father's old woollen socks to keep her feet warm. Facts, facts, no one to query them! They were a solid core in the hysterical shifts of family life. They had insulated her, like her flesh, against the enemy, against the cold.

Out of curiosity she looked it up now, avoiding by experience the scattered mines of irrelevant information.

IMPERISHABLE THOUGHTS OF MEN ENSHRINED
IN THE BOOKS OF THE WORLD
THE GREAT EPIC OF MILTON

Bzz ... bzz ... Here he was, shooting the Lords and Commons full of patriotic darts:

'Is it nothing that the grave and frugal Transylvanian sends out yearly from as far as the mountainous borders of Russia and beyond the Hycernian wilderness, not their youth, but their staid men, to learn our language and our theologic arts?'

No doubt about it. The grandiloquent boom was fractured, like a great bell with a flaw in the casting. What would Partridge or Fowler have to say about the use of a plural possessive adjective referring back to a singular subject?

It was terrible how much one enjoyed being pedantic; it made one feel like a fly climbing up a giant's nose. She read on:

> 'By all concurrence of signs, and by the general instinct of holy and devout men, God is decreeing to begin some great and new period in His Church, even to the reforming of Reformation itself. What does He, then, but reveal Himself to His servants, and as His manner is, first to His Englishmen?'

Superb one-upmanship. 'As His manner is'. Milton's hot line to the heavenly throne. 'First to His Englishmen.' A phrase to savour, that.

It invited no questions. Was that why, Harriet asked herself, dusting off the rest of the set and reluctantly putting them on the bottom shelf, organized religion had atrophied? Like herself, the Church was a great one for telling or for being told. Discussion did not enter into it.

She had one more box left when the door crashed open and Gregg came blundering in, his arms full of small logs.

'Hey,' he called from the door, 'I thought you'd be all tidied up by now and set to make me a mug of tea. Can I stack the logs here? I was sawing some for us, so – dammit, Harry, the fire's nearly out! What a hopeless clot you are.'

'You can take those the hell out of here if you're going to call me a hopeless clot! How dare you come blustering in here calling me names?'

She was furious, torn from her pleasant abstracted world; knocked like a fly from the giant's nose.

'The maid said you were in,' said Gregg placidly. 'Have you filled the boiler with water or is it dry? I'll have to fix up some sort of chain, then you can keep a kettle swinging over the fire like a witch. It'll save you gas.'

He stacked the logs neatly, filled the boiler, using a brass jug she had brought from home. He said pleasantly, as she glowered at him from the painful position of her knees (she had cramp, otherwise she would have attacked him physically), 'Bet you haven't had any lunch.' Harriet groaned from rage and the shooting pains in her kneecaps.

'Put the kettle on, will you? I can't move. I don't need to eat if I'm dining with the quality. And admire these shelves, for God's sake.'

She eased herself up and staggered to the long bunk which now looked like a divan, placed along one side of the main room. It was covered with terracotta linen and had bright yellow cushions; now that it was free of parcels and boxes, it was a civilized oasis. As she lay flat, easing her legs, she watched Gregg. Useless, Magda had called him. But now as he squatted in front of the fire, poking in bits of twig to encourage the flames, methodically feeding it with coal and small logs, he looked fully in control. It occurred to her that it suited him to be useless where Magda was concerned.

Her fury had gone. He had known it would, but he liked to see her flare up, because he accepted that all red-haired women had a temper; in this at least she conformed.

Satisfied with the fire, he set the kettle on the gas and stepped over to shake each shelf in turn. 'Not bad. They're going to stay up, Harry. I can't put up shelves, you know.'

He looked at her guilelessly, and passed his hand along the books. 'Have you read all these?' When she made an impatient noise, he said, 'All right. All I can remember from the poetry I learned at school is "I could not love thee, dear, so much, loved I not Honour more." And that got mixed up with a song they made me sing before my voice broke. "Who is Sylvia?" We used to make feeble jokes about who was Honour, and did all the swains take turns with her and Sylvia.'

'Give me a cigarette,' said Harriet. 'You're a fool, Gregg.' But she couldn't help laughing; it wasn't a bad thing to put poetry in its place. Spell it with a small p.

'Your pal Pritchard fancies himself as a poet,' said Gregg.

'Capital P.'

'I once heard the poor little perisher telling Magda that he was a Po-Po-Poet – in a small way, of course.'

'I don't believe you. He couldn't have said he was a poet in a small way.'

Gregg stood to his full height, held his hands across his chest, bowed his head and said in a high humble voice:

'I am a grocer in a small way of business, ma'am. Nothing too fancy but we aim to please.'

'Well,' said Harriet, blowing out smoke, 'and does he? Is there anything wrong, Gregg?'

'Ah,' said Gregg, 'you must do your skirmishing for yourself. I won't rob you of that feminine pleasure. You may investigate Po-Po Pritchard at your leisure. Now shall I make the tea or will you? I like mine with three lumps, as you know.'

Harriet made tea in a pot this time. Somewhere she had her mother's silver teapot, but after the morning's encounter she did not trust herself to get it out. A china one would do. That silver pot had been another of Magda's favourites.

'Damn, it's raining again,' she said, glancing through the window. 'We can drive up to the house. That's one thing I am pleased about, Gregg, learning to drive. God knows why I left it so late.'

'Illusion of freedom, old dear, that's all it is.' He was holding a book in one hand, and spoke idly, scarcely hearing what she had said. 'Hullo, what's this? I didn't know Scrubbs read poetry.'

Harriet was pouring tea into two cups. When she was alone she used mugs. The tea went all over the tray. She did not need to turn around to see which book he was holding. It had a hard red cover, with a circular coffee stain on the front. All she could hope for was that he would not leaf through it with a wetted finger, with all the slow conscientiousness of a man unaccustomed to handling books.

She made herself clear up the mess, pour away the overflow in Gregg's cup, and then she took the cup and saucer over to him. No one, not even her mother, had mentioned that name to her for ten years.

'Sorry,' he said. 'Shouldn't read other people's inscriptions. Bad form.' And he put the book back away on an empty shelf, propping it up by itself. But his face was full of curiosity.

'I didn't lick my finger,' he said, with a half-laugh. 'I know you're funny about books.'

Harriet was indeed funny about books. She had once overheard one of the young assistants at the library say as much to a parent who had complained about Miss Cooper's sharpness to her child. 'She likes them to have respect,' the girl had said in an undertone, like some kind of informer. 'She's funny about books, you see. But Miss Cooper's all right really. Her bark's worse than her bite.' Harriet had provided the children with bookmarkers. A cut-out of a pink pig with a balloon coming out of its mouth, saying 'Don't be a pig, use me instead'. But the chief librarian had told her that this was insulting. There were markers of a kind in the book Gregg had been holding, and she hoped they wouldn't fall out. Dried flowers were so sentimental, so were old strips from football programmes and cricket score-cards.

Anything hoarded exposed its own, and one's own, frailty.

'You know,' said Gregg, 'Scrubbs once said to me that being a prisoner wouldn't have been so bad if he'd had a well-furnished mind. Didn't sound like him, somehow. A well-furnished mind. A kid he knew would be able to recite yards of poetry if she'd been there, he said. Must have been you. I'd forgotten.'

It had stopped raining and the sun made its last brief appearance, shafting off the raindrops in the hedge and making a dazzle of raised swords between the bus and the field. Along the top of the windows fat drops hung in rows as heavy as mercury.

'It's a long time ago,' said Harriet, staring at them.

'We managed to get hold of quite a few books. Some of us had brought one or two from Singapore and somehow managed to hang on to them. We pooled them.' Gregg was speaking slowly, as if changing slides to project on to a screen. 'When we got back to Chungkai in '44 of course the worst was over. We used to put on plays – we had a shot at *Night Must Fall*. We did revues, and we even got together a scratch sort of band. It's amazing what you can do with a cavalry trumpet and a double-bass made out of a packing-case, helped out by a bugle and some violins.'

'Violins!'

'The Japs sent to Bangkok for new strings. For some reason they liked our music. The boys in the band got a lot of time off to practise.'

'Scrubbs said you did *The White Horse Inn*. He'd taken mother to see it in town and he was marvellous at remembering tunes. There was someone else, he told me, another man—'

'Steve. The Aussie who died the day before we were released.'

'That's it; and Steve could write music. So he and Scrubbs—'

'Scrubbs always had a good ear.'

'They'd go into a huddle and Steve would write down the tunes as Scrubbs hummed them. ...'

'We had to make up our own words. God! But it turned out a funny sort of musical.'

He stared right through Harriet, and several thousand dead men walked over her grave.

❋

It is neither the point in space, nor the instant in time at which something happens which is real, but only the event itself. This was a fact that Harriet instantly recognized, for space and time were always linked with one's thinking. The numbers going up the side and across the bottom of a graph meant nothing by themselves. On the square window she traced a line from the raindrops at the top to a spider's web on the side. That was the significant point, the meeting-place. It was as if she and Gregg had put such a dot, where space and time met and an event was created.

'Well,' said Gregg at last, stubbing out the last of his cigarette. 'That was one hell of a time ago. No use in digging it all up. Let's get these—'

'Why not?' asked Harriet in a low voice. 'Why should the dead be shovelled out of memory and conversation? Is the present so marvellous, the future so enticing?'

'I've often wondered why Magda refused him, he'd have been a better bargain in the long run. Better than me.'

'Only he had a short run.'

'Not if she'd married him.'

'Who knows? Gregg, it's not like you to be like this. Tell me what's happened.' Harriet pulled the curtains against the night that had suddenly eclipsed the sombre fields, and lit the lamps. She pulled out the rest of the books from the last box without examining them closely, and put them up on the shelves. They just fitted.

'I'll take that box outside,' said Gregg. 'It'll do for the bonfire. Would you like to have it out here on the fifth? You could make gallons of soup, we could have a party.'

Harriet accepted defeat.

'That'd be fine,' she said. 'I'll change into a skirt now and we'll go up to the house. Mustn't be late again. Shall we walk up instead? I've got a feeling that the car's bogged down, anyway.'

While she changed, Gregg washed the cups, made up the fire, and stared at the bookshelves. But he did not take up the red-backed poetry anthology again. It dominated the room like an icon.

'I like it here,' he said at last. 'You know, Harry, I'm glad you've come. I hope you'll stay.'

Mockingly, Harriet said, 'I've a gramophone as well. And a selection of 78's that will make your hair fall out. The Mills Brothers and Maurice Chevalier and Noel Coward and something called The Two Black Crows that used to slay my father, and Fred Astaire—'

'You're quite illiterate musically, aren't you?' said Gregg lazily, stretching out a hand to catch her as she passed him. 'That's a blessing. Why are you embarrassed?'

'Oh.' Harriet pulled at the revers of her blouse and coloured up patchily. 'I'm not used to pretty speeches. I thought perhaps that you and Magda might take a dim view of my landing here without a word of warning. Not that I care what—'

'Of course not. You don't care. But don't care was made to care, as some grisly relic from my childhood used to tell me.'

He pulled her to him and kissed her. It was not the kind of kiss that one relative gives to another, and it was the first time they had exchanged an embrace that was not in full view of friends or family. Alarmed, Harriet put up her hands against his chest and pushed.

'You're so big for this bus,' she said, as if this was the only trouble. 'I'd better get my Wellingtons. It'll be wet walking up.'

'Just as you say,' said Gregg, and let her go.

- 36 -

Four

They were walking through the dripping trees of the spinney, their heavy soles leaving criss-cross patterns on the shining clay outcrops that oddly mixed with the chalky ribs of the treacherous path, when Harriet noticed that Gregg's eyes were tightly shut. He strode along without hesitation, long and sure, but his right hand was held out from his side and every fifty paces or so he grasped a white stake that had been hammered in at the side of the path.

It was not quite dark and when they came out on to the lane, Gregg opened his eyes and said aloud, as if it were a game, 'Three hundred.'

'Oh, you're measuring the path. I wondered what you were doing. Is that three hundred paces or yards?'

She was nervous of him because of this new turn their relationship was taking and was therefore uncharacteristically polite.

'Paces,' said Gregg, with a swift and amused side-glance. He shut his eyes again and Harriet noticed that more white stakes had been driven in by the side of the lane between the road and ditch. Gregg strode rapidly along it in the dusk, lightly touching each one as he passed. Each stake was waist high.

'Eight hundred,' they said together as they reached the high scrolled-iron gates at the start of the drive to Uplands. Gregg laughed.

'Guess how many up to the house?'

But he started off before she could hazard a guess. She watched him go, knowing that he wanted to be by himself, and with a small sense of terror watched his left hand this time flick out to touch, unerringly, each unobtrusive white post set at intervals alongside the shrubs and gravel.

She felt absurd striding out along the drive, pacing it, and soon slowed down. This was a private ritual, obviously, and as such, its therapeutic magic would be lessened if shared. Some people counted walls and window-panes, others avoided the lines on pavements, like Dr Johnson. Hadn't he also drummed a stick along iron railings like any schoolboy? Anyway, obsessive behaviour was nothing to worry about, normality was far more frightening. All the same Harriet stopped and looked over to the right, where the long curving lake was outlined by rising mist and the bamboo plantations marched along the far end. From the water came the heavy smell of autumn and she knew without moving a step that the flat leathery water-lily leaves quilted the lake, with drifts of wild plum and willow leaves for stitching. Aunt Esther had always loved to watch these changing colours. She had made, years ago, a patchwork bedcover, matching the silks and velvets to the faded tapestry colours of the tough water-lily leaves, the brilliant drifts of red plum, the frail yellow hair of willow.

Walking on up to the house, Harriet remembered that Aunt Esther had died under that quilt, in her own bed, and not in the lake as she had intended.

✻

There was no sign of Gregg when she reached the house and she hesitated. Then she turned away from the stone porch with its tall Doric columns – an unfortunate addition to the flat Georgian certainty of Uplands – and walked through a shrubbery to the cobbled stable yard at the back. She came this way out of habit, to change her gumboots for house shoes in the big storeroom that lay off a stone-flagged passage and behind the kitchen. In the old days she had often helped her aunt to wash eggs at the great sink, and she had enjoyed working the pump-handle. Magda still kept a few free-range hens to supply the house, but Aunt Esther had done it on a larger scale, selling eggs and birds in the small town below.

She walked through into the kitchen and found Magda supervising the last-minute details of the meal. At the moment she employed a Spanish couple, man and wife, to clean the house and cook. She did not look pleased at Harriet's sudden appearance.

'Hullo, Harriet,' she said. 'Why don't you go into the drawing-room and get Gregg to give you a drink?'

'Gregg's gone off somewhere,' Harriet replied, uncertain whether or not to greet the Spanish girl. 'Anyway, you said this morning that you wanted to have a word with me about him, and I thought that now would be as good a time as any, in case you have people coming later.'

'Lila Merrington might look in for coffee.' Magda turned to the girl by her side, who stood patiently waiting to cut bread. She spoke very slowly. 'Can you manage now, Theresa? Make the toast at the last moment, please. Very thin and crisp. Hold the knife so. There, about that thickness. Serve it with the pheasants.'

Harriet exclaimed how splendid it would be to have pheasant, and smiled warmly at the Spanish girl. At once Magda ushered her firmly from the kitchen. She did not approve of informality before servants. It unsettled them. Harriet had simply no idea how to behave.

'Come up to my room,' she said, 'there's not much time, as you say.'

She and Gregg had not shared a bedroom ever since they moved into Uplands, three years ago. They gave out that Gregg sometimes had nightmares and Magda was a light sleeper.

Magda sat at her chintz-skirted dressing-table with a gesture Harriet remembered from their shared childhood (she had a way of looking into a mirror as if it might attack her). Now, baring her teeth, she wiped off a smudge of lip-stick from one of them. An apple-green cashmere dress set off her fairness; but no, she would never have her mother's dash and elegance. 'I've bad news about Gregg. In fact, your coming here is a godsend, Harry.'

She laughed nervously. 'He's been having trouble with his eyes for some months now. Awful headaches and a feeling of pressure. Then he said he could only see if he looked straight ahead. I think it is because he's terrified of going blind that he let me call in a doctor. You know how peculiar he is about—'

'Going blind? Gregg?'

'No, seeing a doctor. He won't ever admit that there's anything wrong with him. I've known him walk for miles with a skinned heel rather than give up.'

Harriet stared at her cousin stupidly. The white posts, the pacing; these were very far from being a laughable obsession. She wondered whether Magda knew about them. Probably not. She said quietly, to hide her own sense of shock, of pity, of outrage:

'He was blind for about a month once before, wasn't he? In prison camp?'

'Oh,' said Magda easily. 'That was lack of vitamin A or something. Luckily he was treated in time, it was right at the end of the war. The doctor thinks this is glaucoma, but we've got to go up and see a specialist. He may need to operate.'

'He's had such bloody luck all round,' said Harriet, looking with horror at her cousin's complacently poised neck and unworried hands.

'You can't say that, Harry! He just walked into a job at Daddy's firm. Then he married me. He's had a jolly easy life for the past ten years. Anyway, don't let's argue over that. What I wanted to do was to warn you. He trips over things; the dogs, for instance. He can't read, and he's terribly irritable. Just be tactful, that's all we can do. We're seeing this specialist next Wednesday, and if there's anything to be done, he'll do it. Don't look so tragic.'

She held out a box of cigarettes. You never knew how Harry would react.

'Now,' she said briskly, as she lighted their cigarettes. 'This is what I want to ask you to do for me. You're family, thank God. Harry, I want you to keep Gregg company. He gets depressed, you see. He goes up to town three days a week, as he's on the board, but he doesn't do much. He seems to have lost interest in the advertising side. The firm really runs without him. Then down here Everett runs the farm. It's all Gregg's fault, really. He could pull his weight if he wanted to. I wouldn't like to sack Everett; he's useful and so's his wife—'

'Come to the point,' said Harriet. 'Gregg will be wondering where we are.'

'Next Wednesday I've got a Housing Committee meeting. You did know I'm on the local Council now? I'm pretty busy on committees most of the time. You know what it is when they find that a person is willing – and capable.'

Harriet nodded. She was one of the first to shift off uncomfortable jobs on to the willing and capable. It was ironic that Magda was doing the same thing to her.

'Oh, Harry!' said Magda impatiently. 'You'll be at the bus all this winter, so you said. I'd like you to pop in and out of this house, talk to Gregg, even read to him, listen to his damned – sorry, those records of his. He likes music. It makes me nervous. I'll tell Theresa and Filipe to expect you at any time, even if I'm not here. And if the bus gets too damp you can always be fixed up with a permanent spare room here. After all, you can't moulder away on the other side of the spinney in that old ruin. I can't think what mother was doing, leaving it to you – anyway, is next Wednesday all right? I can't miss this meeting, and if the verdict's bad, Gregg'll be feeling pretty low.'

She got up with relief and stubbed out her cigarette, smoothed down her dress, made for the door. Harriet followed her slowly, stopping to puff some powder over her flushed face. There were several things wrong with this little speech, she thought. Firstly, Wednesday was the day that might damn Gregg's chances altogether, and Magda still intended to go out and leave him. Secondly, she had successfully reminded Harry that she lived on sufferance on Magda's land and that the idea was one only to be indulged in temporarily. Lastly, and this for some unaccountable reason stung, she had no qualms in leaving her husband to be entertained by dear old Harry, who never had been – and certainly wasn't now – a sex bomb.

'O.K., Magda,' said Harriet, as they went downstairs. 'Of course I'll do what I can. After all, it isn't as if Gregg and I are strangers.' And waited for Magda's approving smile now that she was assured that her busy, enjoyable routine need not be interrupted.

'I knew I could rely on you, Harry,' she said, and swept on ahead into the drawing-room.

Gregg was busy with bottles as they came in. He was refilling his own glass and asked, without looking at them, 'What'll you have, girls?

Magda fluttered up to him and gave her cheerful little laugh that made Harriet prickle into gooseflesh. Marital playacting was as embarrassing for the observer as amateur theatricals. By calling them 'girls' it seemed to her that he gave away his absolute knowledge of what had been going on upstairs; it was a measure of his hatred. She became aware of an extra sense where Gregg was concerned, and now his humiliation moved painfully in her.

As they ate the excellent food Theresa put before them – she had remembered the curls of thin toast, but received no word of praise from Magda – Harriet told herself that this sensitivity was merely because no man had kissed her for years. She had deliberately shut herself off from all sensual contact, preferring to surrender completely to the dry, sexless world of her widowed mother. It had been easier that way: the Library with its neat cards and its shelves packed with every inflammable emotion tight between covers, and her mother's bridge parties and early nights with hot milk and a water-bottle at ten. Life itself became a capsule to be swallowed, not tasted.

'What are you smiling at, Harry?' Gregg asked.

'I was thinking how unexpected life can be,' she replied truthfully. Then, casting back for an acceptable example, went on, 'There was Mrs Everett at the farm, for instance. She was so surprised to see me drive past yesterday that she got herself all wrapped up in a sheet. Then there was that friend of yours, Magda—'

'Po-Po Pritchard,' interrupted Gregg.

'Meirion Pritchard, Gregg. You are beastly. You shouldn't make fun of him.'

'Why the devil not?' Gregg glared at his wife. 'You should be pleased. The wise man tilts with his peers.'

Not understanding, Magda smiled forgivingly and tinkled her bracelets.

'Meirion's shrewd,' she said, addressing Harriet. 'He likes to have a finger in local politics—'

'But what does he *do*? What's his job? Not local bard, I take it?'

'He edits the local paper.'

'What's he doing here with a name like that?'

'Bettering himself, I dare say,' said Gregg with the thickest Welsh accent he could manage.

'His mother was English. He was brought up in Cheltenham,' said Magda primly. 'Why, he was educated in England. He just goes back to Wales to see his grandmother. Some relative of his mother's owns the paper and gave him his chance. He's worked his way up from reporter on all sorts of local rags. He's had some poetry published, too.'

Theresa brought in a big dish of apple snow, and Harriet found herself coaxed to a second helping. It was nice of Magda to remember that it was her favourite pudding. If she hadn't learned to distrust her, she would have been uncritically fond of her.

They were in the drawing-room, sunk into an amiable lethargy, drinking brandy by the fire, full of food and warmth, encompassed by the dogs, when the door bell rang, and a moment later Lila Merrington came in. Even Magda shifted reluctantly.

Magda's friends always made Harriet feel uncomfortable. Their manners were different from the women of her mother's generation. Courtesy was open to misconstruction. For one thing, she was never sure whether to get up to greet an older woman in Magda's circle, for none of them liked to be reminded of their age. They preferred to be waved at airily when they entered a room, like college girls at a reunion. On the other hand, they did not like cursoriness.

So Harriet pretended to be engrossed with Petronella who, in her soft leather collar, lay in self-conscious abandon on the white goatskin flung over one of the silk-covered sofas. The red-setter pup and one of the dachshunds sprawled near Gregg's chair.

'Oh,' cried Lila, with a wave of her hand, 'what baronial elegance! You don't belong to this age at all, darlings. So this is how a councillor lives. Magda, where's your common touch?'

'I'm her common touch,' said Gregg, rising. From where Harriet sat he looked immensely tall, and at once she was aware that he did not like Lila. She appeared to be a fairly new acquaintance of Magda's, and Harriet had only met her a few times before, either in the Brown Bear on a Sunday morning, or walking up to the house along the lane the previous summer.

She was a small woman, with a long face and thin, short hair, and her relentless curiosity gave her the look of a questing rat. She was a great one for asking urgent questions, and it occurred to Harriet, remembering something that Gregg had once said about her, that she too was on the local Council.

She came over and sat down on the sofa. Not, Harriet divined, to be near her, for Lila was not a woman to waste time on female relatives – and poor ones at that – but to be near Gregg.

She started up a teasing, flirtatious conversation, accepted brandy and black coffee and took one of her own small cigars from a flat tin in the pocket of her tweed dress. Magda watched her with indulgence, sensing that she was no real threat to a marriage. Her age was against her for one thing, although she was certainly sailing through the randy fifties with a brave sail hoisted.

'He is a bloody, bloody man,' she was saying, blowing out smoke strongly, as if into someone's face. 'Everything we suggest he blocks. Some of us on the Housing Committee want to extend Maxmead out towards the aerodrome, the land there isn't much use agriculturally, but he's got his eye in the other direction.'

'Not up this way,' said Gregg. 'We don't want houses up here.'

Lila sent him a purely malicious glance.

'That's what all the landowners say. "Take someone else's land." But the poor bastards have got to live somewhere, I suppose.'

Harriet had been tracing the delicate turn of Petronella's long paw, and the whippet opened her large fringed eyes and blinked at her. Harriet had missed part of the conversation, so now she asked idly who they were talking about.

'Oh, one of the Labour councillors. A man who wants to build a factory and bring prosperity to Maxmead. At the rate his workers will breed, that'll mean about forty more houses to be built. Then you'll get a Woolworth's and a couple of supermarkets and Maxmead will be finished.'

'Perhaps we *are* finished,' said Gregg. 'Perhaps we're living on borrowed time, in a fool's paradise.'

Magda got up briskly. 'Nonsense,' she said, 'we must fight. You fought once, Gregg. Now it's up to people like Lila and me.'

'Are you leaving Harry out of this feminist vanguard?' asked Gregg. 'After all, it concerns her too.'

'Oh?' Lila pounced on his words. 'In what way? I thought she lived in London. That battle was lost years ago.'

'Harry's living on our land for the time being,' said Magda. 'She's got a caravan in Twelve-Acre field.'

'What? That old bus? The green one?' Lila burst out laughing. 'Well, you'd better watch it, Harry pet, or you might be joined one day by an army of squatters.'

'Come on, Lila. Let's go and do some homework on those plans we've got to consider. The meeting's on Wednesday and I want to talk to you about old Major Drew's field. He wants planning permission for two bungalows there, and it's a bit near our orchard. I don't know whether we can block it … anyway, we'll see. Excuse us, you two?'

'Of course,' said Gregg. Harriet did not move, even to lift her head, until the two of them had gone out of the room. As soon as the door closed she felt Gregg's hand on her shoulder.

'Pure bitch,' he said. 'She has mad light grey eyes, did you notice? My God, Harry, if she were a horse, I certainly wouldn't buy her.'

Harriet was shaking. The fear she had felt in the spinney on her arrival swamped her again. They sat on silently before the roaring logs, in a lighted room, and yet a common fear held them in darkness, and they wondered who would be the first to hear the assassin's footstep upon the stair.

Five

The following morning Harriet found herself afloat in a thick white mist that pressed up against the windows and surrounded her with utter chilly silence. Not afloat so much as submerged. She might have been at the bottom of the sea or hidden high up in a cloud, waiting for the sky to break open beneath her. Once, on a flight, she had looked down as the clouds below the plane broke apart and for a moment thought that the ships on the sea below were more planes, queer ones, new ones, moving without wings in a blue sky.

Her watch had stopped, but then it always did: time never conformed to the erratic beat of her pulse, it raced ahead or lagged behind, putting her out of key with the rest of the tidy world. The small travelling clock had stopped at one o'clock, soon after she had gone to bed. And what dreams she had had! Lila Merrington leading a march of would-be squatters up over the rise of the meadow; Gregg marching along his line of white posts, his hand flicking out, out, out, to touch and release each one.

She opened the door, went outside to taste the day. There was a special quality about the silence that surrounded Uplands. It was quite unlike the silence in the suburbs, which was dead and cringing or dead and poleaxed, depending upon the time of year. Usually the silence here was fresh and alive, and under it moved all the impersonal secret sounds of the slackening year. Not this morning; the mist made her blind and deaf and when she walked full into a spiky hawthorn hedge she pulled back with a cry of alarm, stumbling in the soaking grass.

Panic could only be damped down by ordinary actions, so she made up the fire, set a kettle to boil and fried bacon and egg just to sniff the sanity of it and listen to the hiss. She made herself a neat place at the long counter she had put up, and which could be flapped up or down as she needed it. But today there was only her reflection to watch in the blank windows, so she soon turned away and sat facing the fire, holding her plate on her lap. The cats came and drank their milk, then sat on her feet and talked to each other in their light snarling voices.

They could be anywhere, she and the cats. At any moment a space traveller might float past the window, tapping gently on the milky panes, anchored on some long umbilical cord. Suppose all the winter was like this? No one delivered milk to her, or papers. Was she equipped to live alone? She lacked her mother's strong sense of routine, of the rightness of regular occupations. Might she become like Oblomov, not moving, not washing, not caring? Then Bella got up and cried to be let out, and as Harriet opened the door for her she saw that the hedge was now visible and in the field wavy shapes of mist moved and shifted in the light wind. Her panic subsided and she waited for the cat to come back inside. Both the animals had discovered that in wet weather they could do their business underneath the bus in the dry. Animals were admirable; they adapted to circumstance.

All the same, as she tidied up, she thought about the word anchored. Then unanchored. That had a dangerous sound. Aunt Esther's mind had been unanchored in that last year of her life, she had in a sense been turning, weightless, in some dimension of her own making. No, not of her making, for her mind had slipped into some other dimension, where it went hallooing about dark spaces and only knocked up against reality as Harriet had knocked up against the hedge: with a sense of shock and unfitness. And all the time, Magda had said that mother was not quite herself, and had engaged a companion for her.

There was a knock on the door. A child's knock. And when Harriet opened it, there was the smallest Everett boy at the bottom of the steps. He had on a red knitted cap with a pompom, and hugged a pint can of milk to his chest.

He said nothing, only stared up at her out of round unwavering eyes.

'Is that for me?' Harriet was forced to ask after a long pause. 'Would you like to come in?'

The little boy shook his head. 'Mam said is this enough and how much do you want every day and I mustn't come in.' The words sped out as if he had rehearsed them, as indeed he had, all the way through the spinney.

'Well, thank you very much,' said Harriet. She was always formal with children, they unnerved her. She took the milk from him and went inside for her purse. When she came back he had gone.

Oh God! Was she such a witch?

Moving the milk can inside the meat safe she touched its cold sides with pleasure. It affirmed her solid presence here, in the bus, within the life at Uplands. Once again she was anchored. She must go to see Mrs Everett, thank her, make arrangements, tell her the tale. Once she was officially informed, then the danger of embellishments was substantially reduced. Besides, Harriet owed her this courtesy. If good manners were the outward signs of an inward grace, one day if Harriet wore good manners like the Happy Hypocrite wore his mask of virtue, then like him, the mask would in time become her own face. A free flow of grace: that might be something to cultivate for one's old age. Scrubbs had had it while he was young; with him it had been effortless.

When at last she left the bus, settling the cats by the fire with their food, and wedging the door a crack open in case they wanted to go out, she looked quite different. She had put on a clean pair of slacks, a silk shirt and over this she had slung an old suede jacket Aunt Esther had once given her. It looked expensively casual with the yellow silk scarf. Leather shoulder-bag, pigskin gloves, straw shopping-basket; now she could match the small country town and slide into its background without jarring its conception of itself.

Her mood lifted as she emerged from the spinney and saw the sun rising above the long tawny roof of the barn. Under its medieval tiles and the centuries-old rafters the bales of straw were piled high, and small, brightly coloured bantam hens ran and pecked on the dusty earth. Old bits of harness still hung, covered with cobwebs with strands of hay from some long-forgotten harvest floating in them. A tractor stood to one side of the wide archway that divided the barn into two.

Mrs Everett was at home. She usually was. This time she was peeling potatoes in the kitchen and she saw Harriet through the kitchen window above the sink and gestured to her to come in. The kitchen was very clean, for Mrs Everett did her housework as if in a fury to wipe out daily every trace of her husband's existence.

'I wanted to thank you,' said Harriet. 'Young Jimmy came with the milk just as I'd remembered I hadn't asked you to send any down for me. My clock had stopped.'

'Oh yes,' said Mrs Everett, unsurprised. She pointed to a chair with her sharp kitchen knife. 'I thought it funny you hadn't called, being here three days. Still, I'm not to know how long you're staying. Mrs Witheredge dropped me the word this morning on her way downtown.'

Harriet was determined to be pleasant, and fought her way past the hedge of Mrs Everett's displeasure with a display of frankness.

'I've been trying to settle in, you see. You know that my mother died in the summer, so I thought I'd come here.'

She could see Mrs Everett responding to a bereavement, the helplessness of a daughter – unmarried at that – trying to make a new life. Blood called to blood, after all. It was a degrading performance, but Harriet carried it through. This much at least one had to come to terms with, when people were necessary to one's comfort they had to be placated. If they thought you odd, then you must be odd in a nice way, so that they could feel superior and leave you alone. Everyone needed someone to look down on.

All the time small boys ran in and out of the kitchen, eating buns and being told off automatically by their mother.

'Jimmy, here, Jimmy,' Mrs Everett called out, and when he came she pulled down his jersey and wiped back his hair with her damp hand. Miss Harriet would never have children.

'Why didn't you stay for Miss Harriet's message, eh? Silly boy, she won't eat you.'

The little boy looked sideways at Harriet. You never knew.

'Well, then, Miss, I'll see that the boys deliver you a pint and a half every day. They can drop your papers in at the same time. You'll be going downtown to order them?'

She had not missed the silk scarf, the lipstick. 'But you'll have to hurry or the shops'll be shut for dinner. It's nearly twelve.'

'Well, I must go, Mrs Everett. It's most kind. I'll pay you every week for the milk and give whoever brings it a shilling.'

Jimmy had been standing silently by. He raised his head at this, opened his mouth and said, 'I saw your two cats. They're the same colour as squirrels and you get a shilling a tail for them.'

Harriet was glad that he had at last spoken to her as if she belonged to the human race, but she was startled.

'Don't you go mistaking my cats for grey squirrels. I'll have enough trouble with them when the shooting starts.'

'It's started. There'll be a party over tomorrow,' said Mrs Everett, her blue eyes above the hard red of her cheeks fixed on Harriet. 'Keep 'em in, miss. We have to tie the dog, else there'd be trouble from the Hall.'

This was the merest hint of intimacy and it came oddly from a woman whose very breasts seemed hard. Hands, feet, ankles; all busy and bony. She was a woman to bear sons, Harriet thought, as she said good-bye and started off down to the town.

Six

It was very quiet once she reached the beechwood. Dry under foot and thick with beechmasts and fine mould. The tall grey trunks shone like pewter as the sun touched them and overhead was a greenish gold shade. Soon they would be burning to death, wrapped in their bright shrouds. Few people came here, unless, like Meirion Pritchard, they were on their way up to the farm or to the Hall itself. It was one of those tacit understandings that abound in the country; land half-private, half-public. The only person Harriet had ever met in the wood was a small man who had kept a sweet shop with his mother at the far end of the town. He used to walk two large panting alsatians and last spring he had been sent away because of his melancholia.

The memory of those two big dogs dragging their small, hopeless master scuffling through the leaves made her long for some kind of bustle and nonsense. Plenty of words where words did not matter. So she headed for the Brown Bear.

There were two pubs in Maxmead. The Finishing Post, which Gregg preferred, was large and shabby and stood at the crossroads. It was the haunt of the lads from a racing stable near by and in addition to a dartboard and a bar-billiards table, it had a bar game she had not come across anywhere else. This was called Ringing the Bull. Gregg was very good at it, and he could judge to a nicety how to send the heavy ring clunking home on to the hook. Magda, who found the local people alarming and hated public bars anyway, did not like the Finishing Post. She would clamp her lips over the rim of her glass as if daring any common germ to infect her, or any stable-lad to take a liberty.

Harriet preferred pubbing alone with Gregg. They would stand leaning against the bar, drinking beer or whisky according to the day, the people they drank with, or the state of their finances. Magda didn't much like letting them go off alone. She had begun to watch Gregg's drinking habits over the last few years and had dropped a discreet hint to Harriet about it.

'He's drinking too much. He's got into the habit of going farther afield. Perhaps it's just as well. We're too well known in Maxmead.' Twice Gregg had been brought home from a village five miles off. Someone had found him asleep over the wheel of his car and had telephoned to Magda.

Harriet went up the worn stone steps of the Brown Bear, thinking about Gregg. She knew why he didn't like the place. The men who drank there were made uneasy by him. To them it seemed a slight that, even if he drank with them, he drank as if he needed to. After all, one didn't admit to needing a drink any more than one admitted to needing a job, or a woman, or money. One drank because it was the civilized thing to do, because conversation flowed more easily; it was the custom. But necessity, no. So the men drew away from Gregg, as their women tended to draw away from Magda. She had too much money. Her mother was Jewish – well, wasn't she? Not that one minded, but … and her father was a jolly *parvenu* and had made money out of the war. Yes, Magda had a great deal to live down in Maxmead. But she would live it down, this Harriet was sure of.

Harriet ordered a pint from the barrel, because to her that was the only good thing about this pub. Beer from the wood. The fake atmosphere of hunting horns and mounted foxes' heads and beeswaxed beams made her uneasy. The bar was solid oak, beautiful, there was a reddish Turkey carpet on the floor and the air was thick with smoke and voices. Voices? It was pretty crowded for a weekday, she realized, and then she looked more closely. It was full of weekend people. Good God, she had so lost count of the time that she had not realized that this was Saturday. She must have missed the market, walked past it in a dream.

Food. She would have to buy something for the weekend. She lit a cigarette carefully, considering. The match flared near her hair and a weekend, whiskery face eyed her with approval as the voice said jovially, 'Watch it!'

Turning away, Harriet found herself thinking that it was a bit of luck that she had put on some decent clothes; it must have been some kind of atavism taking over, the weekend habit. She was a fool, though. She should have brought the car and taken back quantities of provisions. The cats would want rabbit.

As she drank she listened to the talk. Women with weekend hair-dos and hopeful cashmere and tweed get-ups nibbled at squares of cheese and sipped gin with watchful eyes and amused expressions. Their men, carefully sporty with cravats and moustaches, were already full of drink, bubbling over with that jocular lechery which passed for humour among this middle-aged would-be squirearchy. By Sunday evening, their wives or girl-friends would have given the same small laughs a dozen times over as the stories were passed like currency from pub to pub. Then the painted cottages would be shut up and the long crawl home begin.

'I see you've got yourself organized,' said somebody's voice in her ear, and it was so much an echo of what she had been thinking earlier that she swung around quickly, spilling her beer over a pair of green Hush-Puppies.

Meirion Pritchard's small wedge of a face was hard up against a hairy tweed jacket. He was fighting to get to the bar.

'I'm here. What are you drinking?' Harriet asked him. He waved a pint tankard. 'Draught,' he said. 'Thanks.'

She bought the drink, handed it to him and edged her way out of the confusion of arms and faces.

'Let's get over by the window, it's getting rough,' said Meirion. They sat on the low sill next to the coloured panes of leaded glass and Harriet saw that his face was broken up into reflected colours where the sun shone through.

'That gives you a harlequin-saint's face,' she said. 'I wonder people don't paint their faces different colours. It would be bizarre.'

He had not heard her through the din, so he had to shout.

'So this is the pub you patronize?'

'On and off. There isn't much choice unless you go farther out. The Finishing Post is better on weekdays. How d'you make out at Ringing the Bull?'

'I don't. What on earth is it?'

So he wasn't one of Gregg's cronies. She would have been surprised if he had been. Waving the question aside, she said, speaking into his ear, 'I hear that your spinach soufflé was spoiled that evening. All my fault. So sorry.'

Meirion looked at her, distrusting the meek tone. But she made him feel good for some reason. He felt quite doggish, sitting in this pub with an attractive woman. She didn't seem at all odd today; perhaps her surroundings had civilized her.

'I don't really like spinach soufflé. Can't think why Magda insists it's a favourite of mine. Luckily she grilled us some steak. It was the girl's evening off.'

'Oh God, that reminds me! The shops shut at one. I must get in some meat for the weekend. Look, I'm sorry—'

'Have lunch with me,' said Meirion, inspired. It wouldn't do him any harm to be seen lunching with Magda's cousin. Quite the reverse. 'Come on. The shops will be open again at two. It'll be a change for both of us, living alone. We'll eat in the grill-room here.'

'It's hideously expensive and rather pretentious. There's a café down the road.'

'Look,' said Meirion, 'you don't know me well enough to discuss the price of a meal. Will you eat here with me or not? I'm going to.'

At least the suede jacket deserved a session in the grill-room. Harriet accepted on this ground.

It was a good meal. She hadn't eaten there for years. She and her mother usually went to the Tudor café down the road, where the woodworm had been the only well-nourished visitors. The meat there was pale and parched and the potatoes were like white rugby balls. Harriet's mother had been sorry for the waitress, whose terrible bunions throbbed their way through her snipped-open corduroy slippers.

'That was a very decent steak,' said Harriet. 'I'm not much of a cook myself.'

Now she looked like a big, comforting happy woman, thought Meirion. Like Ceres, goddess of the corn. Following his thoughts of her planting and giving abundance, he said, on impulse:

'And how's your garden? I've often looked at it as I passed. Everything seems to race up out of the ground. You must have green fingers.'

'Oh, I don't know,' said Harriet. 'I certainly like to make the earth say beans instead of grass, like Thoreau. But don't take me literally, I make it say *Coboea scandens* – they're marvellous now. Great purple trumpets climbing over the back end of the bus. Have you seen them? And the nasturtiums—' She broke off. Gardeners could be so boring.

'I know Thoreau,' said Meirion. '"Making the yellow soil express its summer thought in bean leaves and blossoms rather than in wormwood and—" I've forgotten how it goes on, but you could say nettles and ground elder. Still, I imagine that your field is somewhat different from Walden pond.'

'I've never tried absolute solitude. So I suppose I'm cheating, in a way. But I only grow very ordinary things, you know.'

Behind them two people had paused, and Harriet sensed their presence. Looking across at Meirion, she saw that he had half risen to his feet. Turning, she saw that Lila Merrington was dipping her long nose down at her with an amused expression.

'Hulloo, you two,' she said, making the words rhyme in a kind of infantile croon. 'I just happened to be passing, as they say. Do let me introduce my friend the Warden. Bertie sweet, this is Harriet, Magda's cousin. And this is Meirion Pritchard, editor of our local rag, *The Curfew*.'

The Warden (of where they were never told) dropped his lower lip and widened his pale eyes. Obviously he had eaten well, for one large smooth hand caressed his large stomach, covered by an expanse of immaculate turquoise blue sweater. Two chins dropped blandly upon its turtle neck.

'Charmed. Oh yes, charmed,' he said with a groaning splutter. 'May *The Curfew* never be tolled, eh? Must be off, must be off. Cronos calls. The husband of you know who—' And placing his hand flat against Lila's prominent shoulder-blades he pushed rather than led her away.

'Talking of husbands,' said Meirion, sinking into his chair and beckoning the waiter. 'Why is it that one never sees Lila's?'

'Isn't he some kind of don?'

'Let's have some brandy. Lila has that effect on me. His name's Peregrine, by the way.'

'Who? The Warden's? She didn't really introduce him at all.'

'No, her husband's. She just wanted to make an impact. Her mind is a maze of complicated manoeuvres. All we know is that he is a warden, and that to her he is Bertie sweet. Whereas he knows all about us—'

'He didn't want to, though.'

'No. That was the point.' Meirion's very dark eyes snapped with laughter. 'Peregrine,' he went on, his hands clasping the brandy glass prayerfully, 'lives, I believe, in Cambridge. But he's not important enough to make it worth Lila's while to join him. So she lives here in Maxmead in a done-up cottage with over-wrought iron gates and highly unsuitable Spanish arches and tries to run the local Council. This Council business is why she's cottoned on to Magda. She likes power, you see, and if she can't get it through sex – although she doesn't do badly there (have you noticed how many thin women have nymphomaniac tendencies?) she's not above using her social contacts.'

Harriet laughed suddenly. 'Now I know I'm in the country,' she said. 'It crawls with intrigue. Tell me about this threat of building around Maxmead. Lila said something last night that bothered me.'

Meirion looked up sharply.

'There's a meeting of the Housing Committee on Wednesday,' he said. 'I understand that there's a certain amount of pressure at Ministry level to expand Maxmead – oh, not to new-town proportions,' he added quickly, seeing the look on her face. 'But they want to find a couple of hundred acres for light engineering and houses, and to do that they'll have to take a certain amount of farmland.'

'I suppose older farmers with twenty or so acres would be quite pleased. Building land fetches an enormous amount of money. My father made quite a bit out of some allotments he bought before the war. It's ironic, in a way.'

She looked into her empty brandy glass and added abruptly, feeling threatened by the very aura of good living and the smell of good food in this grill-room, 'Gregg's right. It's as good as finished around here.'

Meirion looked at her kindly. Her very rawness made him feel protective. 'My dear girl, it will take years at the rate this place takes to make up its mind. And it won't affect you, so don't worry.'

'I know it's selfish to want to hang on to things. All the same—'

'Can you see Magda selling any of her land? I can't.'

'I wonder,' said Harriet almost to herself, 'I wonder if she'd sell the field to me?'

Meirion leaned back and beckoned to the waiter. He laughed.

'Not unless you put her under a spell or make her a very good offer indeed. Have you any idea how much land with planning permission can fetch around here?' He did not wait for her to shake her head, and went on with relish, 'Between two and three thousand pounds an acre. Imagine that. Wouldn't you be tempted?'

'I can see that you would. I must go, Meirion, thank you for the lunch.'

As they reached the street she touched his arm.

'Don't say a word about the field to Magda, please. I must speak to Gregg first.'

Annoyed that she should grab back the first confidence that she had made him, he gave a curiously derisive laugh. She was enraged. The fear that gave her common ground with Gregg and their combined helplessness, and Meirion's knowledge of it, made her flush with anger. Heaving the strap of her bag across her shoulder she said bitingly, 'You can discount Gregg. I know people do. But, believe me, Magda would be lost without him. So don't be so – so cheap.'

Would Magda be lost without him? In the past, maybe, but not now. As she strode away down the High Street she felt ridiculous.

Seven

'Listen to the phrasing,' said Gregg, educating her.

They sat in his small study that led off from the billiards room. Magda elevated it to 'study', Gregg merely called it his room. He had the essentials there: a fire, complicated hi-fi equipment, a tape-recorder, a desk, bookshelves full of leather-bound unread books which gave a soft brown background, comfortable chairs, a drinks cupboard, a pipe-rack (supplied by Magda, who thought all men should smoke pipes in their 'dens') several well-placed lamps, several dogs, and Harriet.

Earlier on he had said, 'I imagine you've been briefed to keep my mind occupied. Don't bother, I'm fully prepared this time.'

'Pity,' said Harriet. She was on the floor by the fire with Petronella's long pointed face in her lap. She reached into her pocket for a handful of cuttings. 'I've picked out some headlines to read to you, to show you how mad the world is.

'For instance?'

'Well,' she said, 'how d'you like this. "HAT A MUST FOR BALD EMIGRANTS." They're bothered about the sun causing skin cancer. That's in Australia. And there's this one: "THE NAKED OR THE DEAD." That's in the Sudan. The soldiers are ordered to shoot anyone wearing clothes in case they're concealing weapons. And in New York there's a pretty story of the King Kleagle – he's a Klan chief – being exposed as a Jew. He shot himself. He wanted to make the world safe for blond, blue-eyed babies.'

'For God's sake,' said Gregg. 'Let's play some music'

But instead of putting on a record, Harriet saw him go over to a box full of labelled tapes, feel over them, and draw one out. He was still practising being blind, and it was too much.

'Only one thing more,' she said. 'Psychologists say that they can transplant memory from one brain to another. They've tried it with rats.'

'Ah,' said Gregg, 'now that might be interesting. Because no two people remember the same thing in the same way. I'm playing you Billie Holliday because there's no one better. Pretend you've never heard all that treacle and mush and rubbish you were brought up on. And listen to the phrasing,' he said. 'Listen to how she says "weather".'

Harriet watched him sink back out of the light, his eyes closed. Her mind was too busy with him to do as she was told, although her ear caught wincingly at a few discords. She opened her mouth to speak as soon as the last disturbing notes stopped, left the room empty.

'If it's glaucoma,' said Harriet, 'they can operate.'

'Christ!' Gregg exploded on to his feet. 'Can't you *listen?* The world is full of talk and twaddle. You're like Magda – you'd put on a pious face for Beethoven or Mozart but it would still sail clean over your heads.'

'Lenin was afraid of Beethoven,' said Harriet with maddening smugness. 'He couldn't bear to listen to music very often. He said that it made him want to say nice things, be kind, stroke the heads of people who created such beauty while living in a vile hell. You might get your hand bitten off, he said. So you must hit out without mercy.'

'People who can't listen to music cut down trees,' said Gregg, busy with his tape-recorder. 'Trees get in their way and worry them. Music frightens them, too. It's too scouring. There's no defence against either, if you come to think of it. Yes, I can see. Busy with a revolution, creating a new kind of hell, Lenin would find Beethoven frightening.'

The evening was going badly. Gregg was restless, he had had a bad day. The pressure on his eyes had set up a throbbing headache, and he filled their glasses again, with a kind of desperation. What were they talking about? he wondered. It was no good, all this talk. A man had to come to terms with his life.

Since his eyes had started playing him up Gregg had sat in this room by himself for hours at a time. Magda used to say that for a quiet man he surrounded himself with a great deal of noise. It gave him pleasure to record some of the great symphonies which seemed to him to state everything about life, in blessedly non-human terms. But what he liked best was to look through the records he had collected over the years, 78's and some EP's and LP's, and tape his favourites. Men who played their chosen instrument to perfection: Johnny Hodges or Pablo Casals, Sidney Bechet or Moiseiwitsch. Catholicity stretched to unselectiveness, some would say, but he didn't care. After all, it was for his private enjoyment. Every man had a secret period with which he could perfectly tune in, and for Gregg, as for so many of his generation lapped up later by the war and its aftermath, this was the thirties. It was then that he had discovered Bessie Smith and Billie Holliday and Jimmy Rushing, Teddy Wilson and Count Basie and Ellington, and he stuck to them like a don to his classics.

What disturbed him even more than the possible loss of his sight was that strange feeling of life running down. Sometimes he thought back to the time, just after the war, when he had entered with enthusiasm into old Bertie Harrington's firm. That was a laugh anyhow, making plastics and artificial smells to go with them, so that an indestructible rose smelt like a real one – so long as you remembered to spray on your aerosol stink. Even bees homed to Instant Summer. Yes, he'd enjoyed that advertising jag, for in the old days he had had some talent for the quick and lively line; his caricatures in prison camp had done a lot for him – and for the men dying by inches around him. Sometimes he hauled them out, these drawings, to revive those unbelievable days, months, years. Drawings on that thick yellow lavatory paper nicked from the Japs. On the end-pages of the books the men possessed between them. Lamb's *Tales From Shakespeare, No Orchids For Miss Blandish* – he couldn't remember any more.

But he had lost interest after his marriage. Even the move to Uplands had disappointed him. The shade of the old trees, the sun rising over the meadows, a green view: somehow he had expected that such a life would mean a renewal of his belief. He had expected to feel young and fresh and invigorated again. But life wasn't like that. Instead, he had become conscious of decay, and the mushrooming growth that battened on to it. He felt beleaguered even in the woods, and the thud of an axe, the buzz of lorries on the road beyond, the red factories and housing estates blown like spores in the countryside around, underlined for him the random nuisances of the new rural condition.

He truly felt, as he had said the other evening, that they were living in a fool's paradise, that their time – or did he mean *his* time? – was going, going and would soon be gone.

Now he looked with compunction at Harriet, who had come here looking for something she had never had; but did she know what she was looking for? What was she saying now, trying to keep her temper, trying to play fair with an irritable bastard who drank too much and who was no damn good to anyone?

'I know Benny Goodman and Duke Ellington played at Carnegie Hall, but I still can't like jazz. It's just a lot of noise to me.'

Gregg, at that moment, loved her. The spiky honesty that so annoyed other people, being unfeminine, was right for his mood. So although he did not care what she felt about jazz, he wiped a hand over his throbbing eyes and started to talk.

'Look, Harry, it's the living moment they're concerned with. They're singing about being broke and pickled with drink and high with drugs and betrayed and in love. Never mind if it's all a noise to you. They're alive and they're not respectable. They bash it out ...' He walked restlessly over to a cupboard and opened a door. Here were his drawings of prison camp days; oddly enough, he had never shown them to anyone. 'It's not like a five-piece band under the palms of a Grand Hotel, playing Limehouse Blues with a piano, three violins and a 'cello.' There they were, the drawings, in that old black folder, with Second Violin written on it: he'd filched it from a drunken musician in the old days. He and Scrubbs had always been knocking things off; to pinch an ashtray from a pub meant that you somehow got even. 'You've got to let go. Open up. Then it sorts itself out and it's not a noise.'

'What are you trying to say? You're implying something! You're making fun of me.'

He had the folder now. Hell, why didn't he learn? You couldn't talk about jazz, it was like measuring other people's heartbeats. Like putting a welfare worker on to Billie Holliday, allowing the Salvation Army into Basin Street. Too true the devil had all the best tunes.

'Darling Harry, let it drop. I've got something to show you.'

Unplaced, Harriet said sulkily, 'Scrubbs was mad about Sophie Tucker. He took me to the Palladium once to see her.' And she saw her again, immense, glittering up there on the stage, ageless, sentimental and greedy, glad as a child to be greeted by that terrific Palladium yell.

'There you are, then. She wasn't one of the greats. But couldn't you get from her a bit of what jazz is about? She reached out for sex like a child for a jampot. Sex and love and yum-yum-yummy Red Hot Momma smother. Climb back in the womb, baby, 'cos after I'm gone you're gonna miss your red hot momma—'

He sang the words with abandon. Was he drunk or ill?

'I can't quite see what I'm handing you, unless I hold it far away,' said Gregg in a quite different, a flat voice. Merely handling this thick yellow bumph gave him a shiver of apprehension. 'Here. You'll see the name and date on each one.'

Thin, prominent ears, scruffy bandage round one of them: a sane Van Gogh. Even without this clue Harriet would have recognized him. Half an ear shot away at Singapore, lucky it missed his jawbone. Scrubbs Malone in 1942.

'I still had a couple of 2Bs left, that's why it's so black.'

As she still said nothing, merely held the drawing, staring at it, he went on, 'That's how Scrubbs looked when he arrived at Chungkai. They'd come upriver by sampan from Kanchanburi, but they'd walked from Bahn Pong to there. That's the longest twenty miles in the world. God, he looked awful, as if he'd been a prisoner for months. Filthy dirty, and he stank of river mud and fish offal. Careless about his uniform, we had to pull him up about that. Still, he never got any scruffier. Smartened up quite a bit when his ear healed.'

Harriet said thinly, 'You've caught his smile. But his head's bristly.'

'They shaved off all his hair in hospital at Singapore before the Japs got there.'

'Of course,' said Harriet. 'And when the Japs came down the wards they told all the walking wounded to go outside and turn to the right. Scrubbs, being Irish, of course turned left.' She laughed. 'I remember him telling me, and how he belted off when he heard the shots. He said that taught him not to trust his fellow-men.' Her finger rubbed gently over the unfamiliar bristly head. His hair had been long and fine and fair.

'He was a mad devil all right. Liked to needle the Japs. You heard about Tarzan of the Apes?'

Harriet nodded. 'But you can tell me again. Wait – who are these others?'

A group of three, drawn as the wise monkeys. One with a hand missing.

'That's Jocko. He nearly fell up against a Jap officer and put out a hand to save himself. Touched the bastard's sleeve by mistake and that was that. Whipped out his sword and there was Jocko's hand lying in the dust. To teach him respect.'

As she went through the pile, seeing the winks, the obscene gestures, the grins stitched on these gaunt faces, it seemed as if she had never before noticed how many bones the human frame needed to support itself. But in spite of tatters and crutches each drawing had its particular bravado.

'Most of them are dead,' said Gregg, watching her face. 'One or two are at Roehampton. Some may even be successful businessmen like me. Why don't you stop me, Harry? You've heard all this before. You're letting me wallow.'

'We're both wallowing. Tell me about Tarzan and we'll finish for tonight.'

'Well, all their top brass came. We used to put on some good shows, kept us going. Scrubbs, the idiot, was swinging about in the trees we'd set up on the stage, scratching himself and bellowing some nonsense about being a huge hairy old ape. Then the Japs cottoned on that he was taking them off. He'd hit off their voices exactly, you see. High-pitched, hysterical, they were. They stopped the show. Marched out, then sent the guards back in to burn the scenery and get the main actors. They were beaten up with rattan canes, usual thing.'

'He always went as far as he could with everything,' said Harriet. 'When he lived with us before the war he nearly drove mother mad. She even threatened to throw him out, but he always got round her in the end. I remember once—'

She could not go on. Scrubbs beaten with rattan canes. Small men, impassive, hissing with exertion (did they hiss when they beat a man?) obsessed with their own code of honourable conduct; beating out the devil of the white man's wrong thinking.

'Yes,' said Gregg, as if he enjoyed the memory. 'Food and water cut for twenty-four hours, to purify our thinking. What a lot of cock the apologists talk about the oriental soul. And yet there was this common bond – I don't know. You knew what to expect, you knew they were unpredictable, so you were always on your toes; it stopped us sinking into a hopeless stupor.' He took the drawings from her.

'Scrubbs used to say that the beatings were one of the things a public school education prepared you for.'

'He pushed his luck because he didn't believe in it,' said Harriet. All at once she felt bitterly tired. She wanted to be alone, away from Gregg. She couldn't after all share these self-indulgent forays into the past. She got up, saying it was late, she'd go before Magda got back. He did not move, only said:

'I've got a spare tape. Wouldn't you like to know how you sound?'

So, to please him, she said yes, although she didn't really care. His tape-recorder obviously intrigued him; perhaps now it was his only pleasure.

'Let's play a sort of game, then,' she said, sitting down again on the floor and hugging her knees. 'I'll start off by asking you questions.'

Trust a woman to pick a game like that.

'Fine,' said Gregg. 'Right, let's go.'

'What is your most nostalgic sound?'

He was surprisingly quick.

'Cooee. On a misty autumn evening.'

'Saddest?'

'Wait for me.'

'Happiest?'

'I always sheer off that word. Oh – I don't know. Yes. A train's whistle coming into the valley.'

Harriet was intrigued. She asked why, although this was against the rules.

'My cousin was coming from school to stay with us. I was twelve years old and I loved her.'

Without comment Harriet said that she was going on to smells.

Gregg began to laugh.

'Smells? D'you mean, what smells come to mind?'

Harriet nodded, then remembered that on tape a nod would mean a gap. She said yes.

'Let's go for something real, then. Discount the smells that keep this house going. Antiseptic, that's it. The smell of antiseptic.'

'Go on, marry it to mood.'

Gregg put his feet over the arm of his chair, visibly relaxing for the first time that evening.

'Sense of importance. Happiness. Pain. Guess the scene, go on.'

'Small boy with cut knee. Being brave in the scullery under mama's approving eye?'

'Half right. Being brave in a casualty department under the eye of a small girl who had stabbed small boy.'

'Ah ha!' sang out Harriet triumphantly. 'This couldn't tie in with the girl on the train? Happiness and antiseptic go together, do they?'

'You're trying to cheat,' said Gregg. 'No, you *are* cheating. I'm not giving you my childhood in gobbets. Anyway, you're not interested. You're only interested in Scrubbs.'

'Hush, you'll spoil the tape. All right, ask me something then.'

'Have some more whisky and a cigarette while I think.'

That would mean a minute's indecipherable background noise.

'Let's get off smells and on to the weather. That's always evocative. Nostalgic weather?'

'Oh, cold, cold, cold, with frozen fingers!' cried Harriet.

'Dicta?'

'Dicta?'

'Yes, wise saws. You're not as clever as I thought, that's a comfort. Come on. Dicta.'

'My childhood was littered with clichés. Don't go out until the streets have warmed up. Then my mother used to say an odd thing. She told my father that he was like a fiddler who hung up his fiddle outside his own door. I understood that as I grew older.'

'You're qualifying too much. What's the first thing you remember?'

'Having my mother do up my white kid boots. She kept the buttonhook in the second drawer of the sideboard with the odd bits of silver. I was two. How about you?'

'Throwing a spoonful of rice pudding at the cat who ate it. Then getting a big smile from my nurse as she thought I'd finished it without a fuss. First lesson in placating women.'

'Instead of a slap a smile. Life isn't that simple.'

'It is, you know. And childhood's okay if you only take a brief look back. God knows you're acting it out all over again every second of your adult life.'

'All right,' said Harriet. 'That's enough. Switch off.'

He went over to the tape-recorder, ran the spools back. Then after a moment, their voices started again.

'What is your most nostalgic sound?'

'Cooee, on a misty autumn evening.'

'Saddest?'

'Wait for me.'

They listened to the rest in silence, then Gregg said, switching off,

'Your voice sounds deeper. So positive.'

'You sound like a stranger, a countryman. There's a burr one doesn't notice ordinarily. Zummerzet.'

'I was born there. You never asked me. Harry, if Scrubbs had lived you'd have got over him. Married someone else.'

'He never knew me as a woman, as myself. Only as a sort of adoring kid sister, climbing roofs with him and covering his tracks.'

'That cousin on the train, the one who stabbed me, was the one Scrubbs wanted to marry. You know, on the rebound from Magda. It was she he'd motored down to see that last time.'

Maybe he wanted to hurt her, really hurt her. There in the past were two women Scrubbs had loved and who had not loved him. How could she have forgotten? Of course it was Gregg's cousin. That bitch.

'Why did she stab you?'

'You only want to know because of Scrubbs. You didn't ask before. I was in the bath and she'd been reading about Marat. Charlotte Corday, wasn't it? Didn't she stab him? She was only acting it out. She was like that.'

Harriet stared at him. The girl sounded mad if not downright sadistic.

'So what did she tell him, that last time?'

'Oh, Harry, what does it matter? She told him she'd think it over.'

In a small, troubled voice Harriet said, 'But that's just what Magda said that first time, when he was twenty. Before the war. When he came back on one leave, she was engaged to somebody else. Twice is too much, Gregg, with a war between. I think he drove straight for that tree.'

Gregg stood up, very tall, taller than the standard lamp he snapped out. He was about to say something, but he changed his mind.

'Let me walk you down,' he said. 'It's a beautiful night. Moon's up. I can see the stars perfectly. It's because they're such a long way off.'

�֎

The clarity of the moonlight outside was alarming after the firelit room. They paced down the drive with the dogs, the lake lying off to their left, flat and glittering as tin. This light soaked up colour, sharpened the call of the owls. Trees stood about them, black with black shadows. The two figures were swamped and dwarfed by the pouring white. The dogs were multiplied by their shadows, so that it seemed as if a pack moved out of the gates and into the lane.

The only thing that could not wither in this abstract world of black and white was the truth, and although Gregg had once made a promise he intended to break it now.

Harriet gave him the opening, unaware. She asked about his last spell of blindness, out of compunction for her disinterest earlier on.

'I didn't get myself through it,' he said, 'I was scared stiff. There'd been rumours that the war might be ending, but I knew that if it didn't end fast I'd be stuck for the rest of my life, tapping along with a stick. Jocko got me all the fruit he could – banana fritters. Can't touch 'em now. If you're after nostalgic smells, there's another for you. Scrubbs thought that fruit could cure me; papayas and pomeloes, he got the Malays to smuggle them in and paid them in cigarettes.' He stumbled over a root and Harriet put out a hand. He thrust it away. 'I'm all right. I've done this walk with my eyes shut a hundred times. Night doesn't bother me.'

'Will you come in and have some coffee?' asked Harriet, as they came out of the spinney.

'No, let's walk.'

They turned and walked across the unploughed part of the field in front of Harriet's bus. Beyond was a long strip of old apple orchard. He leant up against the sagging five-bar gate, watching the lights of Maxmead away below. They were like the riding lights of boats in a harbour.

'Scrubbs talked to me a lot. He found a hell of a lot to say to stop me going out of my mind and I didn't know whether to believe him or not. I thought he was boasting.'

'What on earth did he tell you?'

'Oh, we had a lot of time to talk. Women and sex and getting on buses and eating Sunday dinner belonged to a world we'd temporarily mislaid. We used to plan evenings in detail. Like meeting a girl at Victoria station, what we'd say, where we'd go for dinner, which theatre, hailing a cab, surreptitiously counting our money to see if it would cover a night club afterwards. And would she or wouldn't she.'

'When he was twenty-one Alec gave him a pewter mug with an absurd verse on it. I bet he quoted it at this point.'

'What? Oh you mean the one that starts "Here's to the girls who do and here's to the girls who don't. ..." I forget how it goes on.' And suddenly Gregg knew that he couldn't say what he had intended. Why, like the psychologists Harriet had told him about earlier, should he transplant this particular memory from one brain to another? They were not experimental rats. Not merely out of loyalty to a friend who might or might not have killed himself but because all of a sudden it seemed wildly irrelevant, at this distance. Unnecessary too to lay a further burden on this awkward unpredictable woman, whose adolescence still showed like a petticoat. A woman whom he oddly enough at the right moment wanted badly to go to bed with. That moment was not now, not while she pitied him.

'I must get back,' he said. 'Magda will be home. And you need some sleep after an evening with a jittery old man.'

'You're exactly ten years older than I am.'

He kissed her worried face, lifted his own, aware that his headache had gone, and that the pressure on his eyeballs had lessened. A faint hope stirred in him, then sank away. As he walked home he was filled with the dread that he might be cured and then he'd really have to do something about himself.

Eight

❈

On Monday Harriet drove into Cambridge. She started off early and got back before dark. It had started to rain, a fine pricking fusillade that had already made the lane through the spinney soft and mushy. Before the gate of the bus, imprinted in the mud, were pawmarks.

She was instantly alarmed, vulnerable as a solitary explorer who on opening the flap of his tent at dawn finds pugmarks of a prowling lion encompassing his tent. On the flower-beds, which she had attempted to tidy up on Sunday, there were more. Pawmarks on the path all around: suppose they came back in the night, stealthily prowling? The tough claws of the dachshunds would click on the paving stones by the step with the same hard drubbing as a thrush's beak busy disembowelling a snail.

Magda.

She had been here: yes, there was a Wellington boot mark, a criss-cross on the floor of the kitchen. Harriet had been invaded in her absence, and had she been in she could only have crouched behind the curtain in the cabin. There was no escape route from the bus: this was disturbing.

The two cats sat in the deep chair by the fire, their paws tucked in, their heads up. Bella yawned, stretched out a paw, jumped down with a cry of welcome. Or complaint. Harriet stood stroking the small batface, tracing the tremor of a purr in the little cat's throat.

The fire had been made up, and recently. Perhaps there was a note. It was on the long counter table, weighted down by a blue mug.

'Do come up to the house tonight. One or two things I'd like to talk over. M.'

Harriet's stomach tightened with guilt for sins she had not yet committed. Ah, to hell with Magda, there were better things to do this evening.

After she had fed the cats and cut herself a huge wedge of fresh white bread, buttered it and covered it thickly with cream cheese and chopped chives, she settled down to drink her tea and read the book of instructions. This book she took from the cardboard box which held the prize for which she had travelled into Cambridge.

It was a tape-recorder, and it had taken her half the day to find one that ran on batteries. Oddly enough, it had cost her about half the amount for which she had sold her mother's rosewood dressing-table and this fact gave her an almost immoral sense of satisfaction. If you thought around these things long enough, there was absolutely no unjustified expenditure.

It took her a little time to digest the instructions and assemble the spools. Then, with a curious feeling of trepidation she began to talk aloud. Her voice was stitched with self-consciousness and was at first draggingly solemn. Later on, it came in high, breathless rushes.

❋

'I'm going to talk about Scrubbs at last, because … well, I want to. I must. And if anything happens to me these tapes are for you, Gregg. You can add them to your collection for entertainment in between the jazz.

'It isn't any use, you see, to sell up furniture and a house and bury the dead, because none of us really ever lets go. Letting go is the hardest thing of all. Really letting go. We hug things, spikes and all, to our bare bloody breasts and wonder why we can't walk upright and be happy. But this isn't about me. I don't want it to be. I suppose we'll all come into it: Scrubbs and Magda and mother and Alec and Aunt Esther and Uncle Bertie. Who'd have thought that one day it'd be me telling it, sitting in a battered old bus by a spinney, the night coming and winter coming and God knows what stretching ahead?

'That's an owl hooting now. Funny how its notes float like thistle-seed on the air. And the dark is a tide over the field and beyond it the town's riding at anchor. Scrubbs said once that he'd like to swamp the town so that we could have a complete illusion of the sea down there. That was a long time ago, before the bus was put here like a retired old war-horse. Just after they'd bought Uplands.

'He didn't come here all that often, he was too dead keen to get into the war. That was the only time I hated him when he said he hoped I'd get out of my pacifist stage, as he called it. The time for him to have fought, I told him, was in Spain. That was the real tragedy of Europe, the beginning of it all. What, with all those pansy poets? No thanks, he'd said. After all, Scrubbs wasn't anything more than an ordinary, decent Englishman – sorry, half-Englishman. I mustn't forget that his father was Irish. I know this, so why does he burn a hole in everything I remember? The kind of young man who makes your hackles rise if you're sensitive and whose breath blasts any emotion that rises more than a yard from the ground.

'I was honest in those days and I didn't mind saying that under every English club tie beats a hard Fascist heart. Be my brother or I'll have you black-balled from every worthwhile club and job in our shrinking empire. Old boy.

'That was why he thought me such a joke.

'Read Housman, he told me. Panacea for a fifteen-year-old with sentimental ideas about the brotherhood of man. I never did, of course. I stuck to Gorki, and joined the Left Book Club.'

※

Bella jumped up with a small questioning cry. She couldn't understand why Harriet sat there talking to herself. She stretched out a paw to touch the spinning spools and darted it away again, then came arching and quivering along the table, drawing her back under Harriet's chin and flicking up her tail sharply. She hated to be disregarded.

Harriet stopped the tape. She supposed that it was only half through, although she had only been speaking for – how long? – three, four minutes? Should she wipe it off, or leave it?

She sat looking at the cat in her lap, stroking its creamy belly, envying its uncomplicated life. No tangles there. A cat's life was like a smooth skein of silk, threads could be drawn easily from it one at a time. A time for claws to be out and a time for them to be in. A time to fast and a time to feast. Bella's as yet un-named daughter had not inherited her mother's patrician looks. Harriet had mistakenly mated Bella with a blue-point, and the kitten (the only one unsold from a litter of five) had her father's pale blue eyes and a lighter mask. She was also of a heavier build. Bella's eyes were as violet as any women's magazine heroine. She was almost depraved in her beauty at certain times. Very Egyptian. Hadn't there been an astronomer, Lalande, who wanted to call a constellation after a cat? After all, he argued, you had the bear and the bull and the goat and a dozen lesser animals. Why not a cat to stretch out in outer space to play havoc with the milky way?

'Do you know that you are the eye of Ra and Shetat?' Harriet asked, as the kitten came purposefully across the floor towards her. It was time she was named. A name was a charm against the unknown. She would call her Shetat, which the ignorant would think was a whimsical version of Shecat. On impulse she switched on the tape, and said solemnly, her hand on the little cat's head, as it clawed its way up her leg,

'I hereby name you Shetat because you are the Eye of Ra and Shetat and the personification of the power of the sun and the moon and a conqueror of the powers of darkness. And did you know that you are mentioned in the Book of the Dead? One of your kin waited by the Persea tree in Heliopolis on the night that the enemies of Osiris were destroyed, and then you bit off the head of the serpent of darkness.'

Which was more than any of us managed to do, thought Harriet as she switched off. The newly named Shetat gave a pink yawn and leapt straight on to Harriet's lap, disturbing her mother, who had slept throughout the ceremony.

Harriet sat very still, becoming aware of the small sounds that filled this hermit shell of hers. The deep rumble of the cats' purring, the scarcely breathing kettle, a moth beating around the lamp. The owl outside had flown farther off and the fields crept with darkness. It ran beside the hedges, hid in hollows, liquid as clouds in the living sky.

'I'm a cricket,' she thought. 'A cricket's home is for itself alone. A place where it can be warm, snug and safe, and it will fight fiercely if other insects enter by mistake. It is not a home where the young grow up, like the bee's hive, and it is not a trap for insects like the spider's web.'

All these were facts which she had once learned off by heart. Facts suited Harriet. 'Grasshoppers,' she said, getting up to make a large pot of coffee, 'grasshoppers sing when it is warm and sunny and on cold dull days they are silent.'

She shifted the cats on to their own chair by the fire. She didn't care about Magda's note. As she waited for the kettle to boil she put the bar across the door, a thing she had not done for years. The last time was when there were rumours of a roving tramp. She pulled the curtains, lowered the lamp, twitched the long curtains between kitchen and main room together, collected her coffee and sat down once again at the long counter. She wanted to be left alone like a cricket, in a cricket's selfish house. Or a hermit crab in a shell of her own choosing. She wanted no one to knock on her shell, for this evening she had ceased to feel human. This evening she wanted to explore the past in her own way, give it a vocal, an easily destroyable shape. The past was surely expendable, it had to be. In that way only could it be controlled. Coffee, cigarettes were by her hand. Switching on the tape, she closed her eyes, sat back and began to talk.

Nine

❧

Track One

'Scrubbs wasn't his proper name, of course. He was given that at school and it fitted him like his freckled skin. He had a lopsided mouth. Thin, untidy, tall. Blue eyes and big ears and all the blarney in the world although he hadn't a trace of Irish in his voice. I expect there were thousands of boys like him, but to mother and me he was always special. He was the son she hadn't had and the brother I'd missed.

'When we first got to know him he was beginning to fit into the pattern: good at games, cheating his way through exams, no apparent fear of anything or anybody. He loved practical jokes. Maybe to other people he was just a self-confident charmer with that hint of a lost child about him that women found irresistible. Women of all ages. Everyone except Magda, of course. She was living with us at the time, while my aunt and uncle were abroad.

'Scrubbs had an appalling temper. I mustn't forget that. So had his father. I think I remember Captain Malone coming to the house for the first time. I was reading the *Just-So Stories* and he reminded me of that one about the rhinoceros. His clothes were wrinkled like another skin around him and by the way he looked I thought cake-crumbs had got under it. Mother said when he'd gone that you could scarcely blame his wife for running off with a motor-car salesman, a quick-tempered man like that. In those days people were so desperate to sell you anything that you could almost wear a car out with trial runs before you decided to buy it. Mrs Malone had a lot of trial runs, and one day she went off on one and never came back.

'Scrubbs was only about five at the time and getting uncontrollable. Of course, we didn't know him then. His mother called him Paddy when she bothered about him at all. Captain Malone was abroad most of the year with an oil company and she didn't press him to take her with him. She played bridge, mother said, in a talkative, apologetic kind of way and left Scrubbs to a series of half-trained maids. He told me once that they used to threaten him with a policeman when he was naughty and when he was good they let him brush their long black hair.

'Scrubbs said a funny thing about his mother once when we were talking in the garden. It was after we'd heard that she was dead and he was trying to drown a fly in a pool of lemonade on the wooden table. There he was, poking away at it with a bit of stick. "She used to come and stare down at me when I was little, to say good night," he said. "You know those big vague eyes of hers. I felt she was like an hourglass and I was tilting her so that the sands ran out too fast. Daft. I used to scream then and pull her hair."

'I loved Scrubbs to talk to me. He didn't do it very often. But I knew what he meant about his mother. Silly Millie we used to call her. She had those big washed-out eyes you find in weak women who suddenly do one violent thing and then fade out. But it all seemed far-fetched to me, at thirteen. He used to dream about his mother at school, too. She turned into an hourglass and cracked open and sand poured out all over him and he woke up choking. But he always swore that he didn't miss her when she went off. I liked Scrubbs to talk seriously, I suppose he thought that he was safe with a priggish schoolgirl with glasses. Foureyes he used to call me. I suppose he had to take it out on somebody.

'I remember this because I remember every single occasion when he really talked and later on he stopped teasing and let me come with him to watch him play football. But he always took Magda to the dances at that ridiculous club. They were about eighteen then and I hated them going off together, Magda in green chiffon with her hair up.

'He always wanted people to notice him. He got several good hidings at his prep school for breaking all the ground-floor windows with a hammer and stamping on the geraniums in the Head's garden. But he soon learned to conform, because it was easier that way. He noticed which boys were popular, saw they were good at games and cribbed their homework, so he did the same. I suppose he was accepted by them in the crude, self-centred way of the young and he began to find his way in the school jungle. He fitted into the simple anarchy and respected the strict tribal rites. Later on, he liked the army, the discipline reassured him.

'It was years later, on one of his leaves – in between coming back wounded from Norway and going off again to Singapore – that he told me how he'd dreaded the school terms ending. He was only six or seven when he was sent away to school. He said he always knew when the holidays were coming; the other boys crossing off the days on their calendars, and at last the sound of taxis drawing up, the hoot of the trains in the distance, the school emptying. Then the fresh smell of the school without boys, without cooking. The way the hall grew bigger and how his footsteps echoed through the corridors. He'd watch the army of cleaners who came to empty inkwells and stack away desks and scrub with carbolic soap and polish the floors. In the lavatories there'd be the swish of distemper brushes as they spread lime green and whitewash over the term's obscenities.

'At the end of the first term he got a postcard from his father in Gibraltar saying that he couldn't get home but the Head would look after him. On his seventh birthday he had a letter from the Pacific, then at Christmas a card and a delayed box of trains. And still nothing from his mother and her car salesman.

'The Head and his wife were kind to him; they knew their duty. When he was eight he spent the summer holidays lying under the trees around the empty cricket field, or pummelling a punchball in the deserted gym. Once he escaped through the gate and went through the streets of that seaside town looking in windows at other people's home lives. Women pouring tea reminded him of his mother. A father on the beach playing awkward cricket with his son. Just about this time he grew thinner – I've seen photographs of him in the family album mother kept. All ears and bones. He started to wet his bed. I don't know how I got to know this – did mother tell me? I didn't get it from Scrubbs himself, that's certain. The Head wrote to Captain Malone. A strong letter. And the reply was even stronger. The Captain believed that schools were not meant to make boys happy but to teach them to do without happiness. Like young fruit trees, they were supposed to grow better and straighter when tied to stiff stakes.

'There must have been a good deal of adult manipulation. Mrs Malone had married her car salesman and was now Mrs Andy Jamieson, so it was all right for the boy to go to her in his holidays. I can almost hear Captain Malone saying that she'd never make a man of him and that she was a slut, but if the Head insisted – well, there was nothing he could do, in New York.

'So the next Easter a small red car drew up at the door of the school, nearly running down a small boy in a canary yellow sweater who dribbled a rugger ball with great concentration. When the woman in the car called out to him, "Paddy, Paddy darling!" he didn't look up. He'd forgotten his name. Silly Millie told us that it cut her to the heart, her own son not knowing his mother. Poor Silly Millie. We got to know her better later on, and I can imagine that just because Scrubbs stood there, indifferent to grown-ups, she tried all the harder. After all, she was his mother, wasn't she? A mother who had deviated slightly, but a mother all the same. The boy was hers just as surely as the earrings in her ears, even if he wasn't so pretty.

'Then Scrubbs asked her why she hadn't come before if she was his mother, if she'd missed him as she said. I expect she laughed at that, thinking him old-fashioned. She was one of those women who are sure that her femininity can deflect all arrows of judgement. She was a very female female, was Silly Millie, but there was no harm to her. She was just utterly unaware of other people's feelings. I've often wondered whether this set a pattern in Scrubbs's relations with women. The more indifferent they were, the more feminine, the more they attracted him. He invited kicks.

'Luckily he liked Andy Jamieson. Andy treated Scrubbs with the easy affability of his calling; awkward customers were nothing to him. Soon Scrubbs was calling him Andy and the two of them went roaring around the countryside in the red car, stopping at roadhouses with swimming-pools. When he was a young man Scrubbs would always finish up at the

Ace of Spades for a swim and eggs and bacon. Andy gave this new son of his a glass of beer every time he dived off the top board. So by his tenth birthday Scrubbs could drink two pints of beer without feeling any effects at all. Soon afterwards he started to smoke. Andy, I suppose remembering his own childhood, gave him a strong cheroot, hoping that it would make him sick, but it didn't, it only gave him a taste for good cigars. Soon the two of them spent the evenings smoking and drinking beer in the patchy, sandy garden of the bungalow that overlooked the sea. Where was it? Pagham, Shoreham? One of those trodden-over places in Sussex, anyway. These evenings were condemned by Millie in a most flattering way. They both knew that her pretended horror masked delight and pride in the naughty waywardness of her two men. It gave Scrubbs a delightful sense of power. He saw then that women loved to be shocked, and he recognized that special indulgent note in their scolding. He began, by the time he was thirteen, to learn that no often meant yes, even yes please.

'Then he met Alec. He was in his last year at the Glebe and ready to move on to Wallington, the elder-brother school, in effect. One of those minor public schools which seems to produce the loudest voices and the filthiest rugger songs. Alec was the son of a friend of mother's, a widow whom I had to call Aunt Mary. A real musical-comedy widow at that. Fat and wispy. She walked with a swimming motion, as if she had an air-filled bustle under her skirts. I longed to get at it with a pin. Alec was a sickly boy; he'd just spent a year in a TB hospital and TB had killed his father, so I suppose that Aunt Mary had some reason to worry about him. He's outlived Scrubbs, though. Where is he? South Africa? He went off somewhere for his chest.

'Alec was given into Scrubbs's care because the Head and his wife were at their wits' ends about him. Here was Scrubbs, tall and shock-haired, with a devil's smile. Captain of rugger, captain of cricket. But not school captain. "Boy," said the Head. Scrubbs used to take him off to make mother laugh. "Boy, your habits preclude this – ah – ultimate honour. Once again my wife has found cigar-butts in the Fives Courts."

'I can't do it like Scrubbs did.

'Anyway, he admitted to the habit, saying that he'd started young. He swore that he'd beat any other boy he found smoking, but couldn't break the habit himself because what with Common Entrance coming up his concentration would be affected. He was just fourteen at the time. I often think that the wretched Head was under Scrubbs's spell: there was in his nature a streak of absolute honesty and vulnerability. No one with those blushing ears could be false, so he got away with murder. Any other boy would have been thrown out of that school years before. Now I think that I would have respected him more if he had been thrown out. Even his acts of rebellion conformed to pattern. He was a sort of Bob Cherry with lapses. "Bob Cherry's cheeky grin made old Quelch relent."

'The Head's wife came up with the idea of making Scrubbs responsible for the new boy. Matron had been complaining about the long detailed list of necessities Alec required, and foresaw trouble. It came quickly. The first night in the dormitory. There were the usual rites. A new boy had to stand up on his bed wearing only his pyjama trousers and recite "Hi Ham Ha Huge Hugly Hairy Hold Hape". If his performance didn't come up to scratch all the other boys chucked sponges filled with cold water at him. If he didn't act up at all then he was tossed up in a blanket and dropped on to the floor. Then he had to start all over again.

'Scrubbs was told about Alec's medical history, and although he thought him a cissy for being so pale and small, he took him aside and warned him to put all he could into his performance. He had no great hopes of him, though, and expected him to burst into tears at the initiation.

'Years later they told me the story. I used to pester them for details about boarding-school life, which I thought was a kind of paradise. I soaked up the *Magnet* and the *Gem*. St Hilda's, in spite of climbs down the ivy, was pale by comparison.

'I can see Alec now, he told the story so vividly. Standing on his bed in the half-darkened dormitory; two candles after lights-out were all they dared risk. The boys repeated the words to him, circling his bed, holding their icy sponges tenderly, longing to throw them at that skinny body. Then to their surprise there was the new boy twisting up his face, swinging his arms along by his side in marvellous mimicry, scratching his armpits, howling with animal conviction the absurd chant, "Hi Ham Ha

Huge Hugly Hairy Hold Hape", and tweaking ears and hair, even daring to snatch a sponge here and there and squeeze it over his audience.

'It was a riot. Sponges, towels, pillows were hurled around the room, and nobody thought of tossing the new boy. Then the lights were switched on, by an angry prefect who dashed in, followed by a master. As if he didn't know there was an initiation rite on he demanded to know the reason for the ghastly row. Then Alec, rather blue around the mouth and wrapped in his dressing-gown, took it on himself to explain.

'"I'm terribly sorry, sir," he said, in true-blue *Magnet* and *Gem* style, "I'm afraid I started it, chucking a sponge about."

'Alec was made. And it started the friendship between him and Scrubbs, and it brought Scrubbs into our lives.'

Ten

❀

On Wednesday Harriet had Uplands to herself, at least until Magda and Gregg came back in the evening. She was glad to get away from the bus, for she felt foolish at having let herself go so completely, and to have the evidence neatly wound up and crouching in its hiding-place was unnerving. And yet, having started this excursion backwards she seemed to see the past everywhere; in the great Victorian hothouse that Aunt Esther had tried to restore and use to grow a vine; in the woods where Uncle Bertie and Scrubbs had cut down and sawn tree-trunks for the Christmas fires; on the lake where several times they had skated. Who were those people who had always been invited over whenever her aunt and uncle had felt obliged to be energetic? Briggs, or rather, the Briggses, that was it. The name suited their family solidarity. Harriet remembered the apple-picking parties, the tennis parties, the skating. With the Briggses around at full throttle one could experience vicariously the exhilaration of sport without the exhaustion of absolute participation, and this Aunt Esther adroitly exploited.

She would stand, applauding gently, well wrapped up in furs while the Briggses valiantly circled to a Viennese waltz on the frozen lake. 'Such a charming outdoor ballroom,' she would call across to them. 'I will take charge of the gramophone and watch.' Aunt Esther did not trust the ice, for the lake was deep.

Walking now through the neglected kitchen gardens where rosemary and rue had run to woody shrubs, where the rhododendron walk had grown narrow and high and was always dank in autumn and winter, Harriet was filled with dread at Gregg's homecoming. Suppose the news was bad, really bad? Blindness, paralysis, any incurable disease, was a total experience. It set a man apart, forced him to live within his own strict confines. How could an unafflicted person jump into the same pit, pretend to an understanding of his disabilities? You did not help an eyeless man by putting out your own eyes; you extended yourself to him. You became, within limits, a blind man's eyes. In the last few years Harriet had grown to believe that other people's troubles were a refuge from one's own. Certainly her mother had kept busy enough since her husband's death, since Scrubbs's death. She had been right.

Harriet found it odd, as she waded through the weeds that beat up against the boundaries of Magda's flower garden (symptom of Gregg's perilous loss of interest) that she, who had left good works to her mother, might now consciously have to extend herself to someone. What of her cricket's selfish house? That she might have, tucked away on the edge of a field, but wherever there were people there was involvement and if she was honest – and there was no point in not being so – what else had she expected, coming here? She still sought the cloak of family protection and for once might be expected to make some return. The pond at Walden was a long way off, and even if he had only stuck it out for a couple of years, Thoreau had faced the challenge of absolute solitude. He had succeeded in making the earth express its summer thought in bean leaves and blossoms. ...

Her mood did not lift as she trod sombrely along the brushed paths. Now she was inside the beech hedge. Around her the day lay like a broken piece of summer, solid gold. Here there was no autumn tangle: Magda was a great destroyer of the unwanted and the unwieldy. She was for ever seeking out ants' nests in order to destroy them with boiling water before the August nuptial flights; torturing the roses in season so that they stood for half the year like gesticulating vines in their circles of dried blood; pruning forsythia, lopping trees. All Magda's annuals were pulled out before they ran to seed and the dahlias always topped with earwig traps. She even tailored the lavender bushes.

Harriet stood in the middle of the perfect lawns, watched over for moss or moles (Euphorbia in the beds kept moles away) and felt supremely uneasy, as if the day were about to topple around her. Four of the dogs lay on the hot stones of the terrace and even they were as perfectly pruned as the shrubs. Magda caught their fleas and cracked them between her thumbnails. She had the dogs mated, or neutered; she fed and exercised them; she brushed and bullied them. As her reward, whenever she was away, they roamed disconsolately about the grounds and in and out of the kitchens. Only the two dachshunds sat with the medieval patience of carved dogs on the front porch between the fake pillars.

She went at last into the drawing-room and Theresa, who had been watching from the kitchen window, brought in the tea and set it down on a low table by the fire. Logs spurted palely in the sunlight, marooned in their pearly ash. When the girl had gone, Harriet restlessly took up one magazine after another. They were laid out on a small walnut table as if in a waiting-room, their edges evenly overlapping; the sort of glossies that served as comics to rich illiterates. For violence, pictures of fox and otter hunting. For romance, the usual debs on the stairs. At least one member of the royal family nidnodding in a toque; a contact with the impossible glitter of real gold. For comfort, the mother figure to all their uncertainties: the Queen mum plumply smiling at a horse.

❋

When she heard the car she went out with dogs surging around her and was waiting with them in the doorway when it stopped. To her surprise Magda got out alone.

'Where's Gregg?' Voice sharp, stretched with anxiety.

Magda came into the hallway, her face pale and tight. Pulling off her gloves, she threw them on to the oak settle.

'He stayed in town. Will you order tea for me, Harriet? I'm exhausted.'

'Of course. In just a minute. They haven't put him in hospital already?'

Magda's glance was half-contemptuous. Honestly, Harry knew nothing of how these things were done. Coat and hat off, she walked into the drawing-room, saying over her shoulder that Gregg was lucky. They all were.

When Theresa had brought the tea and had gone out again they both lit cigarettes and Harriet waited.

'The panic's over,' said Magda. 'My dear husband has gone off to celebrate. He must have forgotten that you were waiting.'

'He didn't know.' What an absurd game this was to play. 'Come on, Magda, don't make a meal of it.'

Magda let this vulgarism pass with the merest flicker of an eyebrow.

'Well, it is glaucoma, but it isn't acute – it's chronic, so he doesn't need an operation. He'll have to wear glasses, of course, and put in eyedrops morning and night. But although it can't be cured it can be controlled. If he bothers, that is.'

'Can't you make him?'

'I can't stop him drinking, you know that. And any high blood pressure is bad. I can't stand over him night and morning with an eyedropper.'

'Why not? You would for the dogs.'

'Dogs are different,' said Magda, meditatively turning her toe under the labrador's genitals. 'Gregg's got to take himself in hand. God, but it's a relief, I thought I'd have him tapping about with a white stick for the rest of his life.'

'I feel quite limp with relief,' said Harriet. 'It's been awful here today. Isn't Gregg pleased? And why are you mad?'

'He couldn't get away from me quickly enough to celebrate, that's why. He did suggest a dinner in town, but I reminded him about the Council meeting this evening and he just went off in a huff. Ten to one he'll be picked up dead drunk in the Edgware Road.'

'I don't think it matters a hoot in hell what he does tonight. He was scared stiff of going blind, and I'm sure he's had more pain than he's told us about. Even if his vision isn't good, he must feel half-way to normal for the first time in months.'

Harriet's heated and hurried words stung Magda into an indiscretion. Her anger had been steadily growing during the long drive home, and now she said, 'I've forgotten what it's like for Gregg to be normal. If it weren't too late, I'd leave him.' Checking herself for an amendment, she went on, 'At least, I'd make *him* leave *me*. I could manage here quite well without him—'

'Why is it too late?'

'Because now I'm taking part in public life. Divorce wouldn't be a good thing at all – you know what locals are.' She looked sharply at Harriet. 'You don't seem surprised. Why not?'

'I don't know,' said Harriet. 'Nothing seems to surprise me today.'

Disappointed, Magda said, 'You couldn't have heard what I said. I wish I'd left him years ago.'

'Oh, nonsense,' said Harriet. 'You've always got along pretty well.' Asinine remark.

'Then you must be blind.' Magda got up, stepped over two of the dogs and walked nervously to the window. 'You sound like your mother. Married people don't automatically "get along". How can you know? You've never been married. You don't learn about life from books.'

'And some people don't learn about life from life, either.'

They faced each other coldly. Yet again the old antagonisms fought their way through the adult façade and darting back into an old grudge, Magda said, 'You never understood how I felt about Scrubbs either, none of you did. You all wanted him and I couldn't bear it. You wanted to slice him up between you like a cheese. Even my own mother made a fool of herself over him—'

Harriet shook her head hopelessly. Her voice, when she spoke, had lost its aggression. 'We didn't blame you.'

Magda laughed. Stretching up her arm she let the gold charms tinkle their way up and then down to her wrist.

'To think that he gave me every one of these. One for each birthday, one every Christmas. Poor Scrubbs, he was like a brother, that's all. I found the man I wanted. A positive man, a serious man, and he was killed. I didn't want a mad boy who couldn't hold down a job for two minutes.'

'Why did you marry Gregg?'

Magda picked up a log, held it unseeingly.

'He was Scrubbs's friend. He was terribly sweet to me when Scrubbs had that accident. They'd been through such awful things together. And he was willing to join Daddy's firm, so I knew we'd be all right. Anyway, he used to be fun, and terribly good-looking. I used to enjoy walking into a room with him—' She flung the log on to the fire, driving it home with her brogue toe. 'I don't expect you'll believe me, but I used to wonder what Scrubbs would be like in middle age. I know now. He'd be just like Gregg. We'd have nothing hi common but marriage.'

�֍

As soon as Magda had changed and left for her meeting, Harriet got into her own car and drove down to the Finishing Post. She badly needed a drink in neutral territory. Because she was alone she avoided the public bar and went instead into what they called the 'posh bar', because it was tricked out with a brick-red carpet, imitation brass warming-pans and bowls of plastic chrysanthemums. The flowers were changed from season to season to prove that the landlord's wife was on her toes.

She asked for a couple of bags of onion-flavoured crisps because she hadn't eaten, and sat munching them in between long sips of a double whisky. No one she knew came in. It was always slack on a weekday night, the barman said, when he could tear himself away from the laughter in the public bar. Most of the lads preferred the other bar where they could play billiards or darts or, of course, Ringing the Bull. Feeling a fool sitting there alone, she made a move to the door, and then heard a voice she knew.

Opening it, she went through into the public bar. Sure enough it was Gregg, flushed, big in his sheepskin coat, squinting along his hand and taking aim. By his side a gaggle of stable lads, half his height, holding pints and nudging one another. A very thin man of military stance straddled the fireplace, keeping score. This man Harriet only knew by ill-repute. Gregg would only be drinking with him because for some reason he needed company. Chidlington was the man's name. And Chidlington never minded with whom he drank, so long as everyone stood him a round. All he wanted was an audience. His wife, more watchdog than companion, stood guard at his side, her dark eyes alert for infidelities.

It was not late and yet both men had evidently had a great deal to drink. Harriet walked over to Gregg and said, 'I thought you were in London. I'm so glad about the verdict.'

'Just a celebration,' said Chidlington, coming up alertly. 'Back from the grave. Deserves a celebration. What'll you have?'

Gregg said, turning his full face towards her, for his vision was playing him up again. 'My round. Large whisky, Harry?'

'Yes, please.'

All this time Chidlington was looking at Harriet with drunken intensity. Tomorrow he would not recognize her. He was a splendid ruin of a man born for wearing a white topee and for sauntering through the more uncomfortable regions of the world in shorts. Because he held himself so well, with a stiffly conscious air of command, one first of all missed the long, slack and self-indulgent mouth, the restless, shifting eyes.

'What glorious woman have we here?' he asked the air about him.

Embarrassed, Harriet said a civil good evening to his wife who was looking at her with another kind of intensity. Did she scent danger or didn't she? Other women to Hilda Chidlington fell into only two categories: those who attracted her husband and those who didn't. This gave her the same kind of alertness as her husband; the only difference being that she was on the defensive and he on the attack. Harriet, not caring for a role of pig-in-the-middle, decided that she must get Gregg away as soon as decently possible. Later on, Gregg would tell her why he was here and not in London, but she didn't intend to ask him in front of these two. He handed her the whisky but made no attempt to introduce her. This meant that either he was very drunk indeed or that his companions were fringe people he did not want her to meet.

However, Mrs Chidlington, expertly putting herself between her husband and Harriet, appeared quite unaware of any snub. She asked straight out whether she wasn't Gregg's sister-in-law, for she had surely seen her in the Brown Bear with Magda.

'Magda's my cousin,' said Harriet. 'I've been coming here for years.'

'Ah, she's not so well set up as you, madam,' said Chidlington, manoeuvring past his wife. 'I like a bit of what you call avoirdupois.'

'I was on my way up from the station,' said Gregg; 'thought I'd call in for a quick one.'

'Have you eaten, Gregg?'

He shook his head.

'Come and have a meal with us,' said Mrs Chidlington eagerly. 'We only live in the next village. We've bought some land there, so that my husband can grow apples.'

'Cox's Orange Pippins. Must do something in one's retirement. Makes a change from growing tea. Now that the natives have overrun the plantations, what's a poor white man to do?' Chidlington turned away from his wife and addressed Harriet with determined gallantry. 'May I interest you in a box? After all, Eve didn't refuse an apple, and look what that led to.'

For a moment Harriet thought that he was putting on an act and she burst out laughing. Then she caught Mrs Chidlington's cold eye and tried to cut it short.

'I like a woman with a sense of humour,' said Chidlington, beaming down at her. 'Where've you been keeping her, Gregg? Private pleasures, what? Lucky man.'

Gregg seemed to gather himself together. He turned carefully to the other man, frowned slightly, put down his glass and shot out his fist. Chidlington went down, still holding his empty glass, leaning on one elbow on the floor. The stable boys were smitten into silence. He gazed up at Gregg, unsurprised.

'Asked for it,' said Gregg briskly, nodding to Mrs Chidlington, who stood calmly by. 'Drink up, Harry. Good night, Hilda.'

Before she knew it, Harriet had gulped down her whisky and was outside in the cold starry night.

'Got your car?'

'You want a quick getaway, is that it?'

'Oh, he won't come after us. Hilda won't let him.'

They climbed into Harriet's car and she drove off in the direction it faced without another word. They were well out of Maxmead when Harriet started to laugh again.

'That was the quickest drink and punch-up I've ever experienced,' she said. 'He didn't mean any harm, Gregg. If one knocked down all the pub bores one met, the bars would be littered with prone bodies. What got into you?'

'I don't like him,' said Gregg. 'He starts the same old trick with any woman when his wife's there. He likes to humiliate her. Anyway, he's not going to use you in his nasty little private war. Man's a bastard. Worst sort of war casualty. Drifter. A leftover. We've a lot in common. That's why I hit him.'

'Well, where d'you want to go now? You'll feel better when you've had some food.'

'Just drive around. Then leave the car somewhere and we'll walk. I've got the hell of a headache.' A little farther on he said, 'You've no right to go drinking alone. You invite that sort of approach.'

Harriet let out an exasperated snort.

'Don't be such a bloody fool. I've had a rotten day, too, worrying about you. I felt like a drink and went into the posh bar. Then I heard your voice and came in to find you.'

She stopped the car near a village green. By day geese walked over this patch of grass, which had been common land for centuries. Somewhere in the darkness was a pair of stocks.

'You're not like him in any way,' said Harriet, when they had got out and walked a short way into the sweet-smelling night. The stars were very fiery and cold, high up in the cloudless sky. 'Anyway, he's just full of nostalgia, you can smell it on him.'

'He's no good,' said Gregg.

'If you must judge people—' Harriet was very angry by now. The numbness she had found enveloping her at the moment of that unexpected melodramatic blow had given way to throbbing shock. 'If you must judge,' she repeated in a shaky voice, 'then try to understand why people end up as they do. It's no use growing older if you don't grow up, Gregg. The only thing worth cultivating is a sense of proportion.'

Gregg said, 'You sound as if you hate me.'

She stopped, turning up her clear shocked eyes to his face. In order to see her, he had to turn his head and bend slightly. Whether or not he was waiting for her to confirm his petulant exclamation he could not be sure. He put his arms round her and she felt his cold cheek on hers. He was kissing her as the headlights of a car caught them, and held them pinioned in the middle of the green, absurdly isolated for the few seconds it took for the driver, Hilda Chidlington, to identify them as she swept past.

'I hope that was nobody we know,' said Harriet. 'They weren't to know that we were indulging our mutual dislike.'

'What we need,' said Gregg, 'is a cup of coffee, hot and strong and instant. Preferably in the bus.'

'The cats are there,' said Harriet involuntarily.

'To hell with the cats,' said Gregg. 'They have their own bed.'

Part Two

❈

Eleven

After his reprieve Gregg took to walking all over the land as if he had returned to it from a long way off, after a long time, and was learning it again. To Magda's surprise, he put in the eyedrops without mentioning them to her; he never asked for help. And although the process was unpleasant, because it made him blind for about half an hour each morning and evening, the relief made him aware of how long he had been compressing himself within a mould of pain. At first he resented having to wear glasses, but the hornrims he chose he wore like a disguise. As Magda said, at last he looked like a director of the firm, and he travelled up to London twice a week safely and capably protected by this new businessman's identity.

On the days he did not need to go up, he and Harriet strolled along the strip of path that curved above the barley field beyond the house, sheltered by a thick hedge of beech and sloes and elderberry. On the other side of the hedge lay a ploughed field, in the middle of which was a crescent-shaped wood, a haunt for badgers. They would turn, followed by Harriet's cats, down a thin chalk lane between the billowing land where the shadows of late afternoon lay milkily in the hollows.

One afternoon they stopped to watch Everett burning off stubble, and the fires ran over the field in the sudden light winds faster than they could walk. Even when the light faded, other fires leapt up on the crests of far-off hills and for some reason they gave Harriet a feeling of pure happiness.

'Surely that's a lump of chalk moving?' she asked, as they walked back, pointing over the field.

'It's Everett's dog digging out a rat. You're the one who needs an eye butcher.'

'Don't boast. He's not after hares, is he? I saw two the other night. I see now. Yes, it's a white terrier.'

'He's after a rat. Aren't they alike, those two? I've always thought that if that man had a tail, he'd wag it.'

'I must say,' said Harriet, 'that he's excessively obliging. He has a positive obsession about putting in electric light for me, but I'm sure Mrs Everett wouldn't like it. She doesn't quite trust me, for some reason.'

'Quite right, too,' said Gregg. 'Coming in? Magda's off to put Maxmead to rights. We must think about this bonfire night party. I've got Everett's boys on to hauling stuff down to your field. The farm could do with a clean-up.'

'Let's go down to the bus,' said Harriet. She had a prudish feeling about spending evenings at Uplands alone with Gregg, even if they only sat by the fire and listened to his records.

They turned towards the house. In a gap in the beech hedge Magda appeared and signalled vigorously. She smelt strongly of some musky scent and looked particularly well dressed and animated.

'I've told Theresa to make you both her delicious *paella*. Harry, you *will* stay and keep Gregg company? I have to dash off now. The Committee are having drinks with some friends of Lila's in Cambridge. They've got some plan on we're going to discuss. You don't mind, darling?' She leaned forward and kissed Gregg on the cheek.

As the car disappeared down the drive, Harriet giggled.

'That'll be Lila's warden. I wonder what brings him in on the Planning Committee? Meirion and I met him by chance in Maxmead.'

'When?'

'We were having lunch at the Brown Bear. I was rude to Meirion, I'm afraid, and I expect he's avoiding me.'

'Good. Now shall we eat Theresa's *paella* or do you want to drive me out to dinner somewhere?'

'We'll stay in,' she said. She was not used to the word 'we'. It filled her with complicated emotions of guilt, pleasure, gratitude, even perhaps love.

Gregg caught her quick blush.

'I'm too old,' he said, 'I wish I'd found you earlier.'

'I wasn't to be found, earlier,' said Harriet.

After dinner Gregg collected some 78's and they walked down to the bus. Sometimes he let her play what he called her thirties' junk, and then he would put on Fats Waller or Ellington. There was something she had grown to like called 'Chant of the Weeds'. It groped with melancholy fingers and caught at her.

'You've no ear,' said Gregg. 'You still can't tell the difference between a saxophone and a trumpet.'

They talked to each other easily now. Not with the rallying heartiness they had used over the years when they had been merely relatives, but as if something troubling had been cleared out of the way. Gregg said later, as he got up to dress and make her coffee:

'I'm glad we're not within the forbidden categories.'

'I wonder sometimes whether Magda felt that about Scrubbs, in an odd sort of way. She said we tried to divide him up like a cheese between us all.'

Gregg looked over his shoulder as she lay on the bed, smoking. Women looked kinder, more bruisable, without make-up. He knew she hated him to praise her body, but what had astonished him that first night was the amplitude and the creamy Rubens texture of her flesh. In clothes she looked nothing much; now, with a kind of possessiveness he had been unaware of, he found that he was glad. Only he knew how beautifully the hips curved down to the full thighs. Round, generous breasts, still good, still firm. He was lucky. He found that she was shy but passionate, and her response gave him back something he had lost over the years with Magda. A profound respect for this curious, essential exercise. Game for two players. Two only, he would not have a third, even as a ghost.

So, risking a great deal, he said, 'Magda was absolutely right. But I wonder if even now she knows who got the biggest slice?'

Harriet sat up and pulled Gregg's huge sweater over her head, wriggling into it while she took the mug of coffee he offered. 'Go on,' she said. 'You stopped the other evening. I thought I knew everything about Scrubbs. But nobody knows everything about anybody.' She looked at him expectantly but coldly and he cursed himself.

'Oh, it isn't important,' he said. 'Look, before I picked up that book in here the other day I hadn't thought about Scrubbs for years.'

'Neither had I. But even Magda's taken to talking about him. Why, she even said—' But it was impossible to tell Gregg what she had said. It had been an extraordinary remark. It was dangerous to repeat it even to herself, and yet here she was gladly and shamelessly having an affair with a man who might – possibly – be what Scrubbs might have become at much the same age. It was a crazy thought, but it was relevant. Oh yes, it was certainly relevant. Women did things for the most perverted reasons.

'Why are you laughing?' asked Gregg. 'Look, I don't care what Magda said. She'd say anything. If you're trying to tell me that she's having an affair with Meirion, don't bother. I can smell it on her. I'm not a fool. And I don't care.'

'You don't care now, but you may care later,' said Harriet.

'You talk too much. Look, I'm not going to feel guilty about this. I can't bear this awful mystical thing women have about sex. I'm at the end of my forties and I'm glad this has happened to us. It decelerates the slide.'

'For God's sake,' said Harriet. 'I don't want to have a great old talk about sex. Let's leave that for the teenagers. But the mystical thing as you call it, is built in. It's part of the pattern to protect the tribe and all that. You can't have the bearers of future generations running amok, so if you can't keep them corralled you've got to have them on some kind of remote control. Like training rats to go through trapdoors for their food. Ping! Touch the wrong door and you get an electric shock. Sleep with someone else's husband and the same thing happens.'

'But women are naturally immoral.'

'Of course they are. It's all a matter of how much they can get away with before society rumbles them. They have to be devious: men have taught them to be, and other women punish them if they're found out.'

'I don't suppose you got those sort of ideas from your mother,' said Gregg, settling down lazily at the opposite end of the divan and tucking his bare feet under the small of Harriet's back.

'No, you're right. Aunt Esther and I used to take the punt out and drift up near the bamboo plantation and lie there looking up through the leaves of that enormous willow tree and she would tell me how to cope with men.'

The thought of those lazy, hot afternoons made her want to cry, not laugh, so instead she lit a fresh cigarette and walked two fingers up and down the silvery scars that encircled Gregg's ankle.

'How old were you?'

'Fifteen or sixteen. She was my godmother, you see. She felt she had a duty towards me; she felt protective because I was so plain. I suppose she thought that I'd be taken in if I was ever lucky enough to be taken out. If you see what I mean.'

Funny sort of godmother, Gregg thought privately. Aloud he said, 'I thought that godmothers were supposed to see you right with God, not mammon.'

Harriet made a comic face at him.

'She was in a bit of a muddle there. She didn't believe in C. of E. confirmation. Some sort of recessive genes, I suppose. She used to say that baptism was only a kind of insurance against witches on Hallowe'en.'

'Careful,' said Gregg. 'It's Hallowe'en tonight.'

Harriet shivered violently, and Gregg grasped her ankles to steady her. The cats, who had both been asleep on the chair by the fire, got up and stretched themselves into tight arcs. Then Bella ran across the room, and leapt on to the counter by the oil lamp and stood by the window, growling in her throat, her tail bushed.

Pale, Harriet said, 'Oh God, she's heard something. Something, someone, I mean, is outside.'

Gregg quietly cursed the cat. Then he said, forcing himself to laugh, 'Don't be idiotic, Harry. She's after a moth. And look, the lamp's smoking. I'll turn it down.'

He got up, twitched the curtains together where there had been a space, turned down the lamp and lifted down the cat.

'I'd feel safer in the cabin, and there's more room,' said Harriet. 'Give Bella to me, she's still scared.'

They were able to lie side by side on the banked-up cushions and look out into the firelit room. A moment ago it had seemed impregnable, but now Harriet was terribly aware of how thin was the skin that stretched between her and the frosty fields outside, how precarious her relationship with Gregg.

Putting his arm round her, Gregg said, 'Do you remember those Hallowe'en parties they used to give? And how your aunt made poor old Bertie fix up a sort of broomstick on a motor-bike so that she could take off, in full witch's regalia, across the lawn?'

Harriet nodded. It was true. Aunt Esther had made Uplands a perfect setting for herself, which was what her husband had intended. She remembered him telling her father that he had found just the house to set Esther off. And her father had retorted that that wasn't what women were for, unless they were king's mistresses. So Uncle Bertie had replied rather grandly that he intended to be a king of industry, so what was wrong with that?

'Did Uncle Bertie ever try out that egg-and-bacon smell on you?' she asked, suddenly remembering her short, shrewd uncle with affection.

'God, yes!' Gregg burst out laughing. 'He had us out of bed and down the stairs in no time, and nothing was cooking. He never sold it, though.'

'My father used to say that he had a vulgar streak in him, or he wouldn't have thought of making plastic leather smell like real leather, and he never forgave him for spraying mother's everlasting peas with a sweet-pea scent. But that was what started him off, really. Pinewood scent for plastic logs in pubs, or applewood – he was an ingenious man. But no gentleman, said my father.'

'We still export that spray-on leather smell,' said Gregg. 'The South Americans go for it, and so do the Israelis. One old rabbi told me once that even when he's in Tel Aviv he can close his eyes and imagine he's in his London club ...'

'The only ungallant thing the old boy ever did was to die before Aunt Esther,' said Harriet thoughtfully. 'She was still arguing downstairs with the doctor over whether to call in the vicar or the priest, or to send for the local Methodist minister, when he died quietly, all on his own. She never really forgave him.'

'She was an extraordinary woman,' said Gregg, with reservation. 'But what did she advise you to do, if she was against the Church of England?'

'Oh, she'd gallop through Buddhism, Mohammedanism, the British Israelites, the Zoroastrians and Mrs Besant in half an hour flat and then tell me to follow up whichever one most appealed to me. She said she hoped I'd avoid Rome – theosophically speaking.' Harriet's inner eye and ear picked up the flowing gestures of her aunt's hands, the strong inflections of her voice, that slightly un-English throatiness. 'She made every other woman look dowdy,' she said without jealousy. 'And for a beautiful woman, she was concerned with other people's feelings. For instance, Uncle Bertie never knew that she was unfaithful.'

'She told you?'

'Oh yes. After we'd got the Zoroastrians out of the way she loved to settle down to what she called a talk between women ...'

'I swear she put that accent on,' said Gregg, interrupting.

'It was difficult to know when she wasn't acting a part,' admitted Harriet. 'But she was always charitable towards men. She used to say that when you were young, that was the time to be idealistic about sex, when it was part and parcel of love. As people grew older, kindness and compromise watered it down. Satisfaction, she used to say, was very different from true consummation. She actually quoted Yeats. I believe that he was the only poet she ever read. You know:

> 'Maybe the bridebed brings despair
> For each an imagined image brings
> And finds a real image there.

'She said that the young could afford to be cruel but the middle-aged couldn't, because they were vulnerable in a different sort of way. They were over the top.'

'Thanks very much,' said Gregg, kissing her neck.

Harriet arched her face away, and laughed, remembering something else.

'She told me once how to end an affair without hurting a man's feelings.

She was always very concerned with men's feelings. She said that if you really liked this man who wanted you and you tired of him, then you should leave him with his self-respect even if you had to sacrifice your own. I didn't really see this, but she was adamant. She was always against reducing a man in his own eyes, she said it made him dangerous to other women afterwards. There was some young man – she'd never tell me who it was – and he fell madly in love with her ...'

'Did she sleep with him?'

'Oh, yes, for a little while. It was flattering to someone of her age – she must have been in her forties, and he was really much younger. Uncle Bertie was away on a business trip and she was bored. I think it must have been some time in the war – and she loved what she called a situation. She did something I could never do. Never.'

'What was that?'

'She made passionate advances. She wrote mad letters. She offered to follow him wherever he went, to wait for him till the end of the world. She swamped him with poems she'd copied out (Yeats again, I bet). All very highly charged stuff. Of course it frightened the poor young man out of his wits and he fell for someone else on the rebound. I expect he's settled down with a wife and clutch of children in Surbiton by now, and in his spare time he luxuriates in the thought that he once inspired an undying love. And his ego is intact. There!'

She turned to Gregg, expecting him to laugh with her, but he was so silent that she wondered whether he had fallen asleep. When at last he spoke his voice was dry.

'That sounds very cynical and – rather risky. When did she tell you all about this? Not in between chats on Mrs Besant, I take it.'

'Oh no,' said Harriet gaily. 'I told you. Long after. After the war, I think. After Uncle Bertie died. Mother and I used to come down here to keep her company. Magda was abroad. You know, I wasn't sure whether to believe her. What do you think?'

Gregg got up and looked at his watch. It was after eleven. 'You'd better give me my sweater,' he said. 'It's getting cold in here. I'll make up the fire.'

While Harriet pulled on her own clothes, he said, feeding the fire: 'She was telling the truth. At least, half the truth, the only bit of it she could face. And the young man isn't living at Surbiton, Harry. He's dead, and you knew him well.'

Twelve

Gregg left soon after; his secret out, his promise broken. Some things he had kept back from the stony-faced Harriet: things that had been told him when death seemed the next step and there was no point in deceit or self-deception. Perhaps everyone should have a spell of imprisonment and blindness in his life. Certainly, in that hot darkness, in those intense conversations of twenty years ago, he had picked Scrubbs clean – or rather Scrubbs had picked himself clean, so far as he was able. So much so, that afterwards, on the ship that brought them home, Gregg had found that, with his sight returning, the one man he could not bear to see was Scrubbs Malone. They had sucked one another dry.

It was not until two years had passed that they met again, quite by chance, at Gregg's cousin's house. Scrubbs had met her the previous summer at a Wimbledon-week party, the first of the revived post-war championships that tried, with strawberry teas and New Look clothes, to cancel out the long and bloody interval. That was the year Louise Brough played in the winning mixed and women's doubles …

He had been shocked, not pleased, to see Scrubbs trying it on with his cousin. Not that he was in love with her any longer, but certain parts of his life he did not care to overlap, and what he and Janet had done with each other as children was finished with. If he had talked about them by the side of that hot stinking river a thousand miles away, that was finished with too. He decided that in civilian life Scrubbs was not the sort of man he cared to know.

But Scrubbs would not be shaken off. As Gregg gradually found his way back to normal living, learning to accept his parents' almost reverential attentions to the returning hero, assume a peacetime identity, Scrubbs remained wildly out of step. Gregg looked for, and found, a job in advertising. Scrubbs went through his gratuity like a madman. He spent his time between Janet's home in Somerset and the Coopers' in London. He bought a fast car, ate the expensive, still insipid meals that London restaurants offered in the late forties: talked about Henley and Wimbledon and Lords as if he could dive back through the bottom of a champagne glass into the past.

Scrubbs was a fool, Gregg decided. But when he met the Coopers, as he did soon after, he realized why. He could have shaken all those women; Mrs Cooper and Harriet, both doting. Magda, defensive, playing it cool but with a sister's intimacy. Esther, enigmatic and detached, but faintly possessive. They wanted him still to be the deprived boy and he made them suffer because of it.

'Esther's a hag, she disgusts me,' he had told Gregg. 'I'm going to join up again, get away from them all.'

So what had attracted Gregg to Magda in those days was purely the feeling they shared about Scrubbs. They had both rumbled him.

Lying awake in bed, listening to the soft noises from Magda's room as she crept in late, he knew that this had not been the basis on which you could build a marriage. And now it was crumbling fast. Once he had been of use: for him, as for so many men, the war had given him a moment of bright glory, soon eclipsed in the long years of captivity. But even that had not quenched it quite. For Gregg, the enemy had to be seen: it had to be a gun emplacement or a Jap guard. Or a physical condition, like constant hunger and jungle ulcers. It was so difficult in peacetime to know who the enemy was, and when at last he recognized that it was his wife, it was too late for him to do anything about it. This was not his kind of war.

Damn Scrubbs. His death made him inviolate. Even now here was he, Gregg, in middle-age, clearing up the mess that that damnable Peter Pan had left behind him. He would rescue Harriet who had been made miserable by them all; plain in girlhood, chivvied, teased by that oaf. Turning on the light, Gregg reached out for a sleeping pill. His head throbbed. But Scrubbs wasn't an oaf. He was far worse; a charmer, feckless, lost, poison to women. And damned lucky to be out of it all.

Back in the bus Harriet had not attempted to go to bed. She sat upright at the long counter, wide awake. She was still in a state of profound shock, as if she had been struck on the head in the mountains and had woken up in the plains. All the signposts had been turned in different directions and now she had to find her way in spite of them.

Aunt Esther and Scrubbs.

'Why not?' Gregg had said. 'It's happened before. Women of forty go for young men. He may have seen something of Magda in her. And it was no go in that direction—'

Then he'd said, in the face of her stony silence, 'Look, Harry, he *told* me. That time I thought I was going blind, going mad. He had to talk about something, and after three years in prison camp you run out of small talk. We never thought we'd get out alive. There was no chance of my meeting his family. Why should he lie?'

Why, indeed?

'And what in hell's name does it matter? They're both dead. Can't you forget them and go on from here? People come and go in one's life. You told me the other evening to grow up. You must too. Because you can't stop growing old.'

Then he'd gone.

But when had it happened? How was it that she had never suspected? It seemed abominable that they had all been victims of a trick; her mother, the whole family. And that honest face of Scrubbs, saying that he was off to Uplands for his last leave. He'd met some people there—

Of course it happened all the time, like having an affair with someone else's husband. But it happened to other people, not oneself, like being struck by lightning. Lightning illuminated many things at once; half-truths and sugar-coated lies and downright self-deceptions that looked like moralities. It was essential to stop making a virtue out of virtue.

Harriet's foot kicked against the half-hidden tape recorder. She had not told Gregg about buying it. And now it seemed absurd to think that he would ever want to play back what she had recorded the other evening.

The whole thing had been a waste of money, an expensive whim. Yet she drew it out of its box and found herself fitting a new spool. There was something powerful about that shiny coil, it invited confidences. It could always be destroyed: it was not a human ear you were speaking into, after all, that could betray you twenty years later. Harriet lifted it on to the counter with growing confidence. It was a friend. It could sort out her thoughts, set the signposts right. So she had had a shock, things weren't as they seemed. How had they seemed, then? Now it was her turn: this was for herself.

Thirteen

�֍

Track Two

'I think that Scrubbs fell in love with Magda the first time he saw her. He said afterwards that she'd looked at him as if he'd come about the smell on the landing. They were both about fourteen at the time. Magda and I went to the same day school, so she lived with us during the week, and at weekends Uncle Bertie fetched her – and sometimes me as well – and took her off to Uplands. They didn't like the idea of boarding-schools for girls, but at the same time Aunt Esther couldn't be bothered with children. Mother kept exact accounts in a Woolworth notebook of how much it cost her to keep Magda and wouldn't take a penny more.

'Magda and I got on quite well, although we were different ages. I copied her slavishly, so that when she cut off her eyelashes and bathed the spiky bits left in champagne – pinched from her father, not mine, of course – I did, too. It was supposed to make them grow long and tangly like those of the heroines we read about. Ours just stayed short and spiky for ages. Aunt Esther made Magda hide hers with false ones when she took her out.

'Scrubbs spent a good part of his holidays with Alec's family, but when Andy Jamieson took his mother off to South Africa to try to save her lungs he moved in with us. Mother thought of him as a son anyway. For an adolescent (and there were adolescents then, the awkward age, we called it, teenagers didn't exist). For an adolescent, Scrubbs had remarkably good manners. As I've said, he had a way with women, and women like good manners. A child's please and thank you are part of its survival kit; later on, the subtleties are entirely its own. His father married again. Some woman in oil, I heard them say. This made no sort of sense to me. A woman in oil? Precociously I'd read about the Chinese pickling babies in oil to make them grow into fat little living buddhas.

'Silly Millie and Andy came over one summer afternoon and told us about going to South Africa. We were playing badminton in the garden and even I saw how Andy had changed. That confident façade of his had cracked at last; he'd fallen victim to the thin thirties. Andy had the look of a man who'd knocked on too many doors and been turned away too often. Trying his luck in the Cape was a last-ditch move for him, too.

'I remember sitting with him under a sort of rose-bower my father had made the summer he died and I liked him better then than at any time before. We watched the others ducking about on the court while an aeroplane buzzed across the sky, very high up, and as it went over it wrote OXO in white smoke against the blue. In a sense it was fitting. It made me think of something our science mistress had said to illustrate the relative distances between certain objects in time. "Imagine an aeroplane high up above a train standing in a station," she told us. "The pilot can see the station, the train and the railway bridge half a mile away beyond a curve in the railway line." The point being that all that the passengers could see was the platform as the train slowly steamed out.

'There doesn't seem much point in it now. But then, watching Andy, and the badminton players and the aeroplane, it seemed overwhelmingly significant. I felt that if I could be as high up and as detached as that pilot in his plane, writing OXO in blowy white capitals, I would know exactly what lay ahead for all of us. It was an eerie feeling, trying to reach that railway bridge ahead of time.

'Scrubbs was in one of his moods that afternoon. He showed off until we were tired to death of him, and his mother coughed and jingled her bracelets in tiny wan paeans of self-praise and forgot to smile.

'Aunt Mary said in her church voice, as we carried out the tea-things, that Alec's father had had a cough like that and it had taken five years to kill *him*.

'It took less than that to kill poor Silly Millie. To my surprise Aunt Mary cried when the news came. She felt, like mother, that the two of them – Millie and Andy – had both paid so patently for their sins. Failure and ill-health had deflated them and they seemed to all of us to be like two forlorn figures in a windswept landscape. But I had known all along, in my insufferable way, just what lay beyond the railway bridge.

'Now I realize that the two of them were utterly of the thirties, the thin thirties. I've said that before. But even a protected schoolgirl could see that much. Thin men in raincoats waving hopeless banners; sombre colours with splashes of red. Well-spoken men coming to the door selling writing-paper and vacuum cleaners. High lost voices calling against a knife-edged wind. It was an awful time.

'Silly Millie died the year Scrubbs left school, and for a time he went berserk. He refused to take the job his father offered him in his new wife's oil company and took himself off for a couple of years, signing on and off cargo boats. Sometimes we'd have a card from Ireland, then from the Balearics, then from somewhere in the West Indies. But he never went to America. It wasn't big enough to hold both him and his father, I suppose. But he got as far as Karachi and sent us back some silk saris and an ivory brooch each.

'Then it was May again. A fine day. The road smelt of tar, yellow laburnums were out by the front gate. And there on the doorstep was Scrubbs. He was twenty now; thin, brown and outlandishly elegant in a new suit, tattoo marks on his left hand. He had come to ask Magda to marry him.'

Harriet switched off, got up stiffly, feeling the keen chill of the frozen fields outside penetrating the thin skin of the bus. She would have to insulate the inside with sheets of polystyrene. Shivering, she became aware once again that it was Hallowe'en, and dropped the curtain on the still, white fields, the changing lights that stretched away past Maxmead, controlling no traffic, lighting empty roads, and made up the fire. Gregg was very good to her, bringing logs and coal and kindling; nobody had done that for Thoreau in the Concord woods. Making coffee, she felt a fraud, desolate at her dependence, and terribly vulnerable through these new feelings she had found for another human being.

At her age, sexual love! But then, if you thought that you were finished at forty, you were already finished at fourteen. She hadn't understood that when Aunt Esther had flung it out, suddenly, one day a long time ago. But then a fool at forty is a fool indeed … and who else had said that a woman didn't know what to do with freedom except surrender it?

'I've surrendered nothing,' she told herself. 'This thing flows both ways. I'm not even cheating Magda, although she doesn't know. All I'm afraid of is her laughter when she does find out. Poor old Harry, creeping up to the vast picked-over field called sex and finding herself one rather chipped stone.'

There had, of course, been other stones in the past. Picked up and soon abandoned, and now not remembered. She had always told herself after these unsatisfactory interludes that one lived a long time, that sex was merely a catalyst in that long life, for one was alive as a child before it started to work and alive as an old woman long after the reverberations died away. Now she would not use the word 'merely'.

She sat, sipping coffee, staring at the brown spools which sat, twin father-confessors, before her, waiting for the truth as she knew it. Only the truth had turned out to be a distorting mirror in a funfair.

Track Three

'Scrubbs came to ask Magda to marry him and she said that she'd think it over. So he came back to live with us and got some sort of job in insurance which he hated and tried to settle down and be the sort of dependable man Magda wanted. Then, luckily for him, the war started and he was one of the first to join up. I was furious. All he said was "My dear infant, when there's a tootling of trumpets, off one goes." And off he went. But not before he'd taken us all out to dinner and the theatre. Frascati's it was, before it was pulled down, because mother had danced on one of the tables there on Mafeking night, or so the story goes. He could be extravagantly morose, and these moods of his upset mother more than his wild outbursts. I think maybe he loved mother more than anyone else. She anchored him but made no claims.

'I wonder now whether Aunt Esther mightn't have been a bit jealous of mother? I heard her once saying to Uncle Bertie that the trouble with Daisy was that she never meant more than she said. Aunt Esther found this disconcerting. It's certainly a very Anglo-Saxon trait. She wondered whether mother was aware of this. I don't think she was. I'm glad now to think that her simplicity confounded Aunt Esther. For once that devious mind had met its match. All the more so, because the duel was one-sided. Mother was utterly unaware of any struggle for supremacy.

'Scrubbs used to get very drunk and come home with things he'd pinched from pubs. The house was full of tankards and ashtrays with names of breweries on them. Before he went off he bought Magda an engagement ring, but she never wore it.

'Then he was back again after being wounded at Narvik. And that was the long leave he spent at Uplands, recovering. It left him with a limp. That must have been when it happened with Aunt Esther, because Magda had joined the Wrens and had met this other man who was in submarines and was drowned later on. I don't think she ever brought him home.

'What I don't understand is where I came in. Because one night Scrubbs came to my room just before he was sent out to Singapore, and got into bed with me and frightened me to death. He didn't smell of drink, he was in one of his morose moods. When he saw that I was really frightened at what he was trying to do he lay with his arms round me and asked me to wait for him. Then he drifted off to sleep and called me Magda and I was bitterly upset and at the same time dreaded what mother would say if she heard all the whispering and came in. And I still didn't know, years after, whether he meant to say 'wait for me', or whether he thought I was Magda, because when I asked him later he said he didn't remember anything about it.

'When we heard that he'd been captured Magda got officially engaged to her man in submarines – I've forgotten his name. She thought, she truly thought, that Scrubbs was dead. But mother and I didn't. When we heard that he was a prisoner – through the Red Cross – we sent him parcels and letters, but he never got any of them. When he came home Magda stayed at Uplands and Scrubbs stayed with mother and me. It was then that we began to talk to each other properly. He only weighed about seven stone, and what with his limp and his ear shot away we scarcely recognized him at first. He knew all about Magda because she'd written to him and he wouldn't talk about that letter. He told me about acting *Richard the Second* in the camp, but the actors kept dropping out. One day they'd be learning their parts and next they'd be dead or dying of dysentery. Still, I wanted to hear all about it – the bits he didn't mind talking about. Once he put his hand over mine and said, "I wish I could marry you, sweetie, but I can't. I don't love you. I'm very fond of you and I trust you. I feel the same way about you as Magda does about me. You're family and that's it."'

'Yes, that was it. We were family. So I took my hand away and talked about the old days, what there was of them. But it all fell rather flat. We kept having to select the safe bits and train our mental telescope on them. The game of Do you remember? can be terribly tricky. One steps on mines. There's so much to remember when you think about it, but you have to let it all drop back again, like catching little fish and throwing them back in the river. Then the little fish grow enormous.

'There was Aunt Mary, dead. Bombed with her careful, clean house all down round her splattered ears. Silly Millie, dead. Andy, God knows where. Magda, lying low; her submarine man full fathom five. Captain Malone and his wife in oil. Looking for oil in the Middle East. Scrubbs wouldn't see him when he came specially to London after the war. Mother had a long talk with him: she liked Captain Malone. Alec, Scrubbs's friend, farming in Rhodesia, married. It was quite a roll-call.

'And good old faithful Harry, still waiting. I suppose I got the habit and I really thought that by a process of elimination he'd at last come around to me. What a fool! Even Gregg's daft cousin rated higher. Even that tree looming up. Solitary object hit at speed.

'Girls didn't like his looks or his silences, he couldn't fit in. He talked once about going back to the army. I got into the habit of training my mental telescope on a target and looking through it the wrong way round, so that everything hurtful or happy was a long way off and very small. Like remembering Sophie Tucker singing "After You've Gone".'

❋

Harriet found that she could no longer speak. And in any case the tape had wound itself to a finish some minutes earlier. She put out a hand and stopped the senseless gyration.

Where in all this damned farrago of self-indulgent nonsense did Aunt Esther fit in? It was not after all as simple as a woman toppling over into middle-age and trying to hang on to her beauty. On the face of it there was no better rejuvenator than a young man going off to war. Most women appreciated the aphrodisiac quality of the tootling of trumpets and off we go.

She must have stepped into what she considered was a tender affair and found herself inexplicably entangled in a passionate infatuation. She had told Harriet about the letters, the poems: to laugh them off, obliterate the rejection, turn it to her advantage ... no, she could not hate Aunt Esther. After all, it was Harriet who had floundered about in the slime and mud and the water-lily stalks like long umbilical cords, slippery, to get her out of the lake. One afternoon Aunt Esther had given her companion the slip (mother needs a companion, said Magda, she's having a nervous breakdown) and had taken out the punt by herself. Calmly, in the deepest part, she had gathered up her skirts and stepped off into the water. There was scarcely a splash. Of course, she had denied it afterwards. The punt was rocky and old, she said. Absurd.

How hard she had tried to make Magda marry Scrubbs and bear him a child! How desperately she had pleaded with her, before she sank into her year-long silence. Saying that she owed it to a man who had gone through so much.

'Just think,' she had said one afternoon, when the three of them – she, Magda and Harriet – were picking apples. "What a child it would be, my darling! With your father's blood and my blood and your blood and Scrubbs's blood – all running together in its veins! What a child you could make for me, Magda!'

And the two girls had dropped the apples into their basket and looked at her in horror.

Fourteen

At the Guy Fawkes' Night party Ted Everett came into his own. For days he had been organizing the bonfire. His boys and their friends had been set to work hauling old rotten fencing staves, half-dead trees, great ruined tyres, worm-eaten chicken-houses, down through the spinney, past Harriet's bus and on to the field where the great fire was to be lit.

The eldest boy, Steve, smitten with boils, thin, but enthusiastic, drove the tractor with a grab on the back and Harriet saw him through the thin drizzle of early morning edging tree-trunks into position with the nicety of a craftsman.

Gregg had been out with Ted Everett slashing down brambles and overgrown undergrowth in the Crescent Wood, clearing out the ditches near the boundary where bedsteads and collapsed armchairs appeared by stealth. 'The detritus of a society on the hire purchase,' he said, and Ted Everett stored up the word to use later.

The farm had never had such a clearing. It would give them several more acres to plough, Ted told his wife. It was nice to see the boss take an interest at last.

'And why is he, pray?' his wife asked pursily. 'Who gets a grandstand view of the goings-on on bonfire night?'

'Well, poor bugger,' said Ted, staring out of his innocent moon of a face as he shovelled in chips. 'Odds were he'd be blind by the Fifth. Now he's not.'

His wife's folded lips told anyone who cared to get the message that some people might be fooled, but not she.

The circle of straw bales was set wide round the great mound; Gregg supervised this himself. Not too near, he told his helpers. He tested the stakes with his foot. They kept the base of the fire solid. He was exhilarated by the clean-out. He had even found an old chain harrow in the same bed of nettles that had hidden the chicken-houses. He felt obscurely guilty at having neglected this land. He planned to run more farrowing sows in certain of the reclaimed ground.

'We'll cut a path through Crescent Wood after Christmas,' said Gregg to Magda as he helped set up the trestle tables behind the straw bales. 'Get rid of the rest of those damned brambles. Let the trees breathe, they're suffocating each other. Even the rides are getting overgrown.'

Mrs Everett and Harriet set the tables with mugs and glasses and a barrel of beer for the men and one of cider for the children.

'You'll keep the soup and coffee going, Harriet?' asked Magda. 'And Mrs Everett and Theresa and I will cook all the sausages in the oven and bring them down hot with the rolls. Don't let Ted forget the potatoes, he'd better wash them first before he lets the children have them for the fire.'

'Wash them, Mrs Witheredge? Potatoes are never washed that are to be baked in the ashes. Leave the dirt on them, they'll taste all the better,' exclaimed Mrs Everett, scandalized, and to show that she knew what was what.

'Oh,' said Magda. She was not used to being wrong. 'Oh, of course. Well, you do as you think, Mrs Everett. And will Stevie bring his guitar?'

'He'll not be parted from it.' Elevated at also providing the entertainment, she went on, with pride, 'Our Ted'll doubtless oblige on the mouth organ as well.'

Harriet had emptied her shed of everything she had been hoarding for years: old ragged deck-chairs she had never mended, rickety bamboo tables for the garden and a broken kitchen chair from her mother's house on which the guy was to sit.

On the day itself there was an early morning mist and her fire was drawing well. That meant that it would be a frosty-night and not a damp one. She was scarcely up when there was a knock on the door. It was Jimmy Everett. He had on his red knitted cap, but had forgotten his gloves and his hands were blue as he held out her milk can.

'Aren't your hands cold, Jimmy?'

'Not really,' he replied, blowing on them. 'But that old guy hasn't got any gloves, miss. You wouldn't have any, I s'pose? We found some boots. They come off of an old tramp, they were in a ditch and Steve's polished 'em up. That old guy'll look funny without gloves.'

'Look in the shed,' said Harriet. 'There's an old woollen pair I sometimes use for gardening, but they're not much use to me, they get too sodden. You can have those.'

She hated guys. Why couldn't people be content with the symbolism of the thing? Winter solstice and all that. A human sacrifice was going altogether too far: she was surprised that Gregg allowed it.

Jimmy came back with the gloves and knocked on the door again to tell her that he had six packets of sparklers and twelve bangers so she'd better keep her cats in.

✖

'Now then, lads, stand back,' cried Ted Everett, everywhere at once with matches and rolls of newspapers. 'Watch the direction of the wind, son! Keep your fireworks well away from the fire.'

Stakes had been hammered in at a good distance to take the Catherine wheels, and a supply of empty beer bottles were stuck firmly in the ground for the rockets.

Small boys wheeled about in the dusk, woollen scarves over their heads and crossed over their chests and pinned behind. They held sparklers in gloved hands and as they jumped over the straw bales the field appeared to be lighted by whirling fireflies. Groups of unknown, unidentifiable grown ups stood about, waiting for the flames to crackle up into something they could applaud. Women shivered selfconsciously, looking behind them, fearing bangers.

Harriet stood over her fire in the bus, the curtains drawn back so that she would miss nothing. Two great saucepans, one of coffee, one of milk, steamed gently on the stove and she watched a third one, full of tomato soup. She had been opening tins all the late afternoon, it seemed. The door opened and Meirion came in; he had on a green deerstalker with the earflaps tied down.

'Everett's in his element out there. Queer chap. Damned cold, can I warm up in here, help you?'

'Nothing to do except to watch the soup. Let's have some whisky, like your first night here. The bottle's over there, will you pour it?'

Meirion watched her with a faint grudge stirring. She owed him an apology for flaunting off like that, after the damned good lunch he'd stood her. But then she never seemed to feel that an explanation was necessary, he remembered. When a thing was done, it was done; nothing afterwards really mitigated it.

'You've weathered how many weeks? Six? D'you think you'll stand the winter?'

He would not mention it if she didn't. It would sound too petty. Even as he realized that he was asking her another question – a sign of unease – Harriet turned and gave him a long look from under her brows which showed him that she was aware of everything.

'I don't see why I shouldn't weather the winter,' she said now, coolly. 'I've insulated the inside, which gives me twenty-five per cent more heat. Oh look! The first rocket.'

She leaned forward, glass in hand, and watched the rocket curve up and away into the windless air, to eject its own exclamation of stars, which twinkled down; red, green, white. They vanished, and somewhere on the dark field below a child stumbled to find the empty reeking case.

'Whenever you're here,' Harriet laughed at him, 'you're always asking me questions. Now let me ask you one. Who's here?'

'The whole boiling. Magda's asked nearly everyone she knows.'

'Her mother used to like bonfire parties. But she gave them round the other side, near the house. We used to have the bonfire on the home paddock and watch it between the box hedges of the top lawn.'

'You're honoured tonight then, *fête galante, fête champêtre*, eh?'

'Hardly the climate. You know, I sometimes long for somewhere really hot and dry where one's feet never get wet. I hate guys, don't you? Gregg said the kids would be disappointed if they didn't have one. But I shan't watch it burn – it's got my gloves on and it's sitting on one of my mother's kitchen chairs. It's so – so terribly domestic'

Meirion came and stood beside her by the window. The cats had retreated to the cabin, where they sat for comfort on one of Harriet's old pullovers. With each bang from outside they narrowed their eyes and twitched their ears.

'It's also got green glass eyes, goblin, and a pair of old sunglasses. I saw two boys heaving it up and tying it in. Under Ted's directions, of course. How that man loves an audience!'

Harriet was glad that she could satisfy Meirion's curiosity in one direction at least. She said rather wryly:

'Before Mrs Everett started not to like me, she told me all about him. She has a great tolerance for him, you know, although he wears her out—'

The faintest disapproval showed on Meirion's face, and Harriet gestured reassuringly. She saw that he was terrified of embarrassing himself.

'And the children, too. He's a man who desperately tries to flow over into everybody else's life, you see. He throve on his eldest boy's homework until it got beyond him. He used to play football with them up here on the farm. We'd hear him shouting and blowing his whistle and taking all the various positions to show them how to play – but then they quietly trickled away and played down in the town with their friends. He talks war to Gregg and dogs to Magda and the joys of country life to me. He wants to make the bus over, he says, being handy. Give him half a chance and he'll write you a poem.'

'Did his wife tell you all that, or did you work it out for yourself?'

'Pure observation. She doesn't know why he is as he is. Except that he was unfortunate, as she puts it. She went round and round and on about how his mother was so young at the time and rightly he shouldn't have been born at all. No, he's illegitimate, and feels it.'

'Poor bastard,' said Meirion, smiling.

'Yes indeed. He's a man who desperately wants to know his place, if you understand me. Apparently an army camp was near by where his mother lived in Norfolk, and Ted thinks that his father may have been a high-up. Top brass, as he puts it. But he doesn't know and neither does his mother – and if she does, she won't say, she's quite a character. So if he's a general's by-blow is he superior or inferior to Gregg? He can't settle it in his own mind.'

'Well, he knows where his own children come from,' said Meirion, 'that's something. But it does explain it a bit. I'd say a lance-bombardier fathered him. All that bounce. Generals don't have bounce. Only travelling salesmen and frightened soldiers.'

❧

Out in the field the bonfire was catching and the children were in anguish, not knowing what to watch; the fireworks that the grown-ups were setting off or the creeping flames sizzling around the old tyres and the paraffin-soaked bracken and brambles.

'Watch my five-shilling rocket! Watch it! There it goes!'

Somewhere off to the left a muffled-up man was setting fire to an involved home-made set piece, with Catherine wheels and Roman fountains all exploding and sizzling down gushes of sparks. It was Chidlington and his brood.

'Where's Harriet?' asked Magda. Gregg, who was by her side drawing beer for the men, looked over his shoulder at the bus.

'In there. There's someone with her. There, at the window. She's watching.'

'I hope the soup's all right. She's drinking, can you see the silhouette of the glass? Who's that with her?'

In a moment Gregg went over to the fire and had a word with Ted Everett, who was gazing up at the guy.

'Looks real, doesn't he, boss? Tied it on myself. No danger, I'll watch it. Clear off, you boys! Something might explode. No, don't you chuck bangers in the fire, you little devil. No, it's not time for the potatoes yet. Go and ask your mother to light that, Jimmy. Flo! Flo!' His round face glowing, his round eyes snapping, Ted Everett was in his element as executioner. Now he yelled across Gregg to his wife. 'Flo! Make sure that those fireworks can be held in the hand. I put 'em into two separate boxes.

Don't let the kids mix 'em up, now. Got to watch 'em. Jacky, you light the next rocket. Then the helicopters.'

Gregg walked off, plunging through the uneven field, head down. Who the devil had she got in there with her?

'Oh, it's you, Meirion,' he said as he stepped inside. 'Whenever I find you, you're swigging whisky with Harry.'

'Here you are, Gregg. Are you cold?'

Harriet laid her hand against his cold cheek. It was a gesture that Meirion did not miss. It was quite unlike the boisterous welcome of six weeks ago, and he smiled quietly into his glass.

'I'm just going,' he said. 'Let me wash up this glass and then it's your turn to swig whisky.'

As he went out of the door Harriet asked him to tell Magda that the soup was hot, so was the coffee, and to give her a signal if they wanted it in the field.

She looked at the scene below her. It was alive with dark figures under the crackling sky. Small coloured helicopters zoomed, rockets whooshed upwards; she could hear shouts. Suddenly the fire blazed up and there was a cheer; the crowd thickened around it. The flames had smelled out the lolling straw figure, and now, purring and shifting around the legs of the chair, were flickering upwards; she caught the glint of light on the sunglasses. Gregg turned her from the window and kissed her.

'Don't look,' he said, his arm around her shoulders.

✻

'Quick, do look,' said Hilda Chidlington to her husband. 'Sentimental cutout. Damn, they've ducked away. I could have sworn – how Magda stands it, I don't know.'

'Lookit the guy, dad! lookit the guy! He's sizzling,' shouted the Chidlingtons' eldest, clapping his hands to his sides in ecstasy. 'I've stuck a dazzler in his boot! Look, Steve, I've stuck a—'

'He's welcome,' said Chidlington, giving his son a savage shove. 'She's not much to look at.'

'You didn't think that the other night when Gregg docked you one,' said his wife. 'Watch the boys, dear, or they'll go up in flames.'

'Come on out of it, you silly little devil!' roared Chidlington suddenly and stepped forward to haul his youngest son from the fire, pulling him out like a hot potato. 'It's too soon yet for you to fry.'

'Rather macabre, isn't it,' said Lila Merrington, her sharp nose alert over her storm collar. 'I hate guys. It's squirming, it looks alive – oh, its glasses are melting all over its face – how horrible! Where's Harry?'

Both women turned and looked back to the bus. The curtains were pulled together again and the lamps were dimmed. Two figures made their way unsteadily over the furrows, bearing large jugs.

'She's bringing the soup and coffee, thank God. My feet are frozen but my face is on fire.'

'Ah,' mused Lila. *'Dans le grand pare solitaire et glace, deux ombres ont tout a l'heure passe …'*

'I've often envied you your French education,' said Chidlington. 'Perhaps I could enliven the evening by flirting with you? I'm only an old tea planter, but that was good enough for my wife at one time …'

'Don't be a bloody fool, Mark. Watch the children.'

'And you can watch me. A charming family piece.'

'Coffee's up,' said Harriet behind them. 'It's on the trestle table. Soup, too, if you don't mind drinking it from mugs.'

'We're having a lovely time,' said Lila. 'Hasn't Gregg laced the coffee with anything interesting? Or did you both tank up while you were making it?'

Harriet was staring at the collapsed guy. She only caught the last few words.

'There's whisky at the bus if you're dying for a drink,' she said.

'I'm never *dying* for anything,' said Lila. 'My desires are always more or less under control.'

'How splendid for you to be semi-detached, then.' Harriet moved away into the deeper shadows outside the circle of firelight. Now she had really made an enemy. Never mind. There was a cruel testing, an absolute finality about an orgy of burning: it made one reckless. The burning of books, of men, of old women; the firing of cities and of ships, petrol poured on the sea. Even in those countries where the sun became a fiery enemy, burning and rendering to ash water and earth and stone. One dealt in ultimates.

Ted Everett ran past her, brushing clumsily against her arm, making her spill some coffee.

'Shift that log!' he shouted. 'The potatoes can go in now. Here, let me.' He seized hold of a pitchfork and heaved at a rotten branch tottering near the top of the pile. But he overran himself and fell on to the flaming brands of the kitchen chair. The pitchfork saved him from toppling headfirst into the savagely glowing centre, but when Chidlington and Gregg pulled him clear the whole of his right sleeve was alight. At once the women were on him, beating it out.

'I'll take him up to the bus,' said Harriet. 'Magda, keep the children occupied with drinking soup, or they'll be frightened.'

For the field was full of suddenly quiet faces and Roman candles grew and blossomed and died unwatched. Ted Everett's face was dead white. Without a word he accepted Harriet's arm and moved away with her. Once he turned and called to his wife to stay and keep an eye on things.

When they reached the bus Harriet was surprised to see that Lila Merrington had followed them. Perhaps she appreciated a challenge taken up, not adroitly turned. More likely, she wanted to see the inside of this palace of sin.

'Lucky you had leather gloves on,' she said, as Harriet sat Ted down in the cats' usual chair. 'Have you any burn ointment or boracic, Harry?'

'I think dry boracic is best. You must keep a burn dry. Does that hurt, Ted?'

They peeled off his coat, but the only injury was to his right hand, which he had flung forward to save himself. The heavy material of his government-surplus duffle coat had protected him. He looked different, somehow, his face appeared naked, and as the two women peered closer they saw that his eyebrows had been badly singed. Also his eyelashes were non-existent. Lila touched one eyebrow and the hairs crisped off in her fingers.

'We nearly had a live guy,' she said, laughing.

'Come on, let's have some whisky,' said Harriet hurriedly.

Shivering, Ted drank half of his down quickly. Harriet opened out the burnt hand and shook boracic powder into the palm and in between the fingers. She worked gently but fast. Then she took two of her large handkerchiefs and wrapped them loosely round the whole hand. Over the top she folded a silk scarf and fastened it with a safety-pin.

Lila watched her, amused and a little impressed. She said:

'You certainly have all the essentials here. This looks like home.'

'It is home. It's all I need. There, Ted, is that better? We'll have a look later to see if we've stopped it blistering. Or we can call a doctor, if you'd prefer.'

'He won't come,' said Ted. 'Not on Guy Fawkes Night. Here, I must get back to the kids. Thanks a lot, Miss Harriet.'

'You'd better stay put,' said Harriet. 'You can watch from here if I draw back the curtains. I'll just go down and tell your wife that you're still alive. She'll probably come up.'

'I'll stay and finish my whisky in the warm,' said Lila. 'I adore your grandstand view.'

'That's what the wife called it, a grandstand view,' said Ted. 'Will you look at that now? My kids have gone mad. Sending up rockets in handfuls …'

'It's good money burning,' said Lila, her pale grey eyes crinkled up with pleasure.

Together they watched the great fire, with the children darting like bats around it, swooping for potatoes at the bottom. The grown-ups were sitting on the bales drinking soup, eating sausages. They looked easy and full of talk. Away from Maxmead other fireworks zoomed up and away, like messages.

Mrs Everett came in in a fluster.

'Are you sure she's done the right thing? Olive oil is what my mother used to put on burns. Or butter.'

'No,' said Lila, now on Harriet's side. 'You must keep a burn dry. That's the modern method. We've put on some boracic powder.'

Mrs Everett, who had been looking all round the bus instead of at her husband, now let her eyes rest on his face. She gave a shriek.

'Look at your eyebrows! You've burnt 'em off! My, you do look a sketch. You look like a burnt pig.'

Lila decided that she definitely did not like Mrs Everett, so she got up to go. As she reached the door, she turned and offered her a tube of yellow burn ointment that Harriet had left on the cupboard top.

'You could put some of that on his forehead, it's beginning to look red. That'll soothe it and keep the air out.'

When she had gone, Mrs Everett sniffed.

'Whisky! I thought as much. Been filling you up with whisky, has she? I've heard that both those women drink like fish. Jimmy said once that he'd seen 'em all in here, drinking. Still, you know what to expect when a woman lives by herself. Asking for it, she is.'

'Asking for what? She's a decent sort,' said Ted. 'A lot gentler than you, Flo. Ow! Be careful, don't get that stuff in my eyes.' He watched as his wife screwed the top back on to the tube, and grinned, 'I bet she wouldn't have to ask twice.'

Luckily Flo did not hear that remark. She was peering behind the curtain into the cabin, noting that *she* slept in a sleeping-bag. Dirty habit. When did you wash it? She wiped her finger over the tops of the books on the shelves.

'Looking for a lover, are you, Flo?' asked Ted, chuckling.

'You've had a drop, that's what makes you cheeky. Keeps everything nice and clean, I'll say that for her. Now, if you're comfortable, I'll be off.' She moved the whisky bottle away ostentatiously. 'Trust you to fall in the fire, Ted Everett. Of all the things! Reckoned on being the guy, too, did you?'

'Out of the frying-pan, that's me,' said Ted. 'Tell young Steve to give us a tune on his guitar, p'raps I can hear it up here.'

'That you can't,' said his wife, hovering by the door. The sink was full of dirty saucepans – Magda's from the Hall – so she couldn't very well condemn her for those. She was disappointed and it showed on her face. She took it out on her husband, lounging back in front of the fire, spectacularly done up in borrowed silk scarves, his forehead a yellow smear. 'Tcch! We're quite the wounded gentleman, aren't we? You've got the use of your legs, come on down and listen for yourself. Now I'm going back to see if any of your children have followed their father's fine example—' And she went off crossly.

The fire had settled to a healthy glow, a replete tiger, by the time Ted came back to sit on a straw bale and join in the singing with his mouth organ. He could not bear to be out of things any longer. About a dozen adults were left, smoking and drinking beer, and Gregg came over to him with a bottle.

'Good man, Everett,' he said. 'That's the stuff.'

Children were still running about in the dark, looking for spent fireworks, or coaxing the last of the hot potatoes from the ashes. The cold made everyone draw the bales closer round the fire and there was a ring of flickering faces as the singing started up.

Ted stopped to draw breath and Steve argued quietly but fiercely with his friends what to play next. In that momentary silence another guitar started up with an authoritative sweep of chords. People looked round and saw that it was Magda's Spanish houseman, Angelo, who sat with his wife. He seemed unsure whether to go on or not, and looked apologetically at Magda.

'Go on, Angelo, let's have some *flamenco*,' she said indulgently, and at once Mark Chidlington brightened up. He had been frankly bored by Steve's discordant strumming. 'Let Theresa dance for us,' he called out. Other voices took it up. The Spanish couple had been unobtrusively busy all evening, looking after children, handing round food and drink, and now Magda's guests felt guilty. Damn it, the Spaniards didn't have a Guy Fawkes Night to celebrate. But if you thought about it, it was fitting that Catholics should help to celebrate the foiling of a Catholic plot.

Angelo nodded to Theresa and she stood up in her heavy boots and slacks and duffle coat. Her hands went up above her head and she clicked her fingers once, twice, with authority and arrogance as the first chords came crisply off the strings. Her hips moved. Angelo started to sing;

strange harsh words that keened across the night air and hovered above the plucked notes.

In the firelight Theresa moved and stamped, the heavy clothes scarcely concealing the grace and control of her movements. People leant forward, Chidlington shouted self-consciously, once or twice, *'Olé!'* Otherwise there was absolute silence.

This annual enaction of an old cruelty had moved on to another level; the primeval quality of firelight in an open field, the celebrant voice, caught an echo of elemental despair. It seemed to Harriet that they were celebrating life itself, for life and death and purification by fire were things these two understood.

'What was the song about?' someone asked. Theresa shook her head, sank down breathlessly beside Angelo, who replied for her with a deprecating shrug.

'It is just that life is terrible, but that love can make it a little better,' he explained. 'Now let me play for you a softer song, one we sing at the orange festival in our village.'

His fingers strolled across the strings, his voice floated caressingly around the firelit circle while his dark eyes smiled at his wife.

After a few encores he acknowledged the clapping, but shook his head and there was an awkward silence. No one cared to follow such a performance, but at last Ted Everett said, 'We'll finish up with "Good night, Irene"; I'll play it on my mouth organ.'

Obedient voices, rounded up by the sheepdog, ambled draggingly along before scattering separately into a limbo of silence.

Gregg, unable to bear it a moment longer, jumped up and called to Angelo to play them all back to the house with a Spanish dance.

In the criss-cross of figures coming and going before the fire, the music drawing them off up the field, Meirion went unnoticed. He walked off in the direction of Maxmead, not wanting anyone to break his mood, for he was pregnant with a poem. Should he call it 'On Hearing Flamenco in a November Field'? or just 'Flamenco and Fire' or simply 'Flamenco on Bonfire Night'?

'I saw the heart of Spain beating in an English field ...'

He might even bring in the Inquisition. Anyway, he must hurry before inspiration died under the snapping white stars. He was so engrossed that when he collided with a dark figure near the gap in the far hedge, he scarcely noticed.

Lila's warden had been among the guests, and now she drew him after Gregg. Chidlington was insisting on helping Theresa carry back a box of bottles. The field had nearly emptied. Harriet, left alone, said quietly to Ted Everett, whose evening had suddenly fallen flat:

'Let me have another look at your hand, Ted. I'll put on another dressing. And I'm dying for a cup of tea, how about you?'

Once back in the bus, she hung the kettle over the fire, poked in a couple more small logs. Unwinding the bandage she found that there was no blister. She shook more boracic powder into his palm and bound it up again. 'Keep it like that for now,' she said. 'Don't use the hand. How does it feel?'

'As good as you, Miss Harry,' said Ted, suddenly lurching towards her and putting his good arm around her waist. 'You're a marvel and I wish you luck.'

'Well, thanks very much, Ted,' she said, stepping backwards in sheer surprise.

'I mean it,' he said, bearing down on her. 'Here, give us a kiss, it's been quite a bit of an evenin'.'

Which of Aunt Esther's strictures on handing off unwanted attentions should she follow? He was too near for the light laugh gambit; indeed, his lips were already on hers, pressing hard. Turning her head abruptly from what felt like spongy leather and emery paper, she said, 'Oh don't be a bloody fool, Ted! You don't have to be all that grateful.'

'I'm not good enough, I s'pose! But you can't tell if you don't know, and I can't tell, that's my trouble. I might be dirt or I might not.'

He had let his hands hang by his side and made no further movement in her direction as she sprang towards the steaming kettle. Making tea, she kept her back to him. His reaction was so predictable that she put a mental Q.E.D. to her conversation about him with Meirion.

The situation was so ludicrous for both of them that she felt impelled to be honest. Handing him a mug of tea she said: 'Look here, Ted, just because I live alone doesn't mean that I'm sending out distress signals. Even if your father had been General Eisenhower it would make no difference to me. You're not my type.'

'You don't fancy me,' said Ted gloomily. This was an idea he could at least grasp. 'That's what it is. It's just not my day, is it? That Spanish chap out there now, mucking about with our singsong, playing all those duff notes. My boy Steve went after him like a bitch on heat.' He paused. 'Begging your pardon.'

'Come on, Ted, drink up your tea. You don't really fancy me either, if you're honest. We've had a drink and we're friends—'

Ted shook his head heavily. 'No, we're not. You're a cut above me, I reckon. You won't let me fix up this place for you. I'd throw out those dirty old lamps for a start. Dangerous they are, specially with cats about. I'd have electric light in here in a jiffy, but you don't want it.'

'I don't want your wife complaining to my cousin that I'm enticing her husband. Because you know that's what she'd do for a start.'

Enflamed by all this straight talk from a woman, Ted Everett gave her a wink with one naked eyelid. The reddened arc lowered itself slowly over the round, sucked treacle-toffee of his eyeball and she could not look away. So she only heard the end of his next sentence.

' … on Hallowe'en.'

'Hallowe'en? What about Hallowe'en?'

'I told you. I saw you and the boss. Stands to reason you've got to fancy somebody, a real nice armful like you—'

He moved towards her again, remembering the quick glance through the chink in the curtains, his recoil, his fear of discovery and the embarrassment it would bring him.

Harriet felt sick. It had come at last and it tasted bad.

'Mr Witheredge and I have known each other for a long time. If you want to spy on us,' she said, feeling absurd and loathing herself and the thick peasant standing before her, 'then do. If it pleases you to creep around this bus and peer in at the windows I can't stop you. You are at liberty to go to my cousin with your tales and see where that gets you.'

This half-threat made her feel sicker and more humiliated than ever. But it worked. His face lost its jauntiness, his shoulders sagged. He stared, not boldly at her, but down into the dregs of his tea. Lose his job, that was it. Bitch.

There was a muffled tap on the door and Harriet moved to open it. Gregg would have come straight in. It was Steve, and, in spite of his thin face, the boils on the neck, it seemed to Harriet that he had more than a touch of his father's brashness.

'Is Dad here, miss? Mam's worrying.'

'Yes, come in, Steve. I've just dressed your father's hand again. He's been having a cup of tea, would you like one?'

The boy shook his head and put one foot up on the floor of the main living-room, openly staring about. Ted Everett put down his mug with a bang and moved towards the boy.

'Well, thanks then, Miss Harriet. Come on, boy. You'll be late for school in the morning.'

The boy shifted his gaze to Harriet.

'Mrs Witheredge said to tell you that there's still a party going on up at the Hall, and would you join them?'

'Oh,' said Harriet, with a great yawn, 'I've had enough excitement for one day, thank you, Steve. I shall go straight to bed.'

The two of them went off through the spinney, their boots sucking at the wet clay. Standing on the step in the quietness she could hear the boy's excited voice praising Angelo, chattering on against his father's silence.

She had had enough of people for one day, as well. It seemed as if an army had come tramping in and out, as well as swarming all over her field.

Before she got into bed she pulled back the curtains and let the cold moonlight rinse around inside the bus, as boiling water scalded a dirty milk pan. Outside in the field the fire still glowed; it would smoulder until morning. For the first time she thought of the future, and she only ever did this when the present became insupportable. It was so unfair, thought Harriet, as she crawled into her sleeping-bag, that when a man really was a bastard, it was the last thing on earth you could call him.

Below the curve of the field, and so out of sight of the bus, the stranger who had knocked into Meirion paced between the hedges. He noted down distances in a small notebook without needing a torch, for the great eye of the moon blazed down on him. When the lights of the bus finally went out, he walked the whole length of the field, coming right up under Harriet's lonicera hedge. More notes, more calculations. Then he went away through the spinney, a soft man in a black hat, to where his car had been left, secretly, in the lane beyond.

Part Three

Fifteen

✻

Rain blotted out the Cambridgeshire plain. From a low grey sky it swept away the last of summer and brought down great quantities of ash leaves into Harriet's garden. It drummed across the leathery skin of the lake and mashed the last of Magda's roses.

On the third day of it, Gregg walked down to the bus, his oilskins streaming. But Harriet was not there. The bus was padlocked and no smoke struggled out of the chimney. When he peered in through the windows there were no signs of the cats, either. With a curious lurch of fear he looked for a long time at their empty chair by the dead fire. He went into the large barn where she kept her car, not expecting to see it, and did not.

He met Ted Everett on his way to feed the pigs and the man stopped, as if he knew what Gregg was looking for.

'Reckon Miss Harriet's well out of it this weather,' he said, knocking a stream of water out of his lashless eyes. There were no eyebrows either to stop the rain from sluicing down off his army beret to divide in streams over his ruddy cheeks. Gregg nodded. If the man had any news he'd wait to hear – but damned if he'd ask.

'The missus said she'd be off up to London when the winter started,' Ted Everett went on, allowing himself the ghost of a grin.

'Business, I expect,' said Gregg out of his sudden rage. He nodded shortly and went off. If she'd stopped the milk, Mrs Everett might know how long she'd gone for. He hesitated at the gates of the drive. Could he call in at the farm on some excuse? Better not. That woman would seize on anything to gossip about.

But when he went indoors Magda met him in the back kitchen.

'Isn't Harry extraordinary!' she burst out as soon as he backed in through the door, shaking his sou'wester at arm's length. 'Really, to go off without a word! I've had Mrs Everett up here with the letters. The postman wouldn't come up the lane any farther on his bike, imagine that. He hurt his leg playing football or something. Dumped everything with her.'

Gregg was easing off his gumboots and looking round for his slippers. 'What d'you mean?'

'Well, Harry went off yesterday. Mrs Everett sent up one of the boys with the milk and some letters. And then later on in the afternoon Harry called in there on her way to London saying that she wasn't sure when she'd be back. It sounded as if she'd been called up there urgently, Mrs Everett thought. Anyway, she took the cats with her.'

'An urgent call,' repeated Gregg. 'Who on earth from?'

He felt sharply jealous, and Magda heard the resentment in his voice. What stupid questions men asked, did he think she was psychic?

'Oh, how on earth do I know? I expect she's got friends, although you wouldn't think it, selling everything up and coming down here. Honestly, Gregg, we'll have to think this whole thing over in the New Year.'

He hung up his oilskins and heard them drip flatly on to the red tiles. He kept his back turned towards her.

As he said nothing, Magda was driven farther in annoyance. 'She can't just settle down in that field and live like a gipsy. What will people say? One or two are beginning to talk already. Harry can be so – so odd.'

'So could your mother.'

Magda was through in the kitchen, putting on the kettle for tea. She had sent Theresa to bed, for the girl had caught a cold. She did not hear what Gregg had said and he did not care to repeat it. But he followed her into the kitchen and sat half on the scrubbed table, one leg swinging, watching her as she arranged the tray for tea.

'Harry was thinking of asking you whether you'd consider selling the field to her. She was a bit concerned about housing development round here—'

Magda swung round. 'Housing development? That's nothing whatever to do with Harry! What a cheek! The Council plans are still fluid. We've got to rehouse about a hundred people, and there's a waiting list of over four hundred for Council houses. And if the Ministry decide to develop light industry around Maxmead there'll be an overspill of hundreds more needing houses. If it came to it, that field would be worth a goldmine to us, the sort of money that Harry couldn't possibly find. And what on earth would she do with it, pray? Let it run wild, I suppose, for her damned cats to roam around in?'

Gregg watched her anger mounting as she opened cupboards and brought out cups, saucers, plates, cake, sugar, milk. Each separate object she put on the tray with controlled violence. If he said nothing he knew that she could come out with something about which she had kept very quiet up to now. She did.

'I've had that field surveyed, Gregg,' said Magda evenly. 'Several of us who own land near the road have done the same. After all, we belong to the community, we must pull together. As Lila says, we must all be prepared to pay our scot and lot—'

'Pay your *what?*

'Oh, you know. Community dues. But with building permission I have it on the highest authority that the price would be between two and three thousand an acre. Twelve acres. That's about thirty thousand pounds at a conservative estimate. Isn't that something? We could do a lot with that.'

'I don't see much paying your scot and lot about that. And what the hell has Lila got to do with it? She doesn't own any land.'

'No. But she's on the County Planning Committee. Of course, I'll wait for an official approach to be made to me, then I'll merely give them first option on the land, subject to planning permission. We work in closely with all kinds of official bodies—'

'That's perfectly good agricultural land. You can't sell it, Magda.'

Gregg, in his agitation, had gone up to his wife and taken her upper arm in a fierce grip. At once she clenched her fist and wrested it away. She stood apart from him rubbing herself.

'If you cleared more of the woodland on the south side of the farm you could extend the twenty-acre field. Use it for fattening bullocks, or build up a bigger dairy herd.'

'You'd want more buildings and more labour. I suppose you've been talking to Ted Everett about this?'

'No. Oh Gregg, of course not. I've just been thinking, that's all. Anyway, the land is in my name. I can do what I like with it. Carry this tray in for me, will you?'

Magda liked people to do things for her. It reminded them – and her – that she was a person not to be discounted. Now, as she preceded her husband to the drawing-room, she was excited by his opposition. The idea of selling the land had only ever been an idea, the way perhaps of establishing herself in Maxmead, of showing up the other members of the Urban Council. Meirion would see to it, when the time came, that her gesture made headlines in *The Curfew*. It would cause a lot of talk. Maybe this was the way to live down the wartime smear of being the child of a wartime profiteer and a half-Jewish beauty. An offer of valuable land near the road, separated from it only by a wood which was already Council property, so that a link-up to a new estate could be made easily, surely this would show her good faith? Pushing more logs on to the fire, stirring the dogs away from the hearth with her foot, she began to work out how many houses could be built there. On twelve acres, say, one hundred and twenty-four houses. Twelve houses to the acre. One hundred and twenty-four families housed. She saw herself graciously accepting the gratitude of these people, and even the gratitude of the Minister himself, when the plan went up to London. And the money would be lovely, too. Money was always useful. She could afford to compensate Harry, although of course there was no legal obligation to do so. She might even let her keep half an acre. It would be an additional barrier, anyway, between the estate people and Uplands. So she and Gregg would still have their privacy.

'It needn't bother Harry,' she said, as she poured tea, smiling across at Gregg. 'She could keep half an acre and we'd put up a high fence between her and the estate. She needn't even know the houses were there at all. And when the bus falls to bits we could offer to build her a nice little bungalow. Her mother would have liked that.' Gregg lighted a cigarette. He was surprised to find that his hand was trembling and the beginnings of a headache stirred viciously behind his eyes. He realized that Magda actually believed in her own benevolence.

'Harry's mother is dead, so a bungalow is scarcely going to mean much to her,' he said. 'And your mother left Harry the bus. It's nothing much, I know, by our standards. Or rather, by yours. But it means a lot to her. And the view.'

Magda looked at him as if he were mad.

'The view?' she repeated. 'And how much do you suppose she will be prepared to pay for this famous view? Five hundred pounds? A thousand? Gregg, we can get at least *two thousand* pounds an acre for that field. And that's not being greedy, as things are today. If we sold to private speculators we could count on getting double that. So if we sell to the Council we're already sacrificing half what we could legally get. We could buy land in the Bahamas – anywhere – and spend the winters abroad.'

Very quietly Gregg said, 'I wouldn't want to spend any time at all in the Bahamas with you, Magda. And if you think of going on with this monstrous idea, I'll divorce you.'

For a moment Magda did not think she heard properly. She stared at him while handing him his cup of tea. The gold border on the white saucer, the position of the teaspoon, took on an overwhelming presence. She would never look at that tea-set again without remembering his words.

'I believe I have grounds,' Gregg went on, stirring his tea, aware that his wife was watching him. 'I imagine it's no secret. I shall cite Meirion Pritchard. But my real reason will be that I can no longer live with a woman who is activated by spite and personal aggrandisement.'

Magda recovered during this speech. She laughed outright, with real relief.

'You'll have to find other grounds that will stand up in court,' she said. 'Meirion and I aren't lovers. Why did you think we were?'

Why indeed? The fellow was always hanging around. She was always late back, creeping into her room. He was the kind of man to attract her, he told her.

'You're a fool, Gregg,' she said at last. 'Meirion and I have a lot in common. I see a great deal of him, I admit. He's useful with that paper of his. I don't need to go to bed with him to get what I want, and I certainly am not going to risk gossip in my position.' She lighted a cigarette for herself. 'We must have grown very far apart for you to have misjudged me so badly.'

His body like lead, Gregg got up and went to the window. He stood stiffly watching the sweeping grey curtains of rain. When had he ever got the better of Magda?

'I could live in London,' he said heavily. 'At least I have a big stake in the firm.'

Magda smiled into the fire, which spat as rain found its way into it down the chimney.

'And what would Harry do then, poor thing? She'd have no champion.'

Guardedly, Gregg said, 'This scheme of yours would take a year or two to get going. That would give her time to make her plans. What makes you think that she wouldn't fight it? She's no fool. Like me.'

More he could not say. Harriet was gone. She might not want a showdown just yet. Magda yawned.

'Harry always manages to mess things up. She doesn't think before she leaps. There's always trouble wherever she goes. Funny, prickly old Harry. People get involved with her, she can't help it. I don't mind her, though. I quite like having her around, don't you?'

Feeling like the last defender in a besieged city, Gregg said, yes, he did. She liked listening to music with him. She was kind. Then he waited for the cock to crow three times.

Sixteen

'I was surprised to get your letter. It's been such a long time,' said Harriet to the huge old ruin of a man sitting opposite her in the lounge of the Oriental Club.

She had found her way through the seethe of Oxford Street to the great stone façade of Stratford House. Now she had been sucked in gently past the ticker tape in the hall, the gun-metal elephant, up past the padded velvet chair in which you sat to be weighed against brass weights. Had Captain Malone ever been weighed here, sitting beside drums of oil?

Captain Malone said now, heavily, 'Your mother was a fine woman. She was straight and she said what she meant. It hit me when I saw her death announced in *The Times*. Caught up with it weeks after, in Abadan. Should have written before.'

'It was lucky the new people in the house took the trouble to find out where I was living, otherwise I still wouldn't have got it,' said Harriet, imagining him going through a pile of newspapers, kept for him in some club in the Middle East. A cool oasis of a place in the hot glare of desert country. She had only put in the announcement because it was the sort of thing her mother would have expected her to do. She never imagined anybody actually grazing on those columns; looking at the Captain, however, she realized that for people like him, this was probably the fullest extent of their reading.

She caught his glance. Still a strong blue, his eyes lurked behind dropping pouches of leathery skin. He was square, like a monolith. His cheeks dropped to a square softening jaw. Thick white hair emphasized his brownness. He still reminded her, after all these years, of a rhinoceros, but this time with the skin filled out. He had not shrunk in old age, his bones and muscles had set like tough lard in a basin. He misunderstood her swift private smile. To Harriet, as yet, he scarcely seemed part of the present at all.

His hand did not shake as he lifted his long rye-on-the-rocks to his mouth.

'Saw all those bits she put in about the boy on his birthday. Every year to the dot. She never forgot him. I did, months at a time. Then I'd see it. Cut me up every year. Women are odd customers.'

Harriet didn't follow and he noticed her quick frown. At once he was on to something, shrewd and alert. The ice jingled as he set down his glass.

'Never forgave me for not coming over to the boy's funeral. Hate funerals. Pointless. It's all over, done with. But she saw to it that he had a Catholic do. That was right. Be buried as you're christened, even if in between you never get the smell of a priest.'

His strong staccato voice pumped the words home. There was no arguing with him, there never had been. What strange duels had her mother had with him in the past, and who had won?

'Do you mean,' asked Harriet, strangely hesitant, 'd'you mean that mother put Scrubbs in the *In Memoriam* column? I never saw them, she never told me.'

And what had mother said? What dreadful sentiment had she dredged up, what rhyming couplets? That she should have done this in secret offended Harriet so much that she looked across at the old man with hostility. He laughed, slapped the table and this startled an elderly waitress, who looked as if she had walked on from the wings in a Lonsdale play. Long white streamers on her cap and an elaborate square collar worked in some kind of *broderie anglaise*. White apron, black dress. Maybe the men here liked a nanny-figure to bring their drinks or coffee. He waved her away as she came towards them. Then he laughed again, showing strong, long yellowing teeth. An old man-eater.

'Short and to the point it was. "In green and loving memory of Patrick Michael Malone who survived the war but lost the peace. From his family. R.I.P." That appeared every tenth of June until this year. I missed it.'

Harriet stared at him. Very much alive he was, swathed and folded in expensive cloth, settled against the back of the tall chair that held him safe as a womb. He committed an offence purely by being there at all; an offence against the past. His attitude disturbed her in some way: something in it she missed. She was familiar with the discomfort with which certain men watched RAF flypasts since the end of the war: she had seen them gazing up at the shrieking, memorial planes with a guilt mixed with some intolerable envy. Her own father had carried the burden of his survival from the 1914 war in the same way; solemnly removing his hat whenever he walked past the Cenotaph and not speaking until he was fifty yards beyond it.

There was nothing of this about Captain Malone. He was glad to be alive although his son was dead. He was delighted to be a strong old man, why not? He still appreciated Harriet's mother's sentiments about the boy: it was a fitting thing for a woman to do. That was all. Harriet was driven back to another grudge; she was jealous of her mother for thinking of doing such a thing. Above all, of saying just the right words: giving nothing away, saying it all, keeping it a secret from her family. As if she had a right to have this private communion between Scrubbs, Captain Malone and herself.

Captain Malone said, standing up:

'Well, there it was in black and white for anyone who cared to look. Let's go down to dinner.'

He stood up, offering Harriet his arm, and she noticed that he smelt innocently of lavender soap. She wondered, as they moved down the rather noble curve of the stairs, whether Scrubbs had found him formidable. In old age Captain Malone was no sort of rhinoceros; not really, for he no longer charged head on. His remark told her this; it made her aware that he had mastered the art of the oblique reproach, and her silence told him that she had taken his point.

Over his avocado pear – his digestion appeared to Harriet preposterous – he asked about her mother. She told him about the commotion in church and it set him back, she could see that. He left a quarter of his pear out of respect. He appeared to be overcome by the fitness of such a happening, just as Magda had been. Had she died in a Catholic church he would have crossed himself in praise and fear.

'My wife's dead, too,' he said after a pause. 'I don't think you ever met her, although Daisy did.'

Captain Malone's second wife was called Babs, she was American and she was in oil. That was all that Harriet knew of her. Babs had usually preferred to stay over in Paris when Captain Malone paid one of his quick visits to London to check up on Scrubbs and wash his hands of him once again.

Over his sirloin, to Harriet's non-committal murmur, he said:

'You'll need a good burgundy with this. Drink up. Yes, she died last year. Odd in its way. Now Daisy died in church, you say. Babs got heatstroke in Palmyra looking over the Great Temple of Bel. Mad on ruins. I had her ashes sent back to New York. Remarkable woman, good business head, kept me up to the mark; that's what a man needs.'

That was what his first wife had never done for him. Poor Silly Millie, thought Harriet, she would never keep anyone up to the mark, because she had never known what the mark was. As if following her thoughts, Captain Malone said sharply, to ward off sympathy, 'The boy took after his mother.'

'He had your temper. And he was independent, which his mother never was.'

Harriet was drinking more than was wise. Burgundy tended to rouse her to a heavy aggressiveness, then sleepy stupor. But Captain Malone took her words as a compliment. He asked her what she was doing, and as she told him she felt disoriented in the comfort of her surroundings. Being waited on made her uneasy. She began to regret that she had responded so immediately to his letter; although it had been so delayed in reaching her that a refusal would have been more trouble than the hurried journey itself. It had come, too, this curious invitation, at a time when she needed to get away from the ceaseless rain of Cambridgeshire, the narrow compass of the bus and the disturbing night of the bonfire. Even as she spoke, she sensed disapproval in the fall of his jowls.

Over the cheese he allowed himself to say that he had never had any time for her Aunt Esther. Too airy-fairy by half. Then he fired at her the same question her mother had done.

'This old hut. Is the land yours, too? Did your aunt leave you that?'

'It isn't a hut. It's a bus. No, the land isn't mine, but as good as.'

It sounded absurd, under these high, painted ceilings, among pussy-footed waiters. Even the elephant outside might well shake its ears in laughter. A bus!

Even as pride of possession made her flash him a look of pure dislike, he rose to his feet.

'We'll take our coffee upstairs,' he said, and they mounted the staircase together once more.

'You've got your mother's look, Harriet,' he said, settling to his coffee and brandy. 'She used to meet me in the other place, before the Club moved here. Very incensed because ladies weren't allowed up the main staircase. Thought that all the doors labelled "Gentlemen" meant that they were lavatories. But they were just private rooms, to keep women out.' He laughed. 'Have a cigar. I suppose we must move with the times. I always carry small cigars for ladies. My wife enjoyed one after dinner. I allow myself one a day, like to smoke it in company.'

Harriet liked the smell of cigars. It made her think of Christmas, the only time her careful father ever drew one from his breast pocket and leaned back from the ruins of the vast meal. It smelt of money, of security.

'Suits you, a cigar,' said Captain Malone, from under half-closed lids and thick, still-dark brows. 'Yes, you've got a strong face. You're no fool, Harriet. Never married, did you? Mug's game. Done much travelling?'

Harriet pulled herself together. In the past she had been frightened by his manner. Now, in a euphoria of brandy and cigars, she merely saw that he wanted to be entertained. He no longer wanted to talk about the dead; he had made a quick genuflection to the past and had turned away from it.

She told him about the extraordinary hotel she had once stayed in with Aunt Esther. Since the war her aunt had taken her abroad several times; Switzerland, France, Germany. But Bad Gastein would amuse him most, she thought. They had stayed at the Emperorhof, surrounded by woods and waterfalls. It was like living in someone else's past – even the tall wall-mirrors reflected the Hohenzollern dream of European supremacy, and the crumbling of those dreams had thickened the atmosphere of decay and airlessness. It was a luxury museum of scarcely animated dolls. She felt that if the elaborate towers could have been lifted off, the guests would crumble into dust.

She did not say all this to the old man, who might be listening, or sunk into an after-dinner somnolence. She told him instead about the guests; or rather it pleased her to talk about them: for she had never forgotten these old ladies with their dyed red curly hair and their pink powdered cheeks, all blazing diamonds and bare bosoms. Diamonds did not change, age did not dim their glitter. They were still an old girl's best friend because they bought the devoted attentions of young, spry men. These young-old men, living like silverfish in the cracks of a rotten society, escorted their patronesses to the Kurhalle to drink the Spa waters, and to their favourite cafés in the afternoons to guzzle *schlagsahne Torte* and drink coffee. In the evenings they stood guard by the bridge tables, listening to the jingle and clash of gold bracelets and the vulpine bidding.

An old man, Harriet remembered, wearing white gloves to match his gleaming hair (even this was suspect), bowed them in to dinner and tinkled out Strauss and Lehar on a vast Bechstein piano. No one listened.

Bed at ten, for at five in the morning began the white-hooded and robed procession to the *Badehaus;* early devotions to the great god of rejuvenation ... the most decrepit to be lowered into the restorative waters on chairs. The attendants were young and handsome and available and all the lifts were heated.

Harriet remembered the tiny dark-brown squirrels the Germans collectively called Hansi, so tame that they would run up your legs and sit on your shoulder as you walked along the wooded promenades. Once, a youngish man who carried with him the stigmata of an uneasy peace had joined her on one of her solitary walks to the big waterfall, and she had realized that he regarded her as a fellow-conspirator, asking her subtle questions about her real relationship with Aunt Esther.

'She is charming, so vivacious,' he had said jealously, as they watched the grey strings of water, so appropriately called the *Schnurlregen.* 'Is she generous with you? *Sympatisch?*' He had no time for girls, he told her, although he appeared on Harriet's balcony one night, hoping to have a little pleasure with a clean young woman. Sometimes, he told her wistfully, he revolted against the spongy flesh of old women. But she had laughed and he had gone away, still corrupt, but sad. He was saving for his middle years when he would marry and settle down on the French Riviera.

Old, shaking men in wheelchairs or walking with sticks, each attended by a nurse, a chauffeur-valet and occasionally a watchful, bored wife. Financial wizards, Lebanese millionaires, Greeks, Arabian kings with their Austro-Hungarian entourages, Jewish wielders of past power who had spent the war in South America and were now drawn back by the beneficial spa waters, the echoes of an impossible, almost unbelievable past. Each having immense possessions, an intolerable nostalgia and a common terror of death.

Captain Malone opened his eyes. She had almost forgotten him. It had almost been like talking to one of her spools of tape.

'Bloody old fools,' he said. 'Europe's finished. Babs and I liked the desert. Syria. Europe's like a dark room after the light out there. And round the edge of the Sahara now, towards Morocco and Algeria, that's the place to settle. Been all over, and it wasn't just for the oil, although we found plenty. Babs was in oil, you know.'

'Yes, I remember,' said Harriet. 'Mother told me that you'd married a woman in oil.'

'I've got some sort of scheme on,' said Captain Malone. 'But it's too late to go into it tonight. You were trained as a librarian, weren't you? Got a good mind for facts; that follows.'

He had recovered his vitality, but Harriet saw that it was a brief revival. She felt guilty about her rather melancholy travelogue. Anyway, it was late and she had a train to catch.

'Where are you staying?'

She told him that she was staying with friends near Hampton Court. Where they used to live. Neighbours. At once Captain Malone pressed a bell, and when the elderly waitress came, asked her to tell his man to bring the car round in ten minutes.

'Bradshaw will take you home,' he said. 'Now, how about lunching with me here tomorrow? I'm off next day.' As she hesitated, he said, 'Bradshaw will pick you up at twelve o'clock. I've enjoyed having you as my guest.'

He came down to see her off, and as the tall, uniformed chauffeur came in through the doors, he said, as if it didn't really matter:

'I suppose you can drive a car?'

She nodded, wondering whether this meant that she after all would be required to drive Bradshaw. But he said, giving her his dry, fleshy hand, 'And you're healthy, I can see that. Off you go. See you tomorrow,' and relinquished her to Bradshaw and the smoothest drive back to the suburbs that she had ever experienced.

Seventeen

It was strange to sleep in a house again. Strange to walk up the short suburban path, swept by rain, where privet hedges dripped and crude rockeries set in the dowdy grass showed a prematurely bald winter face.

They had waited up for her and she could sense the astonished twitch of curtains as the Daimler slid smoothly away from the gate.

'We're having our Ovaltine, Harry,' said her school friend Jean. 'Mother's gone up to bed. I'll heat you some milk in the kitchen.'

'Don't bother,' said Harriet. 'I've drunk enough to sink a battleship.'

But she stayed and talked with Jean and her husband for politeness' sake, as she would with complete strangers. Jean was a model daughter. She had worked at the Bank of England for fifteen years and then left to marry a fellow-employee. Jean's husband had moved into the house near Hampton Court, so that instead of commuting from Streatham, from his own mother's house, he now made a longer journey to the Bank each day from his wife's mother's house. Jean had two small children, so Harriet had been put up in the baby's room, while the cot had been moved into the other child's room.

'Have the cats behaved?' she asked. The two of them sat complainingly on her feet.

'Oh yes,' said Jean, uncomfortably. 'They don't like children, though, do they?'

'They're not used to children. It was good of you to put us up, Jean. Hotels are funny about cats.'

Derek said, turning off the television, 'Come on, let's hear all about your evening. He must be a pretty posh sort of bloke, sending you home in a hired car.'

Harriet told them all she could. She was curiously reluctant to talk about Captain Malone, because she had not had time to draw her own conclusions about him. Also, she disliked Jean's husband, who sang in the Bank's amateur operatics and was steadily working his way up through the grades. He was responsible, safe and deathly dull. Jean had been engaged to him for years before they married; the delay was due to a muted tug-o'-war between the two mothers. Both threatened to die of heart disease if their children left home; in the end it was Jean's mother's palpitations which won, and Derek's mother moved away to share a flat at Bexhill with a disgruntled unmarried sister.

Derek's neat, straightly-set trilby hat had been a feature of Harriet's mother's Saturday afternoons. 'There it goes, bobbing past the hedge,' she would call out to Harriet. 'Regular as clockwork.' Did she perhaps wish that such an unexceptional hat would turn in at number 26 instead of at number 30? 'Such a nice, steady young man.' Which was not strictly accurate, for Derek had never been young.

Harriet lay in her narrow bed with the cats beside her. 'You let them sleep *in your bed*?' Jean had queried, shocked, and Harriet had bitten back a caustic rejoinder concerning Jean's choice of bedmate. Jean had rebelled only twice in her life, both times at Harriet's urging. Once she had gone round the streets with Harriet and Scrubbs, when he had dressed up in Magda's clothes, mincing on high heels and made up to kill. They had called on various houses, asking for subscriptions to a home for fallen women. Scrubbs was supposed to be the fallen woman.

And once, long before, Harriet had made her spend her dinner money on buns, and they had sneaked out of school to eat them on the river, lying giggling in the bottom of a rowing-boat opposite Hampton Church. It was bad luck that both times someone spotted them and Jean's mother had had palpitations and Jean had found out that rebellion wasn't worth weeks of pale reproach.

'Maybe Captain Malone is looking out for another wife,' the horrible Derek had said, jovially snuffling into his Oval-tine and catching the thin beige skin on his upper lip. Jean knew better than to nod encouragingly at Harriet. She was still a little afraid of her. She handled their relationship, such as it was, as tenderly as a recruit a hand-grenade. She was determined to be nice to poor old Harry for Mrs Cooper's sake. Everybody had liked Mrs Cooper and everybody respected her end. Jean's mother often said patiently, 'I expect I shall go suddenly one day, like Daisy. Then you can have my room for a nursery.'

So Harriet lay in bed in what had once been the boxroom. Nowadays people didn't have boxrooms. You weren't supposed to have boxes and trunks full of lovely rubbish for children to rummage about in on rainy days. What on earth did children do when it was wet? The rain, which had brought this question to mind, drummed on the roof, which seemed to be very high above her head. It was odd, and pleasant, to kick about freely in bedclothes, after curling up in a sleeping-bag. Maybe after all she should make up a permanent bed with proper sheets and pillow-slips. Jean's mother would think she was a slut if she knew. Correction. Jean's mother did think she was a slut. And a Disappointment. And a Wasted Brain. At this thought, Harriet, who had intended to use this brain to work out the real reason for Captain Malone's sudden invitation which had come with the letter of condolence, fell fast asleep.

She awoke to Jean's face, surrounded by curling-pins and faintly luminous with night cream. Jean carried a cup of tea and told her that she had been up half the night with the baby, who was cutting a back tooth.

It was to escape her dreadful patience that Harriet offered to push the baby out for a walk after breakfast. Past her old house, now painted up and given a new ground-glass front door with long-stemmed daisies cut into it and a fake lantern in the porch blobbed about with dollops of coloured glass. Harriet was reminded of the wine-gum jewellery they had used at school to fasten their cloaks in the annual butchery of Shakespeare.

The river was swelling gently after all the rain, ponderous as scarcely-boiling porridge, and a few forgotten punts and rowing-boats lay half-submerged at their moorings. Great mats of yellow willow leaves heaved on the dark water.

How had she ever lived here?

Suddenly afraid of meeting friends of her mother's, she started to walk back to number 30. She ought to telephone Gregg, for by now he would have discovered that the bus was empty. What on earth would he think? But the impulse passed. With luck she should be back there – she almost dared to say, back home – this evening. There was no need, and after all, she was independent. She could come and go as she pleased. It was nonsense to say that the first thing a woman did with her freedom was to surrender it.

❀

But Harriet was not back at Uplands that evening. Nor the next. And she was too occupied to telephone.

In the smaller dining-room at the Oriental Club, for women were not allowed into the men's room for luncheon, she sat on one of the feminine tapestried chairs and listened to what Captain Malone had to say.

He cared, so Harriet heard with astonishment, he cared passionately about trees. Planting trees. In starting off a nature cycle that could reclaim the desert. He had taken from the desert long enough, he told her. He – or rather his Company, CORPCO, Consolidated Oil Refinery and Prospecting Company – had done well out of the Middle East. They had sunk great wells down into the sand and pumped up millions of gallons of oil. He had made a fortune out of it. Far more than his father, who had ground down two generations of Birmingham workers making small arms between the wars. Now it was time to give it back.

Did she realize, he asked her, clenching his mottled hands on the table at either side of his plate, did she realize that the Sahara desert advanced thirty miles in a year on a two-thousand-mile front? The desert was the enemy. Man had made the desert, now it was marching on them. With the earth's population increasing, food must be grown in places where before it was thought to be impossible. And it could be.

'We've got the knowledge, we've got the patience. But it all costs money and goodwill and the co-operation of governments. Now I haven't got long to live, Harriet. I'm an old man and I can't sit around and wait for the Jews and the Arabs to divide the waters of the Jordan amicably. I've picked myself a region which is semi-arid, up near the Tunisian border in Algeria, part of what we hope will be the Green Belt. I can't go out into the Arabian desert or the Syrian desert and hope to do any lasting good. It would be like a small boy going off with a bucket and spade. I'm leaving all that for the big boys. They can bore down and tap Savarin's Sea—'

'Savarin's Sea?' Harriet could scarcely follow him.

'There's supposed to be a great reservoir under the Sahara the size of France. The Albienne Nap. That's its real name. The water level sank, you see, now it's trapped – possibly under a clay layer. Tapping it would cost millions. Now, are you free all this afternoon?'

'Why, yes.'

'Good. Then we'll take a ride out to Berkshire. Some friends of mine in another oil company have been making some interesting experiments. I thought you'd like to see them.'

'But why me?' she asked him later in the car, purring busily out of London.

'I'll tell you later, if I think you've caught on. Now for a few facts.'

He gave them to her, and as usual she drank them in, mentally filed them away. Deserts, said Captain Malone, covered one-third of the world's surface. If a human body was one-third burnt, the patient died. The earth itself could not afford such a deprivation of fertility. Then again, one-third of the earth's population lived on a starvation diet. Twenty-odd countries were threatened by what he called the Sahara offensive. Drifting sand kept gangs of workmen busy clearing roads hundreds of miles from the centre of the desert. She'd see what they were doing about that this afternoon. As the car went on smoothly through the drenching rain, Captain Malone looked out greedily at the green lushness of the countryside. Dripping trees, rolling hills covered with green grass, ploughed land. He drank it in while he bombarded her with facts about Lake Chad in Africa, where the sands were choking the waters. It had shrunk in a hundred years to one-eighth of its size. He jumped to the Arabian desert, where goats and camels and nomadic tribes stripped what little vegetation there remained … to India. To what the Chinese were doing, the Russians … her mind was reeling when at last they drew up outside a long building set in parkland.

Then she was watching model sand-dunes built into wind tunnels to judge the drift of sand in quite a mild current of air, then how they moved in a gale. She saw the research assistants spray these dunes with an emulsion distilled from oil, and how the movement was stopped, even in an 80-mile-an-hour gale.

'By this means we can plant eucalyptus trees that won't get drowned in sand, or blasted or uprooted. We've started in Libya and India. But the northern Sahara is my baby.'

The white-coated men lifted their heads from the wind tunnels; one said, 'Some baby.'

On the way back he told her of the travels he and Babs had done together. He talked about Sennacherib's city of Nineveh. A garden city before it was sacked and vanished for ever under the sands. He mentioned Palmyra.

'Babs didn't actually die in the Temple of Bel,' he said, as the outskirts of London appeared through the running windows. The wind-screen wipers had been hypnotizing Harriet for miles. The chauffeur's straight back through the glass panel that divided the car into two emphasized the monotonous to and fro. She inclined her head to listen. Didn't he ever tire?

'Babs felt ill up there, but she died a week later in Damascus. She kept saying, "Tell them back home I died in Palmyra. Tell them, Mike. It's a lovely place to die in. Twist the truth just for once, for me." So I did. Romantic woman, Babs. She'd like me to do this for her, now. She'd say I made the desert blossom.'

No doubt she would, Harriet thought tiredly.

They were too late for tea. But later, over dinner, after Harriet had had time to recover and bathe her face and make up, Captain Malone started once again.

'Oil's a dirty business, Harriet, and some of the dirt rubs off. But if you go through life without expecting some dirt to rub off on you then you're stupid. But now I want to use the money I've made, the time I've got left. If I'd had a son, he could have carried on for me.'

'You had a son once,' said Harriet. The truth was not to be all on his side. She sat up very straight and looked at him.

Captain Malone made an explosive noise.

'Look, my girl. I had a son once. The world's full of people either being destroyed or destroying themselves. Paddy was like his mother. He was a self-destroyer.'

Harriet was filled with fury. The name Paddy set Scrubbs apart, she saw him as a man apart, a boy apart, no proper name even. She did not care that she faced this man in this opulent place, eating food that he was paying for. She said what she knew she had been feeling for years and what was now absolutely, killingly clear.

'That's the whole point. If he destroyed himself he did it because none of us really accepted him for what he was. You didn't. You saw him as a nuisance, to be trained up in schools, to conform, and when he wouldn't be what you wanted you left him alone. You only chucked him back at his mother because you couldn't be bothered. Look, I know we took him in and he shared our life. I know mother loved him. But his own mother treated him like an amusing pet; that was why he grew so wild, and he knew he was too wild for us, for any of us.' She was crying, tears falling straight down her cheeks like the rain on the windows of the car earlier. She wiped them away with a boy's gesture, using the back of her hand, her eyes wide open, fixed on Captain Malone, as if there were no tears at all. 'It's like having a stray dog come in and everyone giving it a plate of food and a pat. Then it's put out at night and they hope to God it'll be gone in the morning.'

He passed her his large clean handkerchief and it fell out of its crisp folds as she thrust it up against her eyes. She had spoken in a low, fierce voice so that people at the near by tables had noticed nothing. Her display appeared to have cemented a bond between herself and the solid figure opposite: he did not seem to be at all embarrassed.

'I'd like to know who does measure up,' she said, taking up her glass again. She passed the handkerchief back to him, damp and crumpled. 'And who's got the right to do the measuring.'

'Whoever it is,' said Captain Malone, 'it's never the parents.'

They finished the meal in silence. Upstairs, as they drank their coffee, he spoke again, reflectively.

'You're not old yet, Harriet, but one day you will be. From what I've seen of the world I'd say that if you think about being old, you're finished. Old men need new interests. Now in the concession at Terazit I've planted all kinds of trees already: acacia and eucalyptus and honey locust and so on. And when they're of a height, I'll put in fig and apricot. I can watch my trees grow ...'

Harriet at last found herself warming to him. The eighteenth- and nineteenth-century landowners had watched their trees grow. They had had their grounds laid out by men like Capability Brown and planted avenues, created vistas which they knew they would never see in their full perfection. That was no longer possible in the England of today, for we had reverted to being a nation of shopkeepers and shop stewards. Government departments wanted trees that gave them a quick return; the time for the planting of oaks was gone. People's parks contained mini-trees like Japanese cherries. In the suburbs avenues of chestnut and elm were destroyed, their roots interfered with the drains, or they were diseased ... the paraffin-driven circular saw could cut through four hundred years of growth in four minutes.

'Of course you're right,' she said. 'It's the best way to spend the last years of your life. But—'

'I'm telling you this, I asked you to meet me because you're Daisy's girl. I'd like you to feel that I'm a friend. I don't even know whether you like me enough to want to come out and work with me, but if you do, the offer's open.'

'Just because I'm mother's daughter.'

He waved his cigar in sudden irritation. 'Because you have character and a trained mind, and because, like me, you're better in harness. I like to see intelligence and energy used properly, and there's a lot to do outside this country. He paused, smiled briefly. 'I'm not romantic about this, although I like the Arab saying that a forest has a moist breath, because it's true. I want to found a place where people can learn about biosylvics, and forest ecology and do practical work in the nurseries and work for the future.' He looked at her shrewdly through his cigar-smoke. 'I said the future. The past's old, done for, finished. It's the future that counts.'

How much could she believe? How much of all this stemmed from his sense of obligation, of guilt? Even if he planted a million damned trees and they all waved their heads in the deserts the wind would blow through them with a single accusation. What was he after all but a bloody old Irish romantic? A million trees to pay for the life of a son. How did he see himself? Marching at the head of a host of green waving lances against the shifting sand, the stony wilderness, the blinding sun? And how would she figure, playing Sancho Panza to his Don Quixote? Why should she be bulldozed by this old man? She could feel his willpower stretching out to claim her; the bus, Gregg, the field of mustard could all disappear in a puff of his cigar-smoke. She forced her mind away from this possibility and said:

'It's a bit much all at once. I've only just moved in, I—'

'But you've no job? You're not working now? In fact, you're doing nothing?'

'That's right,' said Harriet. 'Nothing. And I'm enjoying it.'

They gazed steadily at each other.

'Well,' said Captain Malone. 'I'll be over again at Christmas. You could fly back with me for a holiday. No promises. After all, you're not a prisoner.'

Eighteen

※

The first sound Harriet heard as she drove past the Everetts' farm and on up the lane was the rhythmic thudding of someone chopping down a tree.

Her mind had been so full of planting trees – she had brought back from the British Museum a list of books she would consult in Cambridge on the whole dizzying subject – that this steady chopping sounded to her like an infidel's cry of defiance to a crusader. She stopped the car abruptly and got out. The cats had settled down on the back seat on an old blanket, so she closed the windows and went off in her only decent pair of London shoes, stepping out at right angles to the lane.

Plunging along the soggy field by the hedge she followed the sound. There were shouts in the distance and then they stopped. Silence. She headed towards the tongue of woodland that stretched like a peninsula into the largest field of all, now under winter barley. As she at last squelched her way to the first low bushes and slender beech trees she heard a creaking noise.

'Pull over here!'

It was Everett's voice.

As she stepped into the clearing she saw that there were several people there, all in gumboots and duffle-coats. Gregg leaned on an axe by a pile of wood-chips, some wedges and a hammer. Everett, with one of his boys, had got a rope up among the topmost branches and was pulling on it. Gregg raised his axe to give the tree another cut. It was a straight, well-grown beech. Magda stood watching, her eyes on the sway of the higher branches, but as Harriet came between the trees she caught sight of her and at once moved in warning.

'Stay where you are, Harry. It's going to fall.'

The men turned in surprise and Everett, his attention momentarily wandering, gave a startled pull on the rope.

The tree fell awkwardly, not in the direction they had planned. The branches crashed among the topmost boughs of other trees – they grew very close together in this spit of woodland – hesitated, lurched to one side, hovered.

Gregg called out sharply, 'Magda, move! Go back, quickly!' But even as he moved the tree came down and as the waving branches threshed into stillness she was no longer there. It seemed as if she had been engulfed.

When they reached her she was pinned by a large branch, which had knocked her on to her back on the ground. The lesser branches held her legs in an amorous tangle.

'Don't move,' said Harriet, dashing forward, wading through the fallen branches and leaves. 'We'll do the moving. Gregg, saw through this branch as quick as you can. Steve, run and telephone for a doctor in case she's broken something.'

Gradually they hacked through the springy, living branches and Magda tentatively moved each leg.

'They're all right,' she said at last. 'It's my ribs, I think.' Luckily an elderberry bush had broken her fall, but she had taken the full force of the blow just below her breast. When the men lifted the last of the dead leaves and bits of bark and broken twigs off her, she tried to get up.

'For God's sake stay still or you'll pierce a lung.' Gregg had gone a muddy grey colour. He took off his coat and eased it underneath his wife, in between her and the wet ground. Harriet unfastened the toggles of Magda's thick sheepskin jacket. The bulk had cushioned her against any lacerations, but the force of the blow had reddened the skin and later it would bruise badly. There was no way of telling whether any ribs were broken and when Harriet wanted to probe Gregg spoke sharply.

'Leave it, Harry. Leave it. Keep her covered. I'll go to Everett's place and see whether the doctor's corning. Keep her warm. Everett, come with me and ask your wife for some blankets and some hot tea.'

As they went off, crashing over shrubs and grinding through beechmasts, Harriet realized that no one had thought to say hullo to her.

Now, as she took off her top coat and tucked it around her cousin's legs she smiled down at her and said:

'I seem to have arrived at an opportune moment.'

Magda, growing white now that the immediate shock had passed and the greater shock beginning, said weakly:

'You idiot, Harry! It would never have happened if you hadn't suddenly sprung out at us like that. Out of nowhere! Felling trees is a delicate job.'

Serves you jolly well right, whispered the ghost of a much younger Harriet, sulky at being blamed, unwillingly aware of being in the wrong. Mutinously she felt herself to be the agent of a much-abused Nature hitting back at Magda.

When Gregg reappeared, followed by Mrs Everett, Everett, and the two eldest boys who were carrying a long stable door, Harriet sensed that it was not only Magda who blamed her. Mrs Everett could scarcely bear to look at her; even Gregg spoke to her evenly and coldly.

'They're sending an ambulance. Let's get her on to the door and carry her to the road.'

As Mrs Everett tucked Magda around with blankets and the two men lifted the improvised stretcher, Harriet stared at the pile of wood-chips and thought them as white as the cut flesh of a roast chicken. There was a curious solidarity about the little group as they moved slowly away along the track through the wood. Harriet watched them go with a feeling of pure isolation. What, after all, had she to do with them? They were all strangers to her. Standing in the wet wood beside the fallen tree, squelching in her ruined high-heeled suède shoes, she felt a pull of panic as overwhelmingly as on that first day in the spinney.

Was there ever a last place? Or was there only borrowed time, Magda's time? Following slowly, like some leftover retainer trailing a royal litter, Harriet saw with clarity the number of times she had watched Magda being borne away by devotees. Into sports cars, waving back. On to planes. Into taxis. Followed by a wake of dogs, young men, employees. Some women's lives were like that.

Taking off her shoes and soaking stockings, she picked up her muddy coat from the ground where it still lay, bearing the pressures of some careless boot, and padded back, mud oozing comfortably up between her toes. When she reached the lane, the ambulance was already there. Magda was just being stowed away inside. Courting a rebuff, she went up to the doors. Should she go with her to the hospital?

'Don't worry, Harry,' said Magda, catching sight of her uncertain face. 'Gregg's coming with me. You get on home; the bus will be damp after all this time, the rain—'

Harriet nodded, moved to her car. As she got into the driver's seat Gregg came up swiftly, put a hand through the open window, touched hers on the wheel, said, as his wife had done, 'Don't worry, Harry.' Then he added, 'I'll let you know later.'

As she drove away she saw the ambulance backing into the Everetts' yard to turn, and there were the Everetts busy as ants about a disturbed nest.

In the bus there was the indefinable smell of damp that always sneaked back in whenever she wasn't there to drive it out with warmth and light. She crumpled up the London midday edition of the evening newspaper she had brought back with her and laid a new fire on the raked-out cinders of the old one. She waded through the great wet overgrown clump of mint at the back to turn on the Calor gas. Then she let the water run until the taste of plastic pipe was gone. She set the kettle on to boil. All these things done in the familiar order set the pattern right, made panic out of place. But when she took her mug of tea and sat down to look out of the five wide windows at the harrowed dun-coloured field, the dull green landscape under low clouds, the view failed to move her. It had imperceptibly withdrawn. It crossed her mind that you never returned to the same place twice.

Creatures had moved into the bus: two earwigs ran over the tea-caddy, a spider had spun itself a snug web by the cups. A fieldmouse had nibbled the soap left in the dish. Harriet opened cupboards; even her clothes smelt musty.

She had lighted the lamps, and her sleeping-bag was unzipped and airing at the leaping fire when Gregg at last arrived. She was slumped in the chair, barefoot, with the cats on her lap, drinking tea and gazing silently into the fire when she heard his step. The door opened and closed behind him.

She looked up and reached out to pour him a mug. He shook the fine rain off his coat and sat down on the divan. He started to speak, but she interrupted him.

'Well, was it my fault? Do you blame me?'

Carefully Gregg reached out and caught a daddy-longlegs wavering near one of the lamps. Without thinking, he crushed it in his hand and dropped it to the floor, rubbing off a thin filament of leg from a bruised knuckle. He noticed Harriet's shoes near by, stuffed with paper, her stockings hanging from a wooden airer over the fire.

'Trees are awkward things. Sometimes they fall wrong. Everett gave a tug at the wrong time. He was startled, we all were – but of course, I—'

Why didn't she ask how Magda was?

'Trust me,' said Harriet. 'Appearing like a demon of the woods. I'm sorry, Gregg.'

It hurt to say that she was sorry. It spoilt her homecoming. Having to apologize set her apart again, a stranger to their doings.

'She's all right,' he said, unaware. 'A couple of broken ribs, one more suspected cracked. They're strapping her up and keeping her in for a few days. Nothing serious. God, this is welcome.'

He drank his tea, watching Harriet, and thought she looked wretched. London hadn't agreed with her. Good.

Harriet gazed into the fire. She saw Magda in bed, in a private room, of course, looking fragile, inviting care, turning her head on the flat pillow to smile at a nurse. Tomorrow the flowers would start to arrive, her room would be full of them. Another bower.

Gregg looked down at the crushed insect and rubbed it into the blue-and-white matting so that it quite disappeared.

'I thought you'd gone off for ever without a word. Whatever happened, Harry? Was it the Guy Fawkes party? You didn't come up to the house afterwards.'

He did not like to approach her, to kiss her. London and her unexplained journey made her a stranger to him and the cats had claimed her, their paws stretched right up to her neck. Their pointed faces lay on her bosom.

Harriet had forgotten about the Guy Fawkes party. What had happened? Something. She looked across at Gregg and suddenly laughed, stretching out her hand to him as if there he was suddenly, and she knew him. He caught it and held on to it strongly.

'Get rid of those damned cats and come over here,' he said. 'They're your familiars. That's better,' as the cats fell away from her body and clawed their way back into the warmth she left in the chair as she moved. 'Harry darling, where the hell have you been? And who have you been with? And why didn't you telephone? All locked up, this place, I couldn't keep a fire in for you …' In between each question he was kissing her and she felt her resistance to him, to the bus, to the relentless green wetness of the countryside, soften. Soon, even the self-pity of her guilt would go. If Magda was queening it in her hygienic bower, so could she in hers, damp and insect-ridden as it was.

There was a tap at the door, and gesturing to Gregg to be quiet, she pulled the curtain behind her as she went through into the kitchen and opened the door. It was Jimmy with a can of milk.

'Mother thought you'd like to make yourself a cup of tea,' he said. 'And here's some letters. They came while you were away. The postman's in hospital now. He's hurt his leg.'

The simplicity of the child's speech, his incurious gaze, reassured her. Perhaps he was not a spy.

'Thanks, Jimmy,' she said, not telling him that she had brought a pint of milk down with her from London. 'I shan't be going away again. Here's your shilling.'

'I haven't earned it.'

'Yes you have. You're a kind boy. Good night now.'

'Tell me your news,' said Gregg, settling the cushions for them both. 'And bar that door, we don't want any more visitors. Will you come up to the house and eat with me? I'll be on my own for a few days.'

'Dear old Harry, wife's bane, husband's friend,' said Harriet unkindly. 'Yes, we'll go up later on.'

She would tell Gregg about Captain Malone, but not about Ted Everett. She would tell him later, over the fire in the drawing-room; they would drink brandy and she would smoke a small cigar. Captain Malone had given her a box of twenty-five. But for the moment they would make love as the bus grew warm around them and mice and other creeping things withdrew from this territory they had tried to reclaim. Each of them had things to tell the other, but they would not tell all. Was the creation of taboos the beginning of the withdrawal of love, or did it signal a larger protectiveness, a surer affection?

Nineteen

✖

The small stir that Harriet's unexpected journey up to London had caused was soon forgotten in the greater one of Magda's unfortunate accident. Three of her ribs were broken, after all, so she had to stay, strapped up, lying flat on her back in her private room at the local hospital. Dr Frampton wanted to keep her under observation, he told her.

To the many friends who came to see her and who brought flowers and fruit and magazines she generously laughed off any suggestion that it was Harriet's sudden appearance which had caused the tree to fall awkwardly.

'It was just unlucky,' she would say to Lila Merrington or her other friends on the Council, and Lila raised her eyebrows and drew her own conclusions, as she was meant to do. Lying there, on the second day, Magda had time to think over her plans for the future, and that evening, when Lila visited her again, she confided to her the plan to offer the Council first refusal of the twelve-acre field, and at once Lila offered to deliver a note to the Chairman of the Housing Committee.

'If you feel strong enough to discuss it with him, darling, it would be a weight off your mind,' she said. 'Harry will get over it. Good Lord, she can't stay there for ever. I think your offer is generous enough. Have you told her yet?'

'Oh no. She's being very good, you see. Looking after the house for me and keeping Gregg company. There's plenty of time yet.'

Lila hesitated. She longed to know the real reason for Magda's decision. After all, it was perfectly good agricultural land she was giving up. Surely she knew, she must have guessed that something was going on between Gregg and Harriet? If she did, it would be a very subtle revenge, and a profitable one, too.

She said delicately, casually, 'Does Gregg think it's a good idea?'

'Oh, Gregg doesn't care one way or the other,' said Magda, closing her eyes. 'He doesn't really have all that much to do with the farm. And he isn't getting any younger.'

With which ambiguities Lila had to be content.

When Harriet came to see her, Magda asked about the London trip and was astonished, and not a little put out, when Harriet told her that it was Captain Malone she had gone up to see.

'Captain Malone, after all these years! Captain Malone, of all people! Was that extraordinary woman with him, the one we used to laugh about, the one in oil?'

Harriet had forgotten that Magda had been in on that joke. She told her that she was dead, and out of quixotic loyalty to the dead woman, said that she had died of heatstroke in the Great Temple of Bel.

'You don't die straight off from a heatstroke,' said Magda. 'Why are the Irish such liars? Anything for a good story.'

'She wanted people to think she died there, because it was romantic. Captain Malone told me that she really died about a week later in Damascus.'

For some reason Harriet could not bear to have Magda cast doubts on that tough old man, with his innocent lavender smell and his driving enthusiasm.

'Go on, what else did he tell you? Did he talk about Scrubbs?'

'Yes. And did you know, Magda, that mother remembered him on his birthday every single year? In the *In Memoriam* columns in *The Times*. The old man spotted it, but I never saw it.'

'Neither did I. But we don't take *The Times*. Well, well,' said Magda, thoroughly entertained. 'You know, Harry, I think he was quite keen on the idea of Scrubbs and me getting married. He once told me that he didn't think his son could do any better, that I could keep him straight. What a marriage that would have been, keeping Scrubbs straight!' She stared up at the ceiling, and for some reason blushed. 'Scrubbs would always take what he wanted, or else have a damned good try. Did the old boy mention me?'

Harriet stared at her. He hadn't once mentioned Magda. She smiled.

'Oh yes,' she said easily. 'He said that you were sure to have done well for yourself.'

Magda gave a half gasp, of pain and laughter.

'Well, I've come to terms, anyway. Forget what I said the other evening – you remember. I was cross. Of course I wouldn't dream of divorcing Gregg. I don't know what he'd do. He'd be lost.'

Harriet had moved away to a bowl of dahlias, and Magda had to turn her head to find her.

'Don't fiddle with them, Harry. Nurse has arranged them just how I like them. Well, I'm glad the old devil gave you a good meal. What's he doing with himself? Still making money?'

Not that she cared, and Harriet, with some last-minute instinct she could not quite understand, replied vaguely that she supposed he was. He was going abroad again.

Harriet looked tired, Magda thought. She hadn't had much of a life, always been content with second best. So, to please her, she tried to find something pleasant to say to cheer her up. In the old days, when they were children, her mother had often told her that Magda must be nice to Harriet, as she was less fortunate then herself.

'You know, Harry,' she said now, into the silence, dredging up something pleasant, smiling in retrospective disbelief. 'I think that Captain Malone took a fancy to you when you were a child. I heard him once telling your mother that he wished he had a daughter like you. You had a character and that was what he admired.'

Had he said this? And if so, had he really meant it? It was the sort of remark a man made about a friend's plain daughter. Character as against beauty or wit. But when she saw Harriet's reaction to this small revelation – true or not – she was surprised to see the tired lines on her cousin's face smooth out in an expression of sudden pleasure.

'Captain Malone said that, did he? I wonder if he meant it.'

But Magda was tired now. She had made the effort, that was enough. A sickroom was no place for earnestness. She closed her eyes, murmuring of course he did, why not? Harry had always had enough character for the whole family. Words and smiles should skip pleasantly over the surface when you were ill, Magda told herself, like waterboatmen on a pond. In Harriet's family there was so much rectitude it was exhausting. Aunt Daisy's favourite saying was that foul deeds came home to roost.

Harriet went, still smiling, as if she had scored some sort of victory, and it was then that Magda rang for a nurse to dial the Chairman's number. She spoke to him herself, asking him to come and see her.

❊

Successful men had never liked Harriet. They felt that she would add nothing to their stature. Their positivity clashed with hers, because it stemmed from a different source. Successful men, men with drive like her uncle, required feminine women, decorative women that other men could admire but never possess. Shop-window wives.

Motoring back home Harriet realized for the first time that Captain Malone could count as a successful man, a wealthy one too, and, although he was old, he still had drive. As she fed the cats that evening before going up to have a meal with Gregg a curious feeling sent a wave of pure ice right through her body. It was as if now, long after and too late, Scrubbs reached out to her through his father. 'Wait for me,' he had said in the blackness of the night. 'Wait for me.'

Guiltily, instinctively she looked at the far corner where she had hidden the tape-recorder and the tapes. Anyone might come in and discover them, and what a sick joke that would be!

Making sure that the curtains were closed, she took out the tape-recorder and, setting it on the table, fitted in one of the tapes. She would wipe off everything it contained, every giveaway sentiment. With her finger poised on the button, she wondered what on earth she had found to say, and was tempted to start it off once again, just to hear herself telling the story. But to whom was she telling it? Who wanted to hear it now? Not Gregg, certainly not him. Not Magda. And Captain Malone's square sanity would altogether refute it. For herself, then? Out of curiosity she set it off, keeping her finger ready to stop it when it became unbearable.

But there was nothing. The tape whirled on, spinning in silence. She watched it for a full minute, then stopped it. Was she pushing the right button? She had never been any good with mechanical things; even radios stopped dead or poured out a stream of conflicting languages and music whenever she tried to adjust a set. Now she reached for the instruction book and read it through carefully. Press this button and that, it was absurdly simple. To record press the button at the back. Simple. So much so that she had forgotten to press it. For her it had been enough to have the spools moving hypnotically.

She stared at the machine in absolute disbelief, set the tapes whirling again and watched the full one unwind on to the empty spool. Somewhere the story was being told … Scrubbs's schooldays, Silly Millie, Hi Ham Ha Huge Hugly Hairy Hold Hape, laburnum blossom and the tattoo on his left hand. Scrubbs wounded, reduced, rejected and rejecter. Scrubbs being sorry, Scrubbs being dead.

She pressed the button at the back when there was a quarter of the spool left.

'Testing,' she said. 'Testing. Dead. Dead. Dead.'

She stopped it, started it again, pressed the right knob, and heard the knelling of her voice. She'd got the hang of it at last. Now she could do what she wanted, but there was nothing she wanted. The confessional was indeed sacrosanct.

✼

The next morning she awoke to a cold frosty day that held the rigorous promise of snow. She awoke with a sensation of floating; there was no struggling to the surface, she merely opened her eyes and felt free. It was a simple, uncomplicated feeling, one entirely new to her. Perhaps a convert felt it, discovering God. It was almost as if someone had peeled off a constricting bandage and her limbs were now free to move in any direction. Lying there in her sleeping-bag – she had after all been too idle to buy sheets and make herself up a proper bed – she could not remember feeling this before, except in childhood, before starting school. Floating there, she cast about in her mind for hurtful things. There were none.

There was nothing she could not bear to remember, if she wanted to remember, and this was surely true liberation. Falling out of love, if this was it, was like waking from a confused nightmare, opening one's eyes to the uncomplicated daylight. In this state, if it lasted, one might make a free choice.

Twenty

In the weeks that followed, Harriet sat in the bus amassing facts. The first snow fell towards the end of November, and it was strange to look out over the thinning countryside, with its searing winds and the beautiful denuded trees and read about the great deserts and how they had been caused. She was forced to buy herself an oil heater and keep it on all night. Somehow the cold discovered every weakness in the framework of the bus. Windows proved to be ill-fitting, cracks appeared treacherously between the floor and the four sides, even the roof leaked in one corner. She dealt with all these things herself, saying nothing to either Gregg or Magda.

Wrapped in a rug, she read about man-made oases and concrete canals. The experimental station south-east of Tripoli with its 180-acre botanical garden, where trees were tested and adapted to the rigours of soil and climate, fascinated her. She read about the fertility of the desert soil when only water was added; the great avenues of eucalyptus and casuarina trees that acted as effective brakes on the sirocco and the khamsin. The spineless cactus that could be imported from America as fodder, and from Tunisia the Florence aurore wheat, early-growing, disease-resisting high-yielder to revolutionize the grain production of Tripolitania. …

She absorbed facts about animal breeding in deserts: Barbary sheep (the origin of the myth of the Golden Fleece?) and zebu-humpback cattle from Sudan. How at Sidi Mesri they crossed a British brown leghorn with the 'Roman chicken' to improve the quality of eggs. … And all the time she absorbed the hard facts about the rich harvests that could be got from the green, protected belt around the edge of the great deserts: citrus fruits, almonds, soft fruit, vegetables. All the time a kind of excitement grew in her. She rediscovered the zest which she had had as a child when the local library had been her refuge and no one at home had had the time or the knowledge to answer her questions.

Then, she had walked back from the library in the clear blowy autumn nights with all the facts she had learned hovering protectively above her head; a pulsating aura of positive information. Sometimes she was so full of euphoria that she floated past the cemetery with its gleaming white headstones with no fear whatever. Even if all the ghosts rose up and thumbed their spectral noses at her she could fell them with a ringing tirade:

'Did you know,' she might call across to them through the tall spiked railings, 'Did you know that *Ich Dien* doesn't really mean "I serve"? It's a degenerate form of the Welsh *Ech Dien*, "This is your man!" Edward the First shouted it out to the chieftains in Carnarvon castle in 1283, holding up his son to them. He'd got his wife to come all the way through those awful mountains in winter to bear his son in Wales. Otherwise the chieftains wouldn't accept him …'

And the ghosts would sink down again into their graves and pull the earth and the granite chips and the jamjars full of stinking forgotten flowers over their forgotten chastened heads and be silent.

Harriet at that time had been fat and big. It seemed that when she was most unhappy she gathered flesh as well as facts around her shrinking bones to hide them from the hard, spry laughter of the world.

Now, sitting up at her long counter, flanked with coffee and cigarettes, she was aware that she was shedding weight. For the first time in years she did not have to loosen the fastening on her skirt or her slacks when she sat down to study. Of course, she told herself, she did a fair amount of walking. Up to the house at least twice a day to help Magda, who was still strapped up and had to be careful. Over the farm on fine days with Gregg, learning the contours of the land in winter. Sometimes, if she walked alone, gathering kindling, she took care to entice one of the Everett children to go with her: children were great dowsers of passion, and she did not look forward to fighting off Ted's advances in the woods.

Ted came, though, one evening, soon after she got back from London, to return the two handkerchiefs and the scarves she had wrapped around his burnt hand on Guy Fawkes Night. Flo had washed and ironed them, he told her. He also brought her a present, a hare, skinned and quartered. He had shot it, he said, in the bottom field over by Hollow Lane. The blighters seemed to be increasing.

He stood before her, grinning, the bloody newspaper parcel in one hand, the neat brown paper parcel in the other. There was a certain complicity in his stance. He knew all right, but he thought no less of her for it. He was even offering some sort of sacrifice to prove it. ...

As she emptied the naked segments of hare into a saucepan and covered them with water, she remembered the beliefs that some African tribes held: Once a person has given another a gift, then that person can never again cause harm to the giver. That made sense of the Christian idea of turning the other cheek. After all, one only had two cheeks. Ted Everett, by making a present of himself, his time, his skills, was always propitiating the fates that might strike him down.

Meirion also came calling. Now the bad weather had started, he no longer walked up from the town below; he cycled. He had called in to see Gregg and Magda, he told her, but they were out, off to dinner somewhere.

'Haven't seen much of you lately,' he said. 'I hear you're busy.'

'Well, yes,' she said, unable to hide the fact, since the orderly piles of books and pamphlets and her own notebooks lay under the lamp.

'I never thought you'd just settle for the country life,' he said, picking up one of the books. 'D'you know, I nearly offered you a job on *The Curfew*. Wondered whether you'd like to run a sort of quiz corner.'

'A quiz corner?'

'Yes. You know. Who did what and when. Who said this or that. Who was the first man to wear a bowler hat or run the four-minute mile—'

'The answer would have been no. What an extraordinary idea!'

'Why?'

Harriet could think of no real reason except her own instinctive dislike of becoming an information desk.

'But you like research.'

'That's quite different. There's a logical end to it. I've finished with stuffing myself like a plum duff with unrelated facts.' She added, 'And I hate doing nothing.'

Curiously he asked, 'Well, what's the logical end of this? Gregg said something about your getting interested in deserts. That's not much use to you here.' He paused. 'Unless you're interested in the human kind.'

She stared at him, not understanding.

'Oh come,' said Meirion, 'I take it that you want to cultivate the physical kind, not the human.'

Harriet said carefully, choosing her words:

'I suppose you could say that I believe in trees that can fight against the desert, and that by planting these a person might hold back the desert that threatens his – or her – own life. Yes, you could say that. But one must move from strength, not weakness. These things have to be thought over.'

'Then this might help,' said Meirion, bringing some proofs out of his pocket. 'It'll be in *The Curfew* on Friday, so there's no perfidy in the leak. Go on, read it.'

He watched her as she read:

PUBLIC-SPIRITED GESTURE FROM ONE OF MAXMEAD'S LANDOWNERS

Mrs Gregory Witheredge has offered the Council a twelve-acre field, now under barley, to ease the housing problems of the district. There are three hundred people on the waiting list for Council houses and Mrs Witheredge has said that she wishes to set an example which she hopes that other landowners will follow. The price has not yet been decided, but subject to planning permission being granted, the Ministry of Housing and Local Government will be approached for a loan.

At the Council meeting last week, Mrs Witheredge, who is recovering from an accident which broke three of her ribs, said that in her opinion it was the duty of Council members (of which she, of course, is one) to do all they could to reduce the housing list.

> Mrs Witheredge's father bought the beautiful old house of
> Uplands just before the war ...

Harriet put the paper down, unable to read any farther. Her heart was beating suffocatingly and she looked up from the smudged, uncorrected page to meet Meirion's interested eyes.

'Are you going to fight it? Make any comment?' he asked. 'Here, let me.'

He poured the whisky for her. She had not been drinking for some days, and as she gulped it down like medicine her face flushed up.

'Of course,' he went on, as Harriet began to read it all over again. 'Nothing will happen for ages. You know what these things are. I think it's a bit premature myself. I mean, the very fact that Magda's a Council member might scotch the whole business in the end.'

'I doubt it,' said Harriet. 'Well, so that's how things are. She might have told me.'

'She probably will, before Friday. I've rather jumped the gun, I'm afraid.'

Harriet looked at him with absolute certainty.

'You showed it to me because you want a statement from the squatter,' she said. 'Well, I'm not making one. I've no rights here at all. I only pay the yearly rates. I don't even rent the land.'

'And I shouldn't think that you can move this bus anywhere else. It'd fall to bits.'

'That's right,' said Harriet calmly. 'Well, how long d'you think all this'll take?'

Meirion smoothed the crumpled proof and sat smoothing it without replying. He was disappointed. He had hoped for an outburst, a vitriolic interview which he could print alongside his report. Not much happened in Maxmead which could be handled in the way the big dailies went about the news, stirring it up.

He made a last effort.

'Look,' he said. 'Magda's mother left you this bus. It's yours. That would make a human-interest story. It might even help squash the whole idea. Magda would hate adverse publicity. She lives her whole life as if she were on a public balcony.'

'I thought you and Magda—'

Meirion, unasked, poured himself a glass of whisky.

'That's just the trouble. So do other people. No, Harry, I subscribe to the Platonic idea that to indulge in bodily pleasures is to pour water through a hungry sieve. We use each other in different ways. And at the moment I'm more useful to her than she is to me.'

'And that's what you like.'

He nodded. 'If I could fight this move of hers, I would. I don't want to have to walk up here through a sprinkling of Council houses—'

'It won't be a sprinkling, it'll be a rash.'

'A rash of Council houses, then. With T.V. aerials and plastic gnomes and concrete rockeries and kids on scooters—'

'I begin to see what you mean about deserts,' said Harriet. 'Come on, let's get drunk. It's one of the fringe benefits of the under-privileged, pouring whisky through a hungry sieve.'

❋

'It's perfectly simple,' said Magda briskly. 'It seems to me to be the answer to a lot of problems. If you'd only see it my way, Harry—'

'A bungalow on half an acre for me, and for you the goodwill of the citizens of Maxmead and a fat bank balance. No thanks, Magda, I'd rather move away.'

'I'll still compensate you, of course.'

The two women sat over a scrappy midday meal at Uplands. Gregg was still in town.

'I should have told you about this before, but Council matters are secret, you understand. Anyway, there's no urgency. It won't start moving for about a year.'

Harriet said, shifting her coffee-cup, 'Was it too secret for Gregg to know?'

Magda hesitated, then she said slowly, 'I told Gregg I was thinking about it while you were up in London, but he doesn't know for certain. We haven't discussed it since. I'll have to tell him, of course, before Friday.

It all came up when he told me that you wanted to buy the field. Really, Harry! Wasn't that a bit selfish, twelve acres for one person?'

'No more than the two hundred and twenty-five or whatever it was that your father left you.'

'Two hundred and fifty-five. Anyway, that's different.'

Their separate childhoods, even their joined childhood, rose up in that difference: it was implicit in the look they exchanged. Harriet started to speak as if to fill the ache of pain that had started after she had laid down the smudgy proof of the evening before. She knew it was futile, she knew that anger lessened her and would make no difference at all to her cousin's decision. If anything, it would harden it.

'It's always been different whenever *you* wanted something, hasn't it? You or your mother. And her mental breakdown was different, wasn't it, from anyone else's? You won't look a thing straight in the face, Magda, you never did. You're selling that field merely because Gregg and I are having an affair and you'd like to see us both squirm. Well, I've cut loose once and I can cut loose again. In fact—'

There was a knock on the door, a knock repeated, and Theresa's horrified face appeared. She looked from one furious woman to the other calm one and burst into tears. Someone behind pushed her aside. It was Ted Everett. He was very white, and he looked straight at Harriet and said hoarsely:

'Can you come, Miss Harriet? I've shot one of your cats down in the field. She's in the hall here. I caught her in the leg, I thought she was a hare.'

Twenty-One

It was Bella.

She lay, wrapped up in a piece of much-bloodied sacking, on the oak settle near the front door. She looked up at Harriet with hostility, her eyes made misshapen by the dark film that half-shuttered them whenever she was ill. She looked slowly and carefully at every strange object and it was obvious that she inhabited a personal country, a country of pain, and it made her wary of exploration. Her resignation, her sharp cry as Harriet raised a corner of the sacking to see the shattered back leg, made Harriet herself shake with pain. The little cat had repudiated her. Her suffering look said, 'You are none of mine. You are a stranger.'

It was Magda who ran for her car, leaving Harriet kneeling there by her cat, tears beating down her face, hideously afraid.

Theresa brought a small blanket and Harriet lifted Bella as gently as she could, all the while her tears running down and drenching the animal's fur. She heard nothing of Ted Everett's apologies, explanations, only Magda's voice telling her over and over again that they must get Bella to the vet quickly, and Harriet must get in the car.

Again, it was only Magda's voice she really attended to when they reached the vet, watched him examining the leg, watched him shake his head and speak.

Magda said, 'Harry, it's no good. Her hindquarters are shattered. You can't save the leg, and she's lost a lot of blood. It's the kindest thing, it won't take a minute. Harry, look at her. She's dying anyway. We can't leave her in pain.'

The vet was preparing an injection and as he poised the needle Bella raised her head and looked once at Harriet with full recognition, her pink mouth open in a half-cry. Harriet put a hand on her head, caressing the black ears, keeping it there, moving her fingers at last so that when the little cat's eyes closed, she was still cradling the heavy head.

The vet was asking Harriet something, but she still did not hear, only sat on, desperately cold and shaking, her hand still supporting Bella. Then Bella was lifted away, the vet spoke to Magda and Magda was carrying a box fetched from the back somewhere. Then they were out again in the car, and driving home.

Somehow Harriet was in Magda's bed, swallowing pills, drinking hot tea, saying that she must go and find Shetat, what had happened to her? And Magda saying quietly that she would find out and that it was all for the best, and that these accidents happened on a farm and no one was to blame, and that the cat was out of its misery, and Harry really ought to get some sleep, she'd feel fine when she woke up. ...

Harriet did not feel fine when she woke up. She came to, rather than woke up, with a dry mouth and an aching head. A soft, furry body lay up against her shoulder and for a moment she thought it was Bella, for this was Bella's favourite position. But it was not Bella, of course, it was Bella's daughter, usurping her place.

Stroking Shetat, scarcely questioning why she was there, why they were both there, Harriet found that once again she could not control her intolerable grief. The cats were her kith and kin, she had said once airily to Magda. She would never have left them, however enticing the prospect. That they could leave her she had never for a moment considered. But she was furious with herself for being so completely sent out of control. She had not cried when her parents died. She told herself that this must be the spinster syndrome, projecting feelings on to animals. She had always despised women who bought favours – she had felt a horrified pity for those desperate, done-up old things at Bad Gastein loading their gigolos with presents. She had laughed at Magda with her dogs. Even the other night Gregg had said that he could always tell when Magda was coming, because of the dogs. The disturbance they made was subsonic. What had he said exactly? When an object travels at a speed less than sound, the disturbance created by that object runs ahead of it. ...

It had made her laugh then. It did not seem so funny now.

She lay quite still as the winter dusk darkened the room around her. The half-grown cat, now her only cat, the one she was fond of but had not grown to love as she loved Bella, purred in her ear. Harriet became aware that she had turned to Magda instinctively just as she had done when they were children. Magda had always known what to do. Did one never grow out of dependence, then, however much one disguised it?

Magda had been kind. She had always possessed a practical good sense. She acted always within her rights, as Aunt Esther had not done. It was then that Harriet remembered her own words spoken just before Theresa knocked at the door, and they seemed to her unforgivable. Perhaps Magda had not heard them, perhaps they could be glossed over, perhaps they could be misunderstood. Words did not always mean exactly what they said. They changed with a tone of voice; they were not as irrevocable as words written down. All the same, it was monstrous, thought Harriet, coming here to claim a ramshackle inheritance, clinging to that old bus as once she had clung to her mother, to Scrubbs, and taking Magda's husband for her own pleasure. It wasn't the sort of thing one remembered with pride.

Casting about in her mind for some sort of explanation – or did she mean excuse? – she dredged up almost without effort one of the many facts she had been storing away against an evil time, like a squirrel with nuts hidden in random holes. Hadn't Konrad Lorenz written about the 'imprinting' of newly hatched birds which attached themselves to the first moving object they saw, and remained for ever emotionally fixated on it? She remembered a drawing of the ethologist, an amusing one; he was on all fours, going across his garden, followed by a row of ducklings, and watched over the hedge by an astonished neighbour.

Each human species, Lorenz had posited, had a critical period of maximum imprintability. In human beings, imprinting with a cause (and why not a person, it happened after all?) took full effect only once in an individual's life: this critical period was during or shortly after puberty. What was sauce for the duckling was evidently sauce for the adolescent girl or boy. ...

Well, it was a theory, and as such it lifted the burden of individual responsibility.

Something else came to mind as she lay there, calmed by the unhurried breathing of the cat in her ear. The day before, in the morning, she had received a letter from Captain Malone. This, coming on the day that Meirion had visited her with his smudgy proof and his hopes for fire and vengeance, had unaccountably dropped out of mind. But now she could summon it up before her in the dark, a large piece of smooth thick paper, typewritten and to the point.

It was full of details about the new irrigation canals at Terazit; of the use of ectyl alcohol spread as a thin layer on top of open water in reservoirs to prevent evaporation, of research into the behaviour and nature of desert seeds which appeared to possess chemical inhibitors which prevented them from germinating or withering under unsuitable or hostile conditions. (Each with its little macintosh, thought Harriet. Don't we all have them. Yes, but Meirion's is the most weatherproof of all.) He would be over before Christmas, wrote Captain Malone, and hoped to hear that she would be returning with him, even if just to take a look at the nurseries. Planting time fell between November and March, so he couldn't linger in England long. Money was the last thing to worry about, of course, and he was hers affectionately. ...

Money was the last thing to worry about. If she had been a different sort of woman, thought Harriet, the words would have dripped like honey in her ear. As it was, they made her suddenly stretch luxuriously. She was being handled with tact, with care, she could see that. But it was pleasant, it was a change. All the same, a curious sense of a lack of identity still flattened her to the bed and she was glad when she heard footsteps outside, the door being opened, the bedside lamp being switched on, and she was swamped with hurting light.

It was Gregg. The only person she had not considered, lying there. And he would have to be considered, she saw that at once by his unquiet face, looking down at her.

❋

Later that evening Magda sent them both off to the Brown Bear for a drink. 'To cheer Harry up.' She was going to make up a bed in the guest-room, she said, and Harry was not to go back to the bus to collect anything for the night. She and Theresa would do what was necessary there. Shetat could stay by the guest-room fire until she came back, with a box of earth in case of accidents. There was absolutely nothing to be discussed tonight, so off they must go.

They went. Although the Brown Bear would not have been their choice, Magda's command was so strong in their ears that they found themselves in the bar before they had time to think.

It was half-empty, being a weekday. The new landlord, who sported a wide air-force moustache as a memento of the days when he had found life good, talked about the weather. He thought that the snow might hold until Christmas. He'd like to see a good old-fashioned white Christmas in the country. And thanks very much for the yule-log. He hoped they'd be in on Christmas Eve, to see it blazing.

'Has Magda said anything to you?' asked Harriet, when the landlord had gone off to serve other customers and they could move away to the fire.

'What about? The field? Yes. She told me while you were upstairs. I said that I wasn't prepared to discuss anything while you were so upset. She knows how I feel. She knows where we stand on that.' Gregg had the air of a man who had gathered himself together and was as yet uncertain of the odds against him. 'She doesn't believe me. She doesn't think I'll do what I said.'

'What did you say? You never told me.'

They sat, not looking at each other, scarcely touching their drinks. Harriet felt hollowed out by the earlier storm of grief and incapable of any emotional reaction whatever.

'I told her,' said Gregg in a low voice, for he had seen Meirion come in and make his way to the bar, 'I told her that if she sold that bloody bit of land I'd leave her. Live in London. Go away. I was planning to buy it for you, Harry, but I couldn't raise enough. I'm too tied up with the firm – what I have isn't really mine.'

'But she said – she told me in hospital – that she'd never divorce you.

So what's the point?' She watched his face. His mouth, his eyes, the very way he inclined his head reflected his emotions, like a range of hills which carries the weather on its back. 'I told her today – I was in such a rage – I told her that we were having an affair,' said Harriet coldly.

It seemed as if these words were once again destined to produce their own climax. For at once a voice broke in on them, a voice that bore down from above, from over the rim of a pint of draught bitter.

'You two look very sad and sober,' said Meirion, taking a seat opposite. 'Can't I cheer you up?'

'Try,' said Harriet without a smile. 'You made a good job of it last night, if I remember.'

'I've still got a hangover from that. Never mention hungry sieves to me again. But Harry, just look what I've got here. You're the expert, what do you think of her?'

He lifted up a cat basket from the floor, and from it came a strident familiar cry. Opening it, he drew out a sealpoint Siamese kitten.

'Eight weeks old. Isn't she beautiful? I've always admired yours, so I thought I'd have one. I—'

'Bloody fool, put it away. Put it away!' shouted Gregg, bringing his fist hard down on the table, rocking the glasses.

The companionable hum that had accompanied the filling up of the pub stopped. People turned, shrugged, some frowned.

Harriet went very white, but she put out a hand and touched the kitten gently.

'It's all right, Meirion, don't let him scare you,' she said. 'You should have two, of course, for company.' She saw him staring at her oddly, and gestured. 'It's just that, just that—' but she couldn't go on.

'Everett shot one of her cats by mistake for a hare today. It's dead,' said Gregg. 'Now for Christ's sake put that animal in its basket and get the hell out of here. You've done enough damage one way and another.'

Meirion stood up, leaving his beer. All three of them were pale, but he was shaking. Without a word he fastened the lid of the basket and at once went out. The door swung to behind him on the sudden silence.

'That was a beastly bullying thing to do to the poor little man,' said

Chidlington, sauntering up. 'What's got into you, Gregg? War been declared?'

'War?' said Gregg stupidly.

'I thought you'd heard the tootling of trumpets and off we go,' said Chidlington. 'Thought you were handing the editor of our local rag a white feather. There's always a war on somewhere, old boy, isn't there?'

Harriet saw it coming. For the second time, in slow motion, Gregg put down his glass, stood up and with horrible accuracy knocked Chidlington down. Then, as the last time, he caught hold of Harriet and dragged her with him to the door. As they went through it they heard Hilda Chidlington's voice saying that this time they'd get him for it. The closing of the door cut off the crescendo of indignation.

'Back to the bus,' said Harriet, starting up the car. 'And damn quick too, before they rouse up the local bobby. Let's hope Magda's been down there and collected my things.'

'Anyway,' said Gregg in a tired voice as they turned up the cut between the banks and went slowly along the lane. 'It was in a different pub this time. Now why do I hate that man?'

'You said it was because he was too like you. But you were drunk then.' She drove almost furtively past the drive gates, dousing her headlights, and, as if the car were on tiptoe, turned slowly through the spinney. Her sidelights caught the white posts that Gregg had planted against his feared blindness, months back.

There was no one in the bus. But someone had been in, to make up the fire and tidy the long counter. Using a torch, she saw that her pyjamas were missing, also her toothbrush and other toilet things. Magda had been thorough.

'We're safe,' she said, and suddenly clung to Gregg in the darkness.

�֍

'I'm sorry,' said Gregg, in the tumble of their bodies, and from where they had desperately fallen on the divan it seemed an age before. 'I can't go on. I'm no use tonight. It must be impotence.'

After a moment Harriet said, 'It doesn't matter. You told me you never liked making love in the dark, it was too impersonal. But a light would give us away.'

'We've been rumbled.' He gave what might have been a half-laugh. The word came out of his past. 'Let's have a cigarette. Too much mind over too little matter.'

They disentangled themselves into separate, comfortable positions, lit cigarettes and lay watching the glow.

'It must be my age,' he said at last. 'D'you know, I can scarcely bear to watch films these days. Always two youngsters in bed together, lashing about in a sort of mad stickiness. Funny, we spent years thinking about it when we couldn't have coped anyway. Now it's a recurrent thing, this sudden slackening, this not wanting—'

Harriet was moved to touch him, now that she was calm again.

'It's not the end of the world.'

'It's the end of part of it.'

'Funny,' Gregg said again after a silence, watching the objects in Harriet's bus reassemble themselves into their own separate statements in the amorphous darkness: a lamp, a jug, a jagged pile of books, the cats' empty chair. 'Things catch up on you. They take you unawares. Wish I could explain, but you can't to a woman. For a man it's the final failure. When men say that they learn from experience, they mean failure, of course. It only makes you smaller and meaner, failure. ...'

'It's mad to mix them up, Gregg. Take the prison camp, for instance. That was an experience, not a failure.'

'Ah!' Gregg shifted with sudden triumphant excitement. 'That's just it! It was borne in on us every single day and every hour that we were failures. We wouldn't have been there at all otherwise. Win or lose, that's Jap philosophy, and the loser's a damned nuisance and an offence to the eye. They were the same about illness, even their own people's.'

'For Christ's sake!' said Harriet brutally, swinging her legs to the ground. 'I'm going to make some coffee. Do you have to dig back twenty years to excuse a single occasion of sexual inadequacy? Less chastity and more delicacy, Forster said, and that's the answer. You're not a penny-in-the-slot machine and neither am I.'

Gregg watched her sturdy, affronted back as she went from fire to kitchen preparing the coffee, and for a moment wished that this could be the whole of life. It was containable, and he almost smiled.

'You told Magda that we were having an affair, you said. What did she say?'

'She didn't have a chance to say anything. Theresa came in, and—'

'You didn't tell her that we were in love. If you had she'd have known that we meant to do something about it. She won't think the other is worth mentioning, so long as we're discreet.'

'Well, we're not in love, are we? So we don't intend to do anything about it.'

Gregg reached out a hand as she came to the edge of the divan with two mugs of coffee. He knocked her arm instead and hot coffee streamed down her bare thigh.

'Oh, sorry.' He mopped her up with his cast-off shirt. 'Here, you drink this one and I'll make some more.'

Over by the fire he said, 'I suppose you're right about not being in love. But I love being with you. I suppose that's not quite the same?'

'I would not love thee, dear, so much, loved I not Honour more,' said Harriet, gingerly patting her burnt thigh. 'Hand me the boracic, Gregg, this hurts. What *do* you love more? And no schoolboy jokes about Sylvia this time.'

'Sylvia? Oh yes. Fancy you remembering that.' He sank into the cats' chair, threw a small log on the fire. He was quite a hairy man, Harriet noted again, shaking the powder along her own smooth thigh, and seeing the firelight glint on his bare legs and chest. A big, tender idiot of a man. A man lost. What was she to do with him? For once in her life, reject before she was rejected.

He spoke now, carefully, not to her, to the fire: 'It's not what I love *more*, Harry. It's just – well, look, ever since you arrived and this business of Scrubbs came up again I've often wondered whether any of us really outlive anything. Take that prison camp, for instance. You go through an experience and it seems to last for ever and then by a miracle it's finished. You're out of it. You think you've outlived it but you haven't. It's changed you, it's warped you; it's conditioned you to the impossible, so that you don't want any more to change circumstances, only to endure them.'

'You're Jap-happy, in fact. Still.'

Gregg swung round, his face contorted.

'Scrubbs told you that, did he?'

'Not about you. About some of the other men.'

'Then I'll tell you something about him. He couldn't make it with anyone except Esther, did you know that? He really only came off with her. Girls were too straightforward for him, if you follow me. That's why in the end he loathed Esther, and why—'

Harriet watched him as he stood up, naked, filling the bus from floor to roof. At least anger gave him back his full stature.

'Of course he meant to hit that tree!' he said. 'Throw over my pants, will you? I'm cold.'

'Now I'll tell you something,' said Harriet, flinging them across the space between them. 'Magda was wrong about Scrubbs. I realized it when Chidlington was giving us that crap about the tootling of trumpets.'

'Magda's never been wrong about Scrubbs.'

'She said that he'd have been like you in middle age. God, she was wrong! Scrubbs would have been another Mark Chidlington.

'So that's it,' said Gregg quietly.

Twenty-Two

Snow fell all the next day in large melting flakes. After breakfast Magda and Harriet buried Bella at the bottom of the garden, near where the home paddock began, just inside the hedge. Snow fell on to the wooden box and on to the spadefuls of earth as they covered it up again. This time Harriet did not cry, but she could not speak as they walked back up the garden together and put their spades away in the shed and walked on into the house, slicing snow off their gumboots at the door to the back kitchen.

Upstairs Shetat was restless. She sniffed around the room. When Harriet came in she wound herself round her legs, crying, suspicious and upset. Several times Magda seemed on the point of saying something; giving her advice, maybe, perhaps offering her one of Petronella's puppies when they were born, which would be the following week. About Gregg, about the field, she said nothing.

After lunch there was a telephone call from the local police. Would Mr Witheredge please come down to the station? A Mr Chidlington was preferring charges of assault, on two occasions. He had witnesses.

About this Magda had plenty to say. She prepared to drive Gregg down to the station, tight lipped.

'There'll be headlines about this in *The Curfew*,' she said. 'Of all the idiotic things to do, Gregg! Meirion wasn't to know about Harry's cat, there was no need to be so offensive. You'll have to apologize to him.'

'There was no need for Chidlington to butt in. Meirion just walked out.'

'Look,' said Harriet, 'I'll go and see Meirion and put it right with him, Magda. I'll try and persuade him to keep it out of the paper. You drive Gregg down and see if you can smooth things over at the station.'

'You can try, Harry. But you won't silence the jungle-drums in a small place like this.' She climbed into the driving-seat. 'Twice is once too often, Gregg! You never told me he'd insulted Harry. Knocking people down in Maxmead! You must be out of your mind. And of course you had to wait until I was on the Council to get into the news.'

Harriet made up her mind after they drove away. She fetched the cats' cushion from the bus, and also collected an old sweater that she used to tuck around them in the coldest weather. Then she put Shetat in the car beside her and drove to Maxmead to find Meirion.

He lived in a long bedsitter that stretched over the top of one of the old cottages in the crowded part of the town near the station. That much she knew, although she had never been there. An old woman opened the door to her knock, an old woman wearing an unseasonable straw hat. She stepped back and called shrilly up the stairs.

Meirion came down and looked at her with surprise and in some reserve.

'I didn't really think you'd be in at this time,' she said, 'but I don't know where your offices are.'

'It's Friday. Publication day,' he said. 'I can take a breather. Come in. Come on up and see my room and have a cup of tea.'

'Meirion, may I bring the cat? Will you carry the cushion?'

Obviously, he thought as he led her upstairs, obviously she didn't intend to risk this one getting shot.

He said as they entered his long, whitewashed room with its dark beams, 'Harry, I'm so terribly sorry about Bella. It was Bella, I know, because this is Shetat. It was such a crass thing for me to do, but I didn't know.'

Harriet put the cat down and it stood still, just looking.

'I came to apologize for Gregg,' she said. 'It was such an awful day, we were all a bit mad. He didn't mean it, of course. Do you know what happened after you left?'

'It's knocked the news of Magda's magnanimous offer right out of people's minds,' said Meirion. 'They can't talk about anything else at the Brown Bear. I was in there at lunch-time.'

'Gregg and Magda are at the police station now. Be a dear and play it down, Meirion. It's so damned embarrassing for everybody.'

Instead of replying, Meirion picked up his kitten. It had come walking unsteadily across the floor, mewing.

'Shetat won't hurt it,' said Harriet. 'They'll soon get used to each other.'

Meirion raised his head and looked at Harriet over the kitten's head. He asked no questions, but put the little thing down on the floor beside Shetat, who stretched out her head and delicately allowed her nose to rove around its ears. The kitten shot out a paw, stretching its transparent claws and Shetat at once cuffed it smartly so that it fell on to its back, its four legs spread wide in comical astonishment.

They laughed.

'There are so many dogs at Uplands,' said Harriet. 'I thought if you could bear it, that the two of them might be some company for each other. For the time being, of course.'

'Of course. But you'll have to tell me about feeding and so on. Do look, aren't they enchanting? I've always preferred cats to dogs.'

The kitten was up and bouncing minutely around Shetat, with its tiny tail fluffed out like a white Christmas tree.

'What are you going to call her? Are you going to have her spayed or do you want to breed from her?'

Women always talked so glibly about animals' sexual functions. Meirion turned away. He said, 'I was thinking of calling her Belladonna. The name crops up in her pedigree. One of her great-grandmothers was Martial Belladonna.'

'That's a pure seal-point strain! That's Shetat's strain, too,' exclaimed Harriet. 'How odd. So they're related.'

'Family solidarity always wins through,' said Meirion, a trifle dryly. 'Is that partly why you're here?'

Harriet went over to the window, looking out over his view of snow-covered roofs, and down into the used-car lot below. Even the old cars had an exotic look, giant white mushrooms under their cushions of snow.

'Let me make you some tea,' said Meirion. 'I won't run the story on the front page, if that's what's bothering Magda, and I'm sure it is. It'll only be a nine-day wonder, I expect. All the same, it's news, and unless she manages to talk Gregg into an apology and persuade the Chidlingtons to drop the case it'll have to be reported. Come and see my kitchen. I converted it myself from an old linen cupboard.'

The kitchen was two steps down and while they waited for the kettle to boil, he explained that Mrs Goatley's daughter had had a bathroom put in on the floor below.

'The old lady and I are supposed to share it,' he said. 'But I've yet to catch her having a bath. I think she strips off bit by bit at her kitchen sink. Never takes her hat off. She only has me here to eke out her pension. With any luck I'll be able to buy this whole cottage when she pegs out. I'd like to have a bit of garden for the cats. Or cat rather. One never knows.'

Harriet left him in the kitchen. Meirion was all right.

'You've made this room very comfortable,' she said, partly to please him, and glad that it was the truth. She liked the abstracts on the walls, done in deep greens and blues, the low furniture, the ceiling-high bookshelves. 'It's like you, this room. Tempered austerity. But why does it smell of apples?'

'It used to be old Goatley's attic. He stored his apples up here.' Meirion followed her up the two steps and put the tray on a table by the electric fire. 'The old boy collapsed and died one Christmas while he was up here choosing some specially good eaters. The thought comforts me; I'm not troubled by his ghost.'

'I don't really think that ghosts ever want to trouble people. It's the other way round. People conjure them up.'

Meirion handed her a delicate cup of china tea. He certainly ran true to expectations.

'There's an old woman in a village not far from here,' he said, 'talking of ghosts. She conjured up the ghost of an old man who used to live in the cottage next door to hers. She was sorry for him when it was pulled down, she said. Now he won't go away. Every night he sits and smokes a pipe in front of her fire and vanishes at ten o'clock when she goes up to bed.'

'A nicely-brought-up old man, evidently,' said Harriet.

She watched the cats make their wary acquaintanceship, then she noticed an elaborate hi-fi arrangement in one corner, and a tape-recorder.

Meirion, seeing her interest, said in explanation, 'I like to tape things that interest me. Music and so on. I read poems aloud.'

'You must talk to Gregg about it. He's got a lot of tapes. He loves music. Haven't you ever asked him up here?'

'I've never got to know him. He doesn't really like me, that's pretty obvious. Anyway, I'm not a great one for entertaining. I prefer to be on my own.'

'It's so funny that people can live in a small place like Maxmead and not find out that they share the same interests. How enclosed we all are, Meirion. It's frightening. I must go.'

As if she had been waiting for these words, Shetat ran across and leapt on to her shoulder and for a moment Harriet held her closely. This was how Meirion had first seen her, he remembered, only now she rose from one of his chairs, not from the middle of a field. Then he had felt revulsion. Now he watched both woman and cat with an emotion he could not identify. It had a painful element, this emotion. Something like warm blood invading a frostbitten area of one's body. With the same firm gesture he remembered, too, she now set the cat on the floor. She said just one word, for she could not manage another out of the tightness of her throat.

'Behave,' she said.

❈

Harriet found the house empty when she arrived back. Magda and Gregg were obviously still out, perhaps trying to placate the Chidlingtons, more likely having a private quarrel over a meal somewhere. She had a light supper off a tray in the drawing-room, which she had come to look on as neutral territory; a sort of commonroom for Gregg and Magda to play out their game of marriage in front of friends. Then she went up to bed, tried to read and failed. She felt alien to the room, to the house, and bereft without her cats. She was entirely out of tune with bedrooms, especially this one. But when she heard footsteps and voices on the stairs she switched off her light and pretended to be asleep when her door opened and her cousin's voice whispered questioningly:

'Harry? You awake?'

Then the door closed. Harriet must have dozed off, because when she woke up later the full moon was blazing in from a dazzlingly clear sky and the fire was out. It was impossible to stay here, nailed in bed. Her window overlooked the front of the house; the lake glittered coldly as if under a shadowless arc light. The trees marched with their obedient stand-ins flat on the snow before them. It was a film-set for an epic.

She got up, dressed and went quietly downstairs. She moved softly along the hall, down a branching passage and stopped outside Gregg's room. He was playing some music to himself and she stood in the dark passageway down the single step and leaned up against the oak door to listen.

It was not jazz. It was an old record, a 78. Its slurred notes revealed that it was a very old one, deeply scratched. It was a military band, playing a selection of tunes she had heard often enough as a child, walking in the park with her father, the pom-pom-pom of the trombones beating across the soft summer air as their feet brushed over dried summer grass. It was the kind of windy music one heard at a seaside bandstand, the beating of the waves and the drag of the shingle under the pier adding their own bracing gusto.

She opened the door softly, and saw that the room was in darkness except for the firelight. Gregg sat, sunk in his deep armchair, one hand on the head of his favourite dog, a labrador pup Magda had wanted to put down. The flames lit his quiet, sunk face. She stood watching. The secure world of his own childhood lapped him round, it was strange to realize that she could not even start to guess what memories this vigorous rendering of the 'Merry Widow Waltz' brought him. Evidently it belonged to a time before he had found out that life could be terrible. A time when all red-faced men up there on the bandstand were untouchable beings, gods almost in the proud mastery of their instruments. A time when children had not started to doubt the wisdom and rightness of the adult world. When a hand reaching down to take yours meant absolute and unquestioning safety.

She had nothing to offer that matched this. Magda might make him miserable, but she also made his life real; that was often the unacknowledged relationship between men and women.

Harriet stepped back, inched the door shut, fetched her coat and gumboots from the kitchen, put them on and let herself out of the back door.

It was cold and still in the grounds and as she came through the shrubbery round to the front of the house she could hear the soft sounds of snow sliding down from the meringue-crisp branches. In a fortnight it would be the white Christmas the landlord wanted. She might send them a card from a place where there was no snow. The frozen gravel cracked under her rubber soles as she walked. Gregg was lucky. She looked for nothing now to replace the permanence and security of her childhood: the summer days, the long infatuation for something unattainable, something non-existent that was Scrubbs Malone. She would have to spend the whole night packing if she was to be off at first light, and she needed to be; the time for illusions and renewable passions was past.

❈

Mrs Everett had given the boys their breakfast and had seen them off to school, well wrapped up, when she heard the sound of a car. Only a fool would be out on a day like this, she told herself, that old north wind would bring a blizzard behind it, sure to. It was no surprise, therefore, to see the Hillman travelling slowly down the lane from the spinney. The surface was icy and the car seemed well laden. Where in the world was she off to now? There'd be a man in it somewhere, sure to be. Funny how her sort always caused trouble. Mrs Everett stepped forward, drawing her woollen shawl tightly around her hard little head against the bitter wind, to ask whether Miss Harriet wanted the milk and papers delivered. But Harriet did not stop. She gave a tiny wave from behind the tightly closed window of the car and kept straight on, down to the London road.

Afterword

Inheriting a bus in the countryside, and moving into it with two Siamese cats, sounds a bit like the beginning of a fairy tale. In *Sing Me Who You Are*, Elizabeth Berridge takes this unconventional premise and sets it against a much more worldly 1960s backdrop – where affairs and regrets take the place of any transformative spells, and modern housing is encroaching upon a rural idyll.

Harriet has inherited the bus from her Aunt Esther – though not the land it sits on, as will become important to the plot of the novel. Berridge spoke of a preoccupation with aunts, often giving them significant roles in her novels, although Aunt Esther must content herself with being a catalyst rather than a physical presence in *Sing Me Who You Are*. She is the reason that Harriet arrives in a new home, aged 37, wary of 'the spinster syndrome, projecting feelings on to animals', accompanied by Bella and Shetat her feline companions. In her short stay there, she will get entangled with more than one man, play third wheel in a relationship, and realise that a long-dead loved one has secrets that will be unearthed.

Though the human relationships are at the forefront of the novel, there is something eternal about these. They are dynamics that could have happened in any decade of the twentieth century, albeit perhaps with shifting conclusions regarding Harriet's enthusiasm for participating in an affair. What makes *Sing Me Who You Are* distinctly a novel of its period are the competing discussions of ecology and housing, and the way the war between the two threatens the stability of Harriet's home.

Early in the novel, Harriet walks in woodland governed by 'one of those tacit understandings that abound in the country; land half-private, half-public'. It's the sort of 'tacit understanding' that is falling by the wayside as the value of land increases and its use becomes something that needs to be codified in law. The concept of planning permission was relatively new in the UK when Berridge was writing the novel: the Town and Country Planning Act 1947 had been the first to introduce the idea, with all pre-existing buildings being granted planning titles. Until this point, ownership had also automatically conferred the right to build. While the change was intended to control what happened to land, it also led to a large jump in land value when permission was given for development. And that's why, twenty years after the initial Act was introduced, Magda is very tempted to sell her farmland to the Council for a housing development.

> "With building permission I have it on the highest authority that
> the price would be between two and three thousand an acre. Twelve
> acres. That's about thirty thousand pounds at a conservative estimate.
> Isn't that something? We could do a lot with that."

Thirty thousand pounds when *Sing Me Who You Are* was written is the equivalent of almost half a million pounds today. Concerns about rocketing land prices were raised in the House of Commons on many occasions: in a July 1961 debate, for example, Michael Stewart MP (later Foreign Secretary under Harold Wilson) spoke strongly against 'the continuing sharp rise in the price of building land which enriches landowners and land speculators at the cost of the community'. In his speech he uses a simile that, given the presence of the Siamese cats in the novel, is aptly feline:

❈ ❈ ❈

The fantastic profiteering in land which we now experience is related
to that true right of private property only in the sense that a tiger and
a cat are related. To say that, in the sacred name of private property,
we must not interfere with the profiteering which is going on in the
land market at present is as if we should tell a man that he should
invite a tiger into his house to keep down the mice.

The faction offering Magda this controversial incentive is the Housing
Committee, which, in turn, is supposedly being influenced directly
by the government. "I understand there's a certain amount of pressure
at Ministry level to expand Maxmead," explains Merion to Harriet –
careful to add, "Oh, not to new-town proportions."

The year before planning permission became a concern in the UK,
the New Towns Act 1946 was intended to enable the government to
designate new towns to be developed. The idea was to help alleviate
housing shortages after the Second World War. Initially in the 1940s,
these were largely in the south east. The second and third waves, in
the 1960s, looked further afield. In the year that *Sing Me Who You Are*
was published Milton Keynes and Peterborough were designated 'new
towns' in Buckinghamshire and Cambridgeshire respectively.

Though these new-town levels of development aren't on the horizon,
there is the prospect of 124 houses on Magda's land. She sees the plan
as 'one hundred and twenty-four families housed' and sees herself
'graciously accepting the gratitude of these people'. The expansion of
housing has not removed a sort of deferential class system where Magda
sees herself as a modern-day Lady Bountiful – even though she would
be the one receiving a significant sum of money. (It doesn't seem to
occur to anybody that a woman of Harriet's class could, herself, move
into one of these homes – indeed, unmarried, childless women would
be unlikely to be top of the priority list.) And that is, indeed, the sort of
tone with which the sale is announced in the local press:

❉ ❉ ❉

PUBLIC-SPIRITED GESTURE FROM ONE OF
MAXMEAD'S LANDOWNERS

Mrs Gregory Witheredge has offered the Council a twelve-acre field, now under barley, to ease the housing problems of the district. There are three hundred people on the waiting list for Council houses and Mrs Witheredge has said that she wishes to set an example which she hopes that other landowners will follow. The price has not yet been decided, but subject to planning permission being granted, the Ministry of Housing and Local Government will be approached for a loan.

This was a period when more and more council houses were being built. They were originally developed in the UK in the late-nineteenth century, often part of slum clearance programmes, but (like new towns) also became part of providing housing after the Second World War. This boom for council house construction took place in 1951–55, but the numbers were rising steadily again through the 1960s. This reached a peak in 1967, of 159,300 homes completed in England and Wales and a further 34,000 in Scotland. Under new legislation in 1967, this housing had to adhere to 'Parker Morris Standards', which included requirements for minimum floor area and kitchen storage space, a flushing toilet, and heating systems that kept kitchens at 13°C and living spaces at 18°C.

Magda's contribution might be a small percentage of the national number, but a huge difference to a small community – and to one woman living in a bus on this land. With £30,000 on the table, you can see why sentimental reasons aren't sufficient for Magda to leave Harriet's rural corner in peace. Indeed, her final decision is 'a very subtle revenge' for Harriet's infidelity. Even before this, though, all Harriet wants to do with the land in Magda's eyes is "let it run wild, I suppose, for her damned cats to roam around in". But this was a decade where the concept of 'letting it run wild' was a choice garnering growing respect from some corners.

✳ ✳ ✳

While many were concerned with housing a growing population, others were equally focused on the maintenance of nature. Harriet's epiphany comes when she meets Captain Malone later in the novel – a spokesperson for an ecological point of view that feels very modern. His passion is for trees, and against deserts – or, more broadly, for ecological fertility and against ecological barrenness.

> Did she realize, he asked her, clenching his mottled hands on the table at either side of his plate, did she realize that the Sahara desert advanced thirty miles in a year on a two-thousand-mile front? The desert was the enemy. Man had made the desert, now it was marching on them. With the earth's population increasing, food must be grown in places where before it was thought to be impossible. And it could be.

In 1967, the world's population was 3.5 billion – less than half what it is today. Captain Malone's predictions about food scarcity, and his recognition that the solution 'costs money and goodwill and the co-operation of governments', today no longer cast him as a lone voice in the wilderness. His anxieties are very ahead of their time, and the same questions are being asked more than half a century later. His theory about 'ectyl alcohol spread as a thin layer on top of open water in reservoirs to prevent evaporation' is still actively used in research – presuming he meant 'cetyl' rather than 'ectyl', though it's unclear if the error is Malone's, Berridge's or someone else's. As recently as 2016, a research paper found that a surface covering made of cetyl and stearyl alcohol saw a 19.26 per cent saving in evaporation loss on a reservoir in India.

But Captain Malone's fixation, which he passes on to Harriet, is chiefly with trees. In her mind, it ties together with land ownership, short-sighted government policy, and the erosion of a romantic vision of home that no longer makes much sense in her own life.

– 209 –

Harriet at last found herself warming to him. The eighteenth- and nineteenth-century landowners had watched their trees grow. They had had their grounds laid out by men like Capability Brown and planted avenues, created vistas which they knew they would never see in their full perfection. That was no longer possible in the England of today, for we had reverted to being a nation of shopkeepers and shop stewards. Government departments wanted trees that gave them a quick return; the time for the planting of oaks was gone.

Modern development seems to be in opposition to this arboreal dream, and not just on this specific farmland. In a 1964 House of Commons debate, Charles Loughlin MP asked the Minister of Housing 'if he is satisfied that the present legislation which prohibits the felling of trees in cases of property development is adequate'. Sir Frederick Corfield's response about tree preservation orders under Section 29 of the Town and Country Planning Act 1962 is undermined by the fact that fines for developers found to disobey the orders could be as little as a pound.

Trees are firmly on Harriet's mind when she returns home to find one in the process of being cut down.

Her mind had been so full of planting trees – she had brought back from the British Museum a list of books she would consult in Cambridge on the whole dizzying subject – that this steady chopping sounded to her like an infidel's cry of defiance to a crusader.

This single act of tree felling becomes indicative of something much wider. Is the tree landing on Magda some last gasp of retribution from nature, or is it simply one of a pattern of accidents in a novel strewn with accidents? As well as the tree felling, there is burning at a bonfire and the sad fate of Bella. No reader can finish *Sing Me Who You Are* believing that the rural world is paradisiacal, or even safe. When Harriet tries to decide which animal she is most like, when it comes

❋ ❋ ❋

to making a home, she makes an unusual choice, one which reflects Berridge's thoughtful and unusual take on the domestic and natural worlds:

> "I'm a cricket," she thought. "A cricket's home is for itself alone. A place where it can be warm, snug and safe, and it will fight fiercely if other insects enter by mistake. It is not a home where the young grow up, like the bee's hive, and it is not a trap for insects like the spider's web."

Harriet isn't escaping everything in the modern world. Ironically, one of the elements that feels most dated in *Sing Me Who You Are* would have been at the forefront of domestic technology in 1967 – the tape recorder, on which she tries to record her memories of Scrubbs. But neither retreat to an atavistic version of ecology or attempts to keep up with modern advances can protect her home. She has fought fiercely against the 'other insects', but without success. 'Animals were admirable; they adapted to circumstance', she thinks early in the novel. She has not managed the same feat. The novel ends with her car heading back on the London road, any sort of fairy tale over.

Simon Thomas

Series consultant **Simon Thomas** created the middlebrow blog Stuck in a Book in 2007. He is also the co-host of the popular podcast Tea or Books? Simon has a PhD from Oxford University in Interwar Literature.